THE CONFRONTATION

DePittars hurled himself about with a terrific leap, a great gust of air pouring out of his mouth. All his features were away from the light and obscured—and he broke for the center of the street at a dead run. He yelled: "Travis!" He stopped dead. He emitted one black curse, and afterward his lank body seemed to break in the middle. Clay Travis remained rooted, but his nerves and muscles answered the warning of that fractional moment. His broad palm slapped the protruding gun butt and wove it upward and forward. A wisp of wind touched his cheek, and a detonating roar smashed the thin-drawn silence to fragments; and then his own tardy shot roared out deeply and found its fair mark. DePittars's broken cry went wailing along the street and high over the housetops, and DePittars fell with some short effort to keep his feet. He called again, but it was a small and despairing cry that died in his throat.

NEW HOPE

Ernest Haycox

LEISURE BOOKS NEW YORK CITY

A LEISURE BOOK®

May 2000

Published by special arrangement with Golden West
Literary Agency.

Dorchester Publishing Co., Inc.
276 Fifth Avenue
New York, NY 10001

ISBN 0-8439-4721-7

Printed in the United States of America.

TABLE OF CONTENTS

FOREWORD

My father wrote about three hundred short stories over a career of thirty years, one begun in college and sustained almost without pause until his death in 1950. He may be best remembered as a Western novelist, but on occasion he opined that he was probably better at writing shorter pieces. Obviously, he said, there wasn't enough space to develop characters or situations in depth in a short work; but one could "open doors" by hint and by implication, and in that fashion lead the reader's imagination beyond the written boundaries. The New Hope stories, written between 1933 and 1937, are fine examples of that skill.

Haycox produced a number of short stories that were bound together by characters or locations — in this case, by both. Some were the classic, confrontational Westerns of pulp fiction in which the likes of noble Joe Breedlove and dyspeptic Indigo Bower (who did their damnedest to avoid trouble but never managed it) and others of less good humor brought down God's wrath on villainy. But by 1933, when the author had graduated to the slick-paper market, particularly *Collier's* magazine, the focus of the linked stories — of other works, too, for that matter — broadened to include the land-tillers and town-builders of the Old West. Historian as well as fiction writer, he was fascinated by the transformation that wagons and wire and iron rails brought to this new land in little more than fifty years.

The author's New Hope was a trading town on the Missouri River, at the edge of the boundless, mysterious West —

a place where Eastern culture and prairie custom confronted each other uncomfortably and sometimes explosively. Its stories are, for the most part, told in the first person, a device Haycox probably did not employ a dozen times in thirty years. His first magazine story, a tale of soldiers on the Mexican border in 1916, was one. Another such early work described a sea storm in Alaskan waters, and a third recounted a military funeral. Though seemingly fiction, all three were substantially autobiographical, and this makes one wonder whether New Hope itself was imaginary in every aspect.

My father was born and raised in Oregon and, in his early years, lived in a succession of logging camps and mill towns — occasionally with his restless father but more often with relatives. One of these communities was Clatskanie, on the lower Columbia River. In 1910, when he was still there with his Uncle Frank's family, there was a railroad connection to Portland, seventy-odd miles east, and various wagon tracks, but there was not yet a highway to greater civilization. Supplies arrived twice weekly on the paddleboat, *Beaver*.

The town was a collection of board buildings, many of which were on pilings to escape a daily tidal surge in the lower river. Dry-land streets turned to mud wallows when it rained, which was often. There were lumber and shingle mills nearby and two large logging camps whose population supported a couple of grocery stores and, by one account, eight saloons. Here, in 1904, timber mogul Simon Benson began bundling his logs into one-thousand-foot-long rafts and towing these cigar-shaped creatures — wonders of the day — to Southern California.

Clatskanie may have lacked some of New Hope's commercial or social infrastructure, but it would have been similar in many ways, and a fine stamping ground for any curious young man stoked with energy and ambition. Ernie was in the seventh grade, struggling with arithmetic and grammar but achieving superior marks in other venues, attendance and deportment included. He earned pocket money collecting beer bottles in the camps and "pearl-diving," a skill practiced in restaurant kitchen sinks. He learned then — if he had not already — how to hold his own against the bumptious sons of loggers and mill hands. Cousin Mary Elizabeth said that, on several occasions, Uncle Frank had found it necessary to admonish the young man for fighting. It does not take great imagination to connect this boy with young Tod, New Hope's storyteller.

The writer was fond of saying that he never did come to terms with the rules of grammar and that, when he breached on some particularly complex sentence structure, his unfailing rule was "to back up and try to go around the beast." This was, of course, massive overstatement. It would be fair to say that he did not allow punctuation to interfere with the flow and impact of his thoughts, and that he regarded copyreaders in general as punctilious, unimaginative creatures. In this edition, his original manuscripts, or those subsequent versions that reflected his editing changes in the late 1940s, are generally the ones that were used. Passages that *Collier's* excised, either due to space limitation or to avoid affront to its genteel readership, have also been restored.

Three other stories appear in this collection, all written near the time of the first New Hope episode. "The Roaring Hour" and "The Kid from River Red" are among the last Haycox stories written for the pulp market, and the latter was his wife Jill's favorite among all of his short stories. She was his in-house critic in the early years and would manage the Haycox literary estate for more than three decades after her husband's death, and that would seem substantial enough reason to include this tale of a young man who yearned for the outlaw life. "The Hour of Fury," which appeared in *Argosy* magazine, incorporates several characterizations for which the writer was well known — among them a good man corrupted by the evil power of a frontier town and a villain who could not run when the cards turned against him.

Ernest Haycox
Mosier, Oregon

THE ROARING HOUR

I

"CLAY TRAVIS CALLS"

In Buffalo Crossing, Tom Gilliam's White Palace Saloon was as fixed an institution as the courthouse and its reckonings often more final. All news came immediately to it; much news originated from it. For here, within the comfortable and rather luxurious precincts, bets and disputes and business deals were arranged and settled; and here men, loosened by the easy conviviality of the place, spoke things never designed to be spoken. For a fact, Tom Gilliam had grown increasingly silent and powerful because of the confidences whispered over his bar, and many a time he had gently steered into his back room these half-liquored individuals whose careless disclosures might easily have released the trigger-set temper of the district. Always watchful, always listening, it was only natural that this late afternoon he should be standing beside the counter when half a dozen idle men turned to the subject of young Clay Travis, new marshal of the Crossing.

'Lonzo Bates, cattleman from the Peaks, turned his glass casually between his fingers and said: "Must be gettin' old. My idea of a good time nowadays is to go down and watch the Limited steam through."

"Who got off today?" asked the attending barkeep.

"A drummer," said 'Lonzo Bates, "and Henry Fallis and the Rambeau girl."

"Fallis," explained the barkeep, "will be here to take pay-off money out to his hay crews on the Neversink. Gail Rambeau, she's been to Omaha, shoppin'."

"Shoppin'?" inquired 'Lonzo. "What was it she couldn't buy in the Crossin'?"

"Fixin's for the house she and Clay Travis are goin' to set up in Callahan's old house on Custer Street."

"Oh," mused 'Lonzo. "So they've decided finally to tie up? When's it to be?"

"Day after tomorrow."

"Nice couple," said 'Lonzo. "And I'm mighty glad to hear about it. How's young Travis makin' out as marshal?"

A studied and cautious silence came to the group, the instant reaction of men on the edge of a dangerous topic. The barkeep flicked a glance toward Tom Gilliam and received for answer a faint nod, which was a signal to go ahead. Gilliam liked to use his housemen as pumps to suck out the thoughts of a group such as this one.

"Well," said the barkeep, "he's only been on the job a week. That ain't much time to prove anything."

"Ain't it?" parried 'Lonzo Bates, somewhat ironically. "I'd disagree. In the course of forty years I've seen a good many men go to hell in the sight of sunup and sundown. I've seen these streets turn from peace to bloody war in the space of time it takes to walk between the Longhorn Restaurant and Ray Steptoe's hitch rack. Well, I'm wishin' Clay Travis well. He's square, tough, and full of salt."

Another of the group, a leather-faced hand by the name of Tex Cope, broke in with some evidence of dissatisfaction. "Ever see reform get anywhere in this town? Clay's a sucker for tackling the job."

"Who," put in 'Lonzo shrewdly, "said he was a reform marshal?"

12

"Nobody said it. It don't have to be said. It's for everybody to see, ain't it? Anybody doubtin' why Lou Walsh appointed him?"

"Guess his honor the mayor had good enough reasons," agreed 'Lonzo, chuckling. "Still, if it is a job Walsh wants done, Clay Travis will do it."

"What job?" asked the barkeep.

The question instantly congealed the run of talk, and even 'Lonzo Bates stared at the barkeep with a sort of gleaming speculation in his wise, old eyes. Presently he said: "Are you tryin' to put somebody on record?"

The barkeep fell to polishing the stainless surface of the counter, poker cheeked and without reply. Tom Gilliam, in the background, scowled at his houseman. Tex Cope spoke again. "Nobody'll ever get anywhere in the reform line around here. Sin has sure got its claws sunk too deep. Clay is a fool to be pullin' somebody else's chestnuts outta the fire. I hate to see him get his fingers burnt. And I'm also thinkin' he ain't so wise to be marryin' right away."

"Something in that," said 'Lonzo Bates quietly. "Things happen quick here. It is a deceivin' country and always full of trouble."

"We'll know more about it inside of a week," prophesied Tex Cope.

"Sure. But don't go layin' any large bets against Clay. I've seen him in action."

"Wouldn't give a lead nickel for his prospects," replied Cope bluntly. And then, conscious that his words were being absorbed by a larger audience, he quit talking, paid his whiskey bill, and turned away. So far, Tom Gilliam had said nothing. Now he moved forward into the circle, his soundly built body creating a pathway, and his florid and well-fed face admirably concealing whatever his mind held.

13

"Don't you think," he observed casually, "you're all some premature?"

There was no answer. The group dissolved. Tex Cope swung out of the White Palace. 'Lonzo Bates leaned against the bar and studied Gilliam with a curious, intent scrutiny.

Over on Railroad Avenue, the Limited's six open-end coaches rolled out of town and left a banner of dust behind. A girl stood on the plank walk, surrounded by valises — a slim, young woman with a straight, quick body that somehow gave out the air of quiet pride and self-confidence. Seeing her there, Clay Travis came across the street at long strides. He was smiling, and the effect of it was to break up a kind of studious, gray-eyed gravity; quite tall and quite broad of shoulder, his head lay a little forward from the habit of looking down on smaller-statured men. All his bones were large, and there was about him an air of rough-and-tumble strength. Paused before the girl, he lifted his hat to reveal a shock of Indian-black hair.

"How was Omaha, Gail?"

"I missed the sagebrush growing in the middle of the streets, Clay."

"Was sort of afraid you might like it and stay."

"You're a handsome liar," retorted the girl. Sudden light broke across the even features. She took his hand and said, with a light touch of mockery: "Well, glad to see me, or aren't you?"

Clay Travis looked quickly about him, colored a little, and bent toward the grips. "I don't like audiences, Gail."

The girl laughed — a gay, free-running laugh and watched him adjust the heavy valises in his big fists. Side by side they went across Railroad Avenue and through the center of the Crossing. "How has everything been, Clay?"

"Same as usual."

"No trouble?"

"Shucks, no," said Clay Travis. "Why would there be?"

But the girl shook her head and lifted her eyes to him with a return of soberness. "There was a drummer on the train who seemed to know this country pretty well, and he told me some things about the district I never knew before. It even made me wish you were back punching instead of being marshal, Clay."

"What'd he tell you?" asked Clay Travis quickly.

"Something about Nick DePittars and Sheriff Derwent."

"Drummers," said Clay Travis, "are always full of hot air. Forget it, Gail. This job is payin' me twice as much as any I could get on the range. Say, you ought to see the black suit the tailor's turnin' out for me. I look like a high-class gambler in it."

"Well, a man gambles when he marries, doesn't he?"

But Clay Travis grinned and drawled out a lazy answer. "Tell you more about that tonight. I. . . ." Then he stopped and looked around. Somebody negligently whistled half a dozen notes of a wedding march and a cool voice said: "Ain't they a pretty pair?"

"Gib," said Clay Travis, swinging around, "a horse should've stepped on you years ago."

Gib Smith lounged in the shade of the Longhorn Restaurant's porch, a little man with a shrewd and reckless face and two greenish, electric eyes. "Wish it had," he affirmed with a spurious show of sorrow. "As is, I grieve and pine away. Gail, when you goin' to throw that big lout over and take me instead?"

"Gib," said Gail Rambeau, "you're drunk again."

"That's the first good idea anybody's give me today," replied Gib Smith.

15

"If I catch you botherin' any more solid citizens," threatened Travis amiably, "I'll run you in. Come on, Gail. It's not fitting you talk with such trash."

"I knew him when he was just one of the boys," jeered Gib Smith to the departing pair. And then he cleared his throat, and Travis looked swiftly around. Gib Smith, blank cheeked, made one surreptitious motion with his hand and winked. Travis nodded.

"Listen," said the girl, who had seen nothing of this byplay, "I won't be the kind of a wife that meddles. But if there is something in the wind, Clay, I want you to tell me. Promise it."

"What could happen in a sleepy joint such as this?" parried Clay Travis, and swung in at a porch. Gail's mother came out of the door, and Travis put down the grips while the girl ran up the steps. Travis turned from that scene, a little embarrassed, and fell to rolling a cigarette, his eyes running along the street with a sudden narrowness. Presently the girl called, and he swung around.

"Coming in, Clay?"

"No, I've got to go back to the office. But I'll be around for dinner, if I get the proper invitation. Do I hear one?"

"You do," said Gail. "How would you like steak and onions?"

"Lady, the first forty years of this will be just swell." He lifted his hat then and wheeled off, cutting across this street and turning into another. At a corner he paused to sweep the walk leading by the White Palace and to inspect the hitch racks; and afterward he walked to his office hard by the courthouse. When he went in, he found Gib Smith pacing back and forth.

"Tim Stevak's in town," announced Gib Smith abruptly.

The last vestige of blandness and carelessness faded from

16

Clay Travis's eyes. Across them appeared a shadow that ran from one high cheekbone to the other. "It's coming," he said quietly, "much sooner than I expected."

"I don't get all this," complained Gib Smith. "Let a fellow in on it. I know he ain't a friend of yours, and I know he's made passes about bracin' you. But, I don't get the caper. What for?"

"I knew it was coming," answered Travis, "but I figured they'd give me a few days to get squared around. Well, they don't mean to. The ball starts now. Gib, keep this under your hat strictly . . . there's going to be hell to pay."

"Stevak squarin' a common grudge?"

"Stevak's only a white chip. Nick DePittars undoubtedly told him to ride into town."

Gib Smith's homely cheeks wrinkled up with mental effort. "Yeah, I know he's one of DePittars's gang. That's public information. You mean DePittars is sendin' him in to get you?"

"No," said Travis. "Stevak isn't bright enough or fast enough to get me. DePittars knows that. I think Stevak knows it."

"Spill it . . . spill it," grunted Gib Smith.

"Remember to keep your mouth sewed up, Gib," warned Travis. "Here's the story complete. Mayor Walsh gave me this job and put the proposition up to me plain. He's lost his grip on the town. He's sittin' high and dry without a man to support him. The crooks come and go as they please. They use the Crossing as a supply point and a playground. Nobody stops 'em. The last marshal didn't. Sheriff Dan Derwent won't . . . for reasons of his own."

"Derwent's crooked," said Gib Smith succinctly.

"Try to prove it," pointed out Travis. "Any warrant for the arrest of DePittars or for any one of DePittars's men dies

17

right in Derwent's office. Sheriff won't serve those warrants. DePittars rides into town, free as air. Nobody does anything. Nobody can prove anything. How does that read? Plain enough . . . DePittars is boss. So Walsh gives me a job. And DePittars is sendin' Stevak here to see what I'll do about it. Clear to you?"

But Gib Smith remained silent, still puzzling, and so Travis went on. "DePittars sends Stevak in to put it up to me. If I don't arrest Stevak and throw him in the jug, I am admitting I can't do anything and that DePittars can continue to ride free as air in and out of the Crossing, raising all the sin he pleases."

"Then find Stevak and lock him up," said Gib Smith promptly.

"If I do that," explained Travis, "it will mean that I am challenging DePittars's strength. And he will come into the Crossing with his toughs and thresh it out with me. Like I said, hell's going to bust loose around here, but I didn't think it would come quite so soon."

Gib Smith looked curiously at his friend. "What you do is your business, Clay. But I'm going to be in town, if that's any help to you."

"Sit tight and say nothing," said Travis, and turned out of the office. Paused on the sidewalk, he saw Henry Fallis come wheeling along in a rig. Sighting Travis, the cattleman drew in and halted the team.

"Clay," he said, "I heard you took the star. Another good rider ruined. You damn' fool, why?"

"I'm marryin', and I need the hundred and twenty a month," drawled Clay. "Where you heading this late in the day?"

"Going out to pay off my haying crews."

Travis looked up to the westering sun and then out along

the sweeping flats to southward. "It's going to be dark before you reach the Neversink, Henry," he said slowly.

"I know . . . I know," said Fallis. "I've been hearin' plenty lately. But I've done this for fifteen years, and I'm damned if I pull in my horns now for a bunch of alleged sagebrush jumpers." Lifting the reins, he called out — "See you tomorrow." — and drove off.

Travis walked on in the direction of the White Palace. Shadows were crawling across the western side of the street while the second-story fronts on the eastern edge were aflame with the last, long rays of the sun. In front of the Prairie Hotel a stage was loading for its night trip to Pistol Gap, sixty miles yonder in a wild land; and Sheriff Dan Derwent stood by the stage's door, jovially talking to some rancher about to embark — building up his political fences, Travis thought. The sheriff's hat was pushed back, and the play of humor tightened and accentuated the rather slackly shrewd lines of the cheeks. He was a tall man, a rather impressive man, and his voice had a touch of grating command about it that reached out through the sultry air. But Travis studied this scene only momentarily, for he was in front of the White Palace now, and he recognized Tim Stevak's horse along the saloon rack's jaded row of beasts. Gib Smith sauntered nonchalantly by and halted near the saloon door, saying nothing yet making an obvious play out of his move. Clay Travis shook his head, dropped his cigarette, and entered.

It was at that short half hour before the lamps were lit, and the gray, smoke-ridden interior bothered his eyes for a moment. There was a desultory game of stud going on nearby, and the bar was filling with men in for their before-dinner whiskey neat. Tom Gilliam strolled out of his back room, skirted the counter, and saw Travis. Instantly a certain indifference fell from him. Wheeling, he made directly for the marshal. But Travis passed him half a glance, pivoted on his heels, and pinned his eyes on a flatly muscular figure midway along the bar, the figure of Tim Stevak. Tom Gilliam called out with a definite carrying power in his words.

"Hello, Clay. Seldom see you here. Step up with me."

The immediate effect was to bring Tim Stevak face about; and then the humming confusion of talk began to drop lower and lower. At that moment Travis knew what he had only hitherto suspected: Buffalo Crossing was aware of what went on beneath the placid surface, Buffalo Crossing understood what his job had to be. The sense of it lay in the deepening silence and on all those cheeks swinging around toward him. Tom Gilliam halted in his tracks and said quickly: "Here, let's have some lights in this dump. Johnny, get busy. It's dismal around here. Have a drink, Clay?"

Clay kept his eyes on Tim Stevak. "Howdy, Tim."

"Hello," muttered Stevak, and rolled his shoulders forward. Yellow hair straggled down from his hat brim, across a rounding forehead. His long arms hung limp, with the hint of corded muscles in them. His answering inspection was flat, without much imagination, yet on guard and a little sullen.

"Didn't expect to see you in the Crossing," said Travis conversationally and stepped nearer.

"I'm here," was Stevak's pointed reply.

"I guess you didn't see the Keep Out sign at the street-end. Let's have your gun, Tim. And come along to the judge with me."

Such small murmur as was left ceased, and a quality of breathlessness came to the White Palace. Stevak remained idle, and he said — "What for?" — in a laconic manner.

"If you've got to have a reason," observed Travis, "I guess disturbin' the peace will do as well as any. The gun, if you please."

"No," said Stevak. "I don't think so."

A harder, more metallic sound filled the marshal's talk. "I wouldn't make that mistake if I was you. This is only a small move in a much bigger game . . . as you ought to know. It's a sort of formality we've got to get over. Don't mess up your part of it. Nick DePittars might not like that."

Stevak stood dumb, the hulking frame immobile, his eyes flat. Tom Gilliam broke in quickly. "I see no disturbance, Clay. Appears entirely high-handed on your part."

"Why, of course," drawled Travis. "That's what I was appointed to be. Tim, I'll not be asking you another time for the gun."

"No trouble in here," called out Gilliam. There was command in it, a peremptory order to Stevak. "I'll have none of my glassware busted. Get it over with, Tim."

That seemed to settle Stevak's pondered uncertainty. Slowly, very slowly as not to be mistaken in his gesture, he lowered his right arm and lifted his weapon half out of its holster. Then he reached across with his left hand, gripped the piece, and offered it reversed to Travis. Travis accepted it and stepped aside. "We'll go along to Judge Pinkham's," he said.

Stevak went out and turned toward the courthouse, Travis following. Part of a crowd came. At the courthouse door Travis looked around and saw Sheriff Derwent break clear of the stage and advance diagonally across the street with a measure of haste. He threw up an arresting arm, but Travis only shook his head and went on after Stevak who stolidly took the corridor down to the Justice of Peace's room and there entered. Travis smiled somewhat grimly to himself as he came through the same entry. All this went smoothly enough — Stevak was performing his part well. For a moment he wondered if the J. P. — old Shad Pinkham — had also been given

21

his lines in advance to read; but, when he saw Pinkham's eyes turn color, he knew it to be otherwise. Pinkham was startled and showed it. He cleared his throat; he rose half out of his chair and settled back again. "Clay," he muttered, "what's this for?"

"Disturbin' the peace," said Clay Travis.

"I heard no sound of trouble," replied Pinkham, at once revealing himself. "Was you disturbin' the peace, Tim?"

"I was drinkin', mindin' my own business," answered Stevak.

Pinkham shook his head at Travis. "That ain't enough, Clay. Mind my advice and don't try to make a reputation too early. There'll be more fittin' occasions later on."

Sheriff Dan Derwent turned in hurriedly, made one brief survey. "What's up, Travis?"

Pinkham looked relieved. "Clay's got Tim here for disturbin' the peace. I find nothin' disorderly about Tim."

Derwent looked long at Travis and was about to speak when Tom Gilliam walked casually in. The sheriff stepped back toward a wall, and Pinkham slowly rose from his chair. Stevak turned with something like a question on his face.

"Now I have no feelings in this one way or another," explained Gilliam. "I'm not hostile at you, Clay. But I think you was high-handed, and I thought I'd just add my word to the judge. As a matter of truth, Tim never turned a hand. It seems all damned funny to me . . . I'll say that much straight out, Clay."

"You're dismissed, Tim," said Pinkham, as if the case were closed. "You'll get a bad reputation if you go in for this kind of foolishness, Travis."

Stevak turned with a veiled amusement in his eyes and held out his hand. "My gun, Mister Marshal."

"That appears to be the end of that," was Travis's cool

answer. "But I'm sorry, Tim. I'll have to arrest you again for carryin' a gun inside the city limits."

"Why, thunder!" exclaimed Pinkham. "Everybody does. What's the matter with you? Sure I know there's an ordinance against it, but that ain't been enforced for twenty years."

"It will be now," stated Travis. "You know the law on it, Pinkham. Slap ten dollars on him."

Pinkham looked his defeat and raised his hands toward Sheriff Derwent. Derwent's eyes took on an odd glow of anger, and the heavy creases of his face sagged downward. "The star seems to've gone to your head, Travis. How long do you expect to get by doin' this tomfoolery?"

"Hit him with a fine, Pinkham," pressed Travis.

"Why, I'm darned if I do!" shouted the judge.

"All right," decided Travis. "If you refuse to do it, I'll arrest Tim every five minutes all night long and drag you out of bed each time. I want this thing settled now."

Derwent muttered under his breath and cast a glance at Tom Gilliam. But Gilliam was silent, his features impressed with a thoughtfulness that was somehow covert and dark. So Derwent swore aloud and let his anger run. "Listen to me, Travis . . . you'll end up in the junk pile! I know this country better than you do. Somebody will have his feelin's hurt at your confounded heavy fist and pot you. I can't say I'd blame 'em, either."

"That's why you quit arresting anybody?" inquired Travis.

Derwent flushed. "None of that sarcasm on me, Travis! Am I to infer you're out to buck me?"

"Use your judgment."

"By God, I can damn' soon crush you!" yelled Derwent.

Travis suddenly swung on the silent Gilliam. "What do you think?"

"Me?" asked Gilliam. "No . . . . I'm out of this. I've got

23

no part in it. All I came for was to put in my word for Tim. There's something behind all this monkey business . . . and it's none of my affair. I'm leaving." And saying so, he turned out of the office. Derwent's eyes followed, jerked back to Travis. "You'd better take my word for it, boy. Play it easy around here. Better marshals than you have been busted."

"Hurry up, Pinkham," said Travis. "Give him the fine."

Pinkham stared at Derwent. But Derwent only glowered and pressed his lips together. So the judge snapped out: "All right. Ten dollars, Tim, and I'm sorry."

Stevak hesitated until Travis prompted him. "Pay it." And then Stevak reached into his pocket and threw a handful of silver on the desk. Morose and irritated, he pulled himself about.

"All right . . . you've got your way this time. Now give me my gun."

Travis broke the gun and kicked out the cartridges. When he handed it back, it was with an accompanying warning. "Don't bring that thing into the Crossing again, Tim, unless you're looking for me. Now go back and tell DePittars this is his answer. He sent you here to get one . . . and he's got it."

Paused in the doorway, he waited for an answer that never came. The sultry hostility thickened throughout the room, seeming definitely to link those three men together in a common animosity. Stevak only stared out of his dull orbs. Pinkham would not lift his head. Derwent's lips were thin with wrath, and a heavy, dangerous light flickered in his eyes.

Seeing all this and marking it exactly for what it was worth, Clay Travis went down the courthouse corridor and out into a suddenly arrived dusk. A six o'clock bell rang somewhere over on Railroad Avenue, and its echo rolled through the hush of the town. There was a small crowd waiting curiously at the courthouse door, and, when Travis appeared, it fell silent. He

24

passed on, turned through Hogan's alley, and came into Custer Street. At the porch of Gail's house he found her father waiting. The elder Rambeau rose from the steps, speaking cautiously: "I saw that play, Clay. In case you don't know, you made some mighty powerful enemies, and this ain't the end of the transaction."

"I expect not," agreed Clay. "Now, say nothing about it to the women. Nothing at all."

Tom Gilliam walked back to his saloon, the florid cheeks more enigmatically set. Instead of going through the front way, he slipped along the side of the building and entered a private door to his office behind the bar. Lighting a lamp, he took up a slow pacing of the room. Once he paused to trim a cigar, and with this dry smoke clamped between his thick jaws he resumed his restless moving. Somebody began picking out a tune on the barroom piano, and there was a freshening sound of activity yonder as the unattached men of the Crossing drifted in for the night's pleasures. Swinging abruptly about, Gilliam went to the wall nearest the bar and slid open a small paneled peep-door.

"Tell Mack Setters to come to me," he said, and pushed the panel shut.

It was a good five minutes before the man came, sliding through the alley doorway with a swift and somehow surreptitious twist of his smallish body. He closed the door and leaned against it, waiting.

"Mack," rumbled Tom Gilliam, "you saw the business in the barroom?"

"Yes."

"Well, he took Tim to Pinkham and forced a ten-dollar fine on Tim. It was a deliberate call, Mack. Travis meant it for a deliberate call."

"Don't underestimate Travis," said Mack Setters. There was a professional tonelessness in the words that was a part of the man's repressed, watchful manner. All that he was showed plainly on him from his white and flexible gambler's fingers to the pinched monotony of a thin face. He was dressed in a broadcloth suit, and a diamond pin flashed out of a white shirt's starched front. And as Gilliam kept on with his endless marching around the room, Mack Setters's eyes followed.

"I'm not," said Gilliam. "I'm not underestimating him. He's wise. He knows exactly how the situation stands, and he's making his position clear. He's called me."

"Called you?"

"Oh, well, he doesn't know it's me. At least, I don't think he does. He lays it on DePittars. But he's smart enough to find out it's me if he continues on the job. I sort of doubted he'd cave in. I know he won't now."

"Walsh picked him," suggested Setters.

Tom Gilliam paused and said heavily: "And Walsh can bury him. Travis has got to go before he does any damage. I'll show Walsh who is master. First, I want you to go see Derwent. Tell Derwent he's exposing his hand. He's a little too careless how he shoots off his face. The whole county knows he's crooked. He might have avoided a great deal of that reputation if he'd played things a little smoother. Tell him I want him to mind his own business strictly and say nothing at all. If the county gets too set in its convictions, it'll vote him out, and then I'll have to go through the trouble of buyin' another man's conscience."

"If," pointed out Setters, "Travis makes a record, he'll be next sheriff."

"Don't you think I see that? Don't worry. He won't make a good record. He goes down before this gets much further. But you tell Derwent to keep out of it strictly. I'll handle it.

Nick DePittars will do the job. Go on now."

"Tom," said Setters, "lend me five hundred."

"What for?" challenged Gilliam.

"I've got to have it," answered Setters a little sullenly.

"No," said Gilliam. "What's the matter with your luck at the tables?"

"Rotten. Listen, Tom, I've got to have that money."

"Not from me," retorted Gilliam. "Go do what I told you."

Setters started to speak. But he changed his mind and closed his lips tightly. A strange mixture of defeat and moroseness appeared on his thin cheeks, and, as silently as he had entered the office, he left it.

That evening in the White Palace there was some betting that Clay Travis would not last out the week as marshal of the Crossing. Nobody could be found to take the other end.

II

"THE QUICKENING TIDE"

At nine o'clock that night Clay Travis left the Rambeau house and turned down Hogan's alley, bound for the office. Halfway along the thick dark, a shadow unexpectedly detached itself from the massed gloom and idled forward. Travis wheeled around, at once alert and suspicious.

"Just goes to show you," came Gib Smith's casual voice, "what could happen. You blasted idiot, why ram around like this?"

"What are you?" drawled Travis. "My official bodyguard?"

"I'll be around," said Gib Smith grimly. "Now don't ask me how I know this, Clay, but there's a funny thing down

27

Railroad Avenue you ought to look into."

"What?"

"Come with me."

Travis fell beside his partner, and they reached Main Street and crossed it by the courthouse, pressing on through the deserted darkness again. "Don't you know I'm not on duty after six o'clock?"

"Wait," said Gib Smith and led into Railroad Avenue. It was a dismal, gloomy end of town, occupied by gaunt warehouses, stables, and a few frowzy rooming houses. Gib Smith crossed the tracks and turned sharply up the steps of a small, slattern, two-roomed house. Here he stopped. "You go in," he said briefly. "Doc Medal's there. It's a girl, Clay, just a girl."

Puzzled, Travis opened the door and found himself in a miniature hallway, at the far end of which spread a thin glow of light. A man's voice came out, kindly and patient; and, when Clay reached the end of the hallway and stepped inside the back room, he found Medal bending over a bed. The doctor turned and said bluntly: "What are you doing here, Clay?"

"Blessed if I know," answered Clay, and paused astonished. There was a girl of around twenty beneath the shabby covers of an iron bed, a frail, peaked girl with enormous eyes that turned toward him and showed the most lusterless indifference he had ever seen. All the spirit was out of her and most of her vitality. Doc Medal said something, but she only shook her head, at which the doctor straightened and slowly put his instruments back into his case and snapped it shut. "Lie still," he told her. "Even if you can't sleep, don't be getting up. I'll see you have some breakfast brought in. Come on, Clay."

Travis followed Medal back to the street. "What's the matter with her?"

28

Medal shook his head and seemed impatient with himself. "I don't know. Half starved for one thing. On the edge of tuberculosis for another. But that isn't all. She's quit cold. Doesn't care. Something on her mind."

"Leila Vale . . . old Henry Vale's girl," said Clay Travis, profoundly regretful. "A pretty kid and a wild one . . . and here she is now."

"Don't blame it all on her," put in Gib Smith quickly. "She's had a tough run of luck. A certain fellow in this town made a fool out of her. After that, she had to eat and she didn't care. But if she was as bad as the rest of her class, she'd be over in Lu Hannigan's place."

"No," said Doc Medal, "that's not her style, boys. Nor is her present life. It's on her mind pretty hard. She's quitting. You know, it might help that girl if some decent woman would only talk to her a little. But . . ." — and Doc Medal said it somewhat bitterly — "decent women don't do those things. Well, that's all. Good night."

"I'll go along," said Gib Smith, and walked off with the doctor, leaving Travis alone. Somebody came around the railroad depot and paused momentarily in the light. Half interested, he recognized the gambler, Mack Setters — and then forgot him. For he was thinking of the barrenness of the girl's room and the tragedy, stark and staring, that pervaded it. And thinking of it, he turned slowly across the tracks and went on to Custer Street. When he tapped on the Rambeau door, Gail came out.

"This is out of my line," explained Travis, having difficulty with the words. "But there's a girl in some sort of trouble, and Doc Medal thought if some other woman. . . ."

"Why, yes," broke in Gail. "Where?"

"Across the tracks," said Travis quite slowly.

The girl murmured a faint — "Oh." — and looked intently

29

at his face. A moment later her small shoulders squared. "Certainly I'll go."

He waited till she got her coat and led her silently back along the deserted side street. In front of that shabby little house he halted. "I'll wait out here. It's Leila Vale. You knew her."

"We're too late, Clay," said Gail Rambeau sadly. "Two years too late. But wait for me."

After she had gone in, Travis rolled a cigarette and lit it abstractedly. The prairie air bit crisply through his clothing, and the shadows along Railroad Avenue seemed deeper and grimier than before. Nothing lovely lived on this edge of town; the wreckage of objects and animals and people gravitated here and soon or late were junked. He heard the women talking in the house, and he heard the Vale girl cough and cry. It made him swear under this breath. Somebody walked slowly along the rough boardwalk, came abreast, and stopped. Mack Setters's sharp face became definite above an upturned coat collar — definite and strained.

"You're a long ways from a poker table, Mack," drawled Travis.

"What's up?" asked Setters roughly.

"Sick girl."

"She's in bad shape?" questioned Setters and bent nearer. A small suspicion crossed the marshal's mind. "Who?"

"Leila Vale lives there, doesn't she?" parried Setters. "She's bad off? What did Medal say?"

"Not encouragin'," was Travis's brief answer. He was watching the gambler's face closely through that woven screen of darkness, and he distinctly observed the thinning of the other's features. Setters said something under his breath and went on, idling along the loose boards. His steps died out for a while and then came tramping back. Once

30

more abreast Travis, he grumbled: "I can't sleep. Asthma or something."

"Or something," said Travis dryly. The door opened, and Gail Rambeau walked down the steps, pulling her coat more tightly about her. She was on the point of speaking when she discovered Setters. The phrase died in her throat, and she slipped one hand inside Travis's crooked elbow and pulled him gently away. Halfway up Custer Street she uttered the checked thought.

"She fell asleep . . . that sad, little girl. But I think I helped. I think I did, Clay. What did the doctor say?"

"Starvation, maybe tuberculosis, and something on her mind."

"Medal is a wiser man than I thought. There is something on her mind. A man."

"Who?"

"Do you suppose she'd tell, Clay?"

"There's been a lot of men, as far as she's concerned," observed Travis bluntly.

"She's still woman enough to want one particular man," said Gail and turned on the porch of her house. Both hands caught the marshal's coat lapels. "When I see a thing like that, I think how lucky I am! Clay, there must be a chance for her."

"Maybe," said Travis gently. "Cold out here. Good night."

He went back towards Railroad Avenue, but saw Mack Setters come quickly out of it into Main Street, and so he turned and intercepted the gambler within the glow of the jail's office door. "Mack," he said, "I want to see you. Come in here."

Setters followed through and stood with his back to a wall, all emotion pinched out of his face.

"You must be the man," challenged Travis.

Setters's eyes widened a little, and after a long pause he said wearily: "What of it?"

"When did you talk to her last?"

"I've had nothing to do with her for a couple years, if it is any of your business."

"A lot of things appear to be my business now that I've got a star. Something's bothering her pretty bad. Something's bothering you . . . or you wouldn't be trampin' the street in front of her door. What's the matter . . . are you ashamed of her?"

Setters said angrily: "She's common property!"

"Who was first responsible for that?" asked Travis.

"My God, man," cried Setters, "don't you think *I* think of that! We made a serious mistake, long ago. Then we quarreled. When I came around to the point of makin' up, it was too late. She went bad."

"But still she's got you fast enough," pointed out Travis relentlessly, "to make you walk up and down in front of her door."

"Yes," admitted Setters doggedly. "But I've got some pride left."

"What for?" grunted Travis. "You're no better than she is. Well, I can do nothing about it. But you know what I think, Mack . . . you'd be pretty dull if you didn't. Good night."

Setters turned through the doorway, halted, and swung around. "Travis, it may seem funny to you, but I'm in your debt for doin' what you did tonight." He let the phrase sink into silence, then added bitterly: "Kindness is not such a frequent thing around here. So I'm remembering it . . . and maybe I'll be able to pay back before long."

Travis watched the man disappear. A little later he rose, walked to the street, and looked along it to where the lights of the White Palace brilliantly blazed. Revelry flooded from the saloon; all the life of the Crossing seemed concentrated there. Travis studied the scene thoughtfully for a short while and afterward went on to his lodgings.

As soon as he was gone from the street, Gib Smith made his appearance from a nearby obscure angle of the buildings and limped back to Ray Steptoe's stable, meaning to make a bed in the hay. Gib had forty dollars and might have afforded the comforts of a hotel room, but to him the idea seemed silly; he was more accustomed to the hay. Dragging out the last of his cigarette, he loitered in the stable's entry and presently saw a fellow come out of the alley that ran beside the White Palace, mount a pony, and canter from town. At that, Gib tossed the cigarette to the dust. "I'm too old a party," he grumbled, "not to recognize the smell of immediate trouble."

III

"THE ROARING HOUR"

At eleven o'clock of the following morning, Henry Fallis drove into Main Street as far as the courthouse, thrust the brake handle forward, and wrapped the reins around it. He sat a moment, looking straight ahead of him, appearing troubled; and then he got down stiffly, one hand clinging to the buggy. Here again he paused, his big body swinging from side to side. Dropping his hand, he started across the walk. Two paces onward he buckled at all his joints, as if a heavy weight had struck him from above, and pitched head first to the boards without a word.

Along the whole of that drowsing street there was no single soul to see him fall; and it was Clay Travis, turning in front of an alley, who first found Fallis lying there unconscious with his arms outstretched as if he were trying to crawl. The cattleman's hat was knocked off, and the bent-over Travis looked straight at a head bruised and blood clotted. At that moment Gib Smith ambled into view, discovered the scene, and ran forward.

"Dead to the world," said Travis. "It's lucky he's alive. I was afraid of it. He was carryin' a couple of thousand out of here last night. Pick up his feet, Gib."

They got him into the marshal's office and propped him up in a chair. Gib Smith hauled a pint flask out of a hind pocket and nursed a stiff drink into the cattleman who came strangling out of his stupor and began to swear. He made an ineffectual effort to fight off Clay's restraining hand, but, when he saw who it was, he relaxed and closed his eyes. "Well," he groaned, "I should have minded your advice, Clay. They ran into me five miles out of town. Jumped me before I could make a move. But they wasn't satisfied with robbin' me. They beat me over the skull till the lights went out. I been lyin' out there ever since."

"Who?" asked Clay Travis.

"Didn't catch sight of but one man, and he wore his neck-piece over his nose."

"You've got some ideas about it?" pressed Travis.

"Who would you think?" grunted Fallis, trying to work the stiffness out of his neck. "Give me that liquor, Gib. And, Clay, send for Sheriff Derwent. Those tracks are fresh enough to follow."

A considerable crowd had collected by the marshal's door. Travis relayed the order to one of the bystanders, but the fellow only moved aside. Derwent had heard. He came through now with a shouldering impatience and absorbed the situation at a

34

glance. "Henry," he boomed out, "this is tough on you."

"Save that for those hounds," growled Fallis. "You get a posse and move out on the trail. It'll be fresh to follow."

"They got your money?"

"What the hell else do you suppose they was after?"

"Careless on your part to ride onto the prairie with so much coin," said the sheriff.

"Look here, Derwent," snapped Fallis, "I've done it for twenty years, and nothing ever happened before. The trouble is, you've let a bunch of toughs get the upper hand. The country is wilder now than it was when I was a young man. You don't do anything."

"What do you want me to do?" inquired Derwent with an air of repressed anger.

"Follow that trail."

"Hell, don't you know it'll peter out in the rocks inside of fifteen miles? Then what'd I have for my trouble but the horse laugh?"

"Find Nick DePittars and bring him in," said Fallis.

But the sheriff shook his head. "After I bring him in, what proof have you got? No, you were an easy mark, and that's about the story."

Fallis got to his feet, full of hard temper. "It's about what I expected from you, Derwent! And there's only one of two things the matter . . . either it's more profitable for you to stand idle, or else you're composed of yellow soap!"

"Be careful!" boomed Derwent. "I won't take that from you!"

"You took it," said Fallis grimly. "Now I'll tell you something else. I've got fifty hands in the Neversink. Tomorrow mornin' I'll put 'em on this trail, and I'll follow it. If it runs out, I'll keep on till I locate DePittars and his toughs. And that'll be the end of DePittars!"

The sheriff's slack face tightened. "You start any vigilante stuff in this county, Henry, and I'll slam you behind the bars for the rest of your life. Put that in your pipe." Then he swung on Travis and stared at him with a scowling, contemptuous disfavor. "Too bad our young marshal can't go out for you, Henry. He'd just rip the land wide open and make a name for himself."

"With a clear conscience," said Travis quietly.

Derwent's under jaw shot forward. "What's that mean?" he ripped out. But Travis only stood against the office wall and let the silence ride. Derwent visibly struggled for control. After a while he said — "You won't last long." — and shouldered his way to the street.

"Bought out . . . body and britches," grunted Henry Fallis.

Travis said casually: "What else did you expect, Henry? Now, hear me. Don't you leave the Crossing today. Don't try to reach your haying crews. Send a man to bring them in."

"Why?"

"It's a lonely prairie for one man," observed Travis. "I'll get Doc Medal for that head of yours."

Meanwhile Mack Setters detached himself from the group about the marshal's office and went idling back to the White Palace. After a moment or two at the bar, he slipped unobtrusively around it and entered the back room. Tom Gilliam was waiting for him.

"Well?"

"Fallis asked Derwent to line out. Derwent put up excuses. Said it was no use. Fallis got mad. Derwent lost his head and spoke like a fool."

"He never had much of a head to lose," observed Gilliam, frowning. "Remember this as a lesson in human nature, Mack. When you buy out a man, you always buy trash. If he wasn't trash, he wouldn't sell."

36

Gilliam was ruthless with his tongue. The remark applied to others besides the sheriff, and Gilliam knew it. Mack Setters's mouth thinned, but he stood in silence. Gilliam lit a cigar, turned about the room. "I want Derwent out of town tonight. He'd only be in the way for what is coming up."

"What's that?"

"I said I'd take care of Travis, didn't I? Well, Nick DePittars and his boys will be in after dark tonight to do what I want done. You go tell Derwent to gather a posse and ride. Tell him not to come back until morning. Tell him to get a big posse . . . couple dozen. The more he takes, the fewer there'll be around tonight to interfere with DePittars."

"Think of a great deal, don't you?" remarked Setters. He said it more or less idly, but there was a certain inflection that drew Tom Gilliam's cool, hard glance swiftly to him.

"That's why I'm boss," said Gilliam shortly. "What of it?"

"Nothing. Gilliam, I've got to have that five hundred."

"Not from me." Then the saloonkeeper's attention grew sharper. "Look here, Mack, are you tryin' to shake me down?"

Setters shook his head. "No. But I need that money."

"You live," pointed out Gilliam, "in the hollow of my hand. If I close it, you're done. Go do what I tell you and don't bother me any more about money."

Setters left the room, closing the door softly behind.

After noon Clay Travis came out of Railroad Avenue to see Sheriff Derwent leaving town with a string of men behind him, bound southward, and, when he reached his office, he found Henry Fallis sitting perplexed at the desk.

"He changed his mind," said Fallis. "He's going out to look at that trail. Came here and told me."

Travis said thoughtfully: "Something behind that, Henry."

"I know. But what?"

Travis shook his head. "Something. Every act of Derwent's is another move in the game."

"What game?"

"The game of gettin' me, Henry."

Fallis straightened. "I'll have my hands in here tomorrow. They'll stay in here as long as you want 'em."

"Better lie down on that couch till you feel organized," admonished Travis and returned to the street. The full, blazing sun crossed westward, and heat layers began to cushion the street. Men moved more slowly; the vitality of this town seemed to withdraw back into the darker and cooler recesses. A high cloud of dust drifted across the building tops from the direction of the loading pens. Doc Medal, looking more tired than usual, emerged from the drug store.

"They've arranged at the restaurant," said Travis, "to take the girl her meals. So that's settled."

"Who's payin' for them?" demanded the doctor. And when Travis said nothing, Medal went on rather gruffly. "Don't interest yourself too much in the grief of this sinful town, Clay. It'll make you old before your time. Only a doctor is supposed to work for charity."

Travis moved on, chuckling. He wheeled into the tailor shop, tried out his new suit, and found it satisfactory. But as he looked in the mirror, it appeared clear to him he was changed — that something reckless and impulsive and carefree had gone for good. The glance returning to him was measured and infinitely watchful and imbedded in deep gravity; it was, he realized, the face of a hunter alert and listening for an unexpected break. Going out, he made his rounds while he pondered over it. *All town marshals,* he reflected, *seem to look the same, but I never understood till now why that was. Well, for me the old, easy days are gone. I can say good bye to that. I guess I've grown up.*

When he roused himself from this line of thought, he found his feet had carried him to the neater side of the Crossing. He was standing now in front of a trim, little house surrounded by white pickets, the Callahan house he had rented against his marriage. The windows were freshly washed, and new curtains hung over them. On the point of going in, he caught sight of Gail moving from one room to another, and he was stricken by an odd sense of confusion that turned him about and put him on the tramp again from one street to another while a tension slowly increased within him. And, as the day gradually settled, he watched Buffalo Crossing go through its changes. The Pistol Gap stage rolled out of town. At five, men came slowly from various buildings and walked toward the White Palace, marking the turn of the day. The heat diminished by degrees. Around six, the sun went down, and past seven the long dusk came off the prairie with an accompanying touch of breeze. He met old man Rambeau walking homeward.

"Come along, " said Rambeau. "It's your last supper as a free man."

Travis looked down Main Street, wondering what it was that he missed — and the next moment he knew. So he said: "I'll be a little late. Ask Gail to keep something warm for me."

Rambeau studied Travis's concern in the glance. "It's to be tonight?"

"I don't know," answered Travis. But he did know. For Rambeau's question was the same question all Buffalo Crossing asked — and the answer lay along the street in the shape of emptiness. At this hour the streets should have been alive; instead, they were abandoned, and there was little show of traffic except the passage of men in and out of the White Palace. The word was published; the wise ones knew. It would be tonight, in one manner or another.

"Wish you didn't have this job," murmured Rambeau.

"Say nothing about it to the women," warned Travis and started down Main Street as dusk collapsed beneath darkness. Sudden light lanes passed out of the windows into the dusty roadway.

One lamp burned dimly on the center table of Gilliam's office, and the saloonman stood away from it, half obscured in the shadows. Mack Setters retreated from the glow until he, too, was only a blurred form in a dismal corner. A pair of men went down the alleyway, boots scraping the packed dirt; the grate and murmur of the saloon crowd sifted through the thin bar wall. There was a faint, spaced tattoo on the office's side door, and Setters moved toward it, only to be checked by Gilliam's quick word.

"Leave it alone. It's only a signal. DePittars and his boys are in."

"Got it all arranged, I see," muttered Setters with a sort of dry-throated effort.

"When I want a thing done, I arrange it myself," rumbled Gilliam and took a pace toward the light. His burly shoulders rolled forward; the full face slowly took on a mask of impenetrable hardness. Unlovely angles of light refracted from the pale, blue eyes. "Now, Setters, go find Travis."

"What for?"

"To bring him into circulation, you fool. He may be inside for the night. He may be where nobody can see him. Find him. Fix up your own story, but lead him into Main Street for DePittars to see. When you have done that, get out of the way."

"A public execution," said Setters tonelessly.

"What's that?" rapped out Gilliam.

"Nothing."

But Gilliam came nearer to the light and stared over to his henchman, seeking to read Setters's face. "If you are gettin' soft, Setters, I'll have to drop you. I've got no place in my affairs for misfits. Go do what I tell you."

The courthouse clock struck eight as Clay Travis left Custer, crossed Main, and went on as far as Railroad Avenue. All the darkness here seemed more pronounced; the barren angles had a quality of dripping gloom at once dense and suggestive. He went as far as the loading pens on the extreme eastern margin of town, retraced his way. Abreast a lightless stable he heard the muted whisper of men inside and caught the shift of a body. But what he looked for was not to be found — the evidence of DePittars's men being in town. That they would come, he no longer doubted. His reasoning had arrived at that conclusion half an hour ago, and all his instincts subsequently had verified the thought-out belief. The feel of it was in the air; the sense of it lay on men's faces as they passed him, stepped away from him. Off Railroad Avenue a few paces he went into another gridironing alley of the Crossing and found it to be twenty minutes past the hour. Going over, he entered the saloon.

He realized then all Buffalo Crossing was sitting expectant. His entry did something to that heavy crowd. There was a reaction that reminded him of dropping a stone into still water. All those men watched him — slowly turned and watched him. At the tables the games stopped, but he had the feeling that those games were all this while being fitfully played, without attention. Gilliam was not to be seen. Nor was Gib Smith. The inspection completed, he swung about and left the White Palace, heading for his office. The disappearance of Gib puzzled him. He had not seen his partner since noon, and, as unimportant as the fact was, it somehow added mystery to

41

this evening so full of threat and secret scheming. Between the White Palace and the courthouse only one man besides himself walked abroad. When he reached his office, he found Mack Setters waiting.

For the moment Setters said nothing, but Travis got the hint of a troubled, confused mind behind the fixity of the gambler's expression. Setters stared up, his body motionless against the wall. His clothes, Travis noted, were marked by bits of hay chaff. Setters lowered his eyes.

"I am going back to her, Travis."

Travis nodded gravely: "I'd hoped you'd work it out that way, Setters."

"But we can't stay here in the Crossing," muttered Setters. "We'd never live it down."

"Go far enough away so that Buffalo Crossing and your mistakes won't ever catch up," said Travis.

"I wish," went on Setters, "you'd walk to Railroad Avenue with me."

"Sure."

Travis went out ahead of the gambler. They swung abreast and followed the walk back towards the White Palace, entirely alone on the street. Across from them a second-story window fell with a report that was like a gunshot, and Setters flung up his head with an accompanying sharp intake of breath. Close-eyed, all his nerves cool within him, Travis saw a woman pass behind the window and then lower a shade. Setters whispered something, looked straight ahead, and spoke rapidly.

"I was told to bring you out here. I'm going through with it for the sake of appearances. Listen . . . DePittars is in the alley behind Ray Steptoe's stable. It's the best I can do for you . . . and Tom Gilliam's behind all this. Derwent and DePittars are nothin' more than monkeys on his chain. I'm leaving. Get out of sight in a hurry."

Saying it, he stepped back and aside. When Travis looked around, Setters was gone — vanished down a narrow runway between the Buffalo Hotel and the Longhorn Restaurant.

Travis walked on with an unvaried stride for another dozen paces. At that point the black mouth of Steptoe's stable opened on his flank, and, still holding a tight rein on his acts, he swung deliberately and went in. He was at once plunged in pure darkness. Sidestepping, he placed himself in a corner of the opening and looked down the street. At once he saw the mark of the trap out of which he had just moved. By the courthouse stood a man, obviously posted and waiting. Another figure idled forward from a different angle and came openly on until he had reached the hotel porch, and here he made his stand.

"Cold killing," said Travis, and felt a first warm stream of anger break through the chill tightness of his body. He faced about, cat-footed the length of the stable, and paused at the back doorway. Horses moved in the rear compound, but, as he loitered, he concluded all of DePittars's gang had spread to other points for the ensuing play; and, acting on that belief, he stepped out, circled the little compound, and followed the consequent alley to Custer Street. Facing back toward Main, he saw the loose, shackling form of a man leaning against the exact corner of a building and obviously waiting for something to show up on Main. Light came across from the White Palace sufficiently strong to identify him. This was Nick DePittars.

The anger died out of Clay Travis, and some chemical change passed through his veins to leave him isolated and cool and indifferent. It were as if part of him went away and left only the essentials of the fighting machine behind. He stepped soundlessly over the tricky boards and traveled down the silent dust until he had come within forty feet of the turned and waiting Nick DePittars. And at that point he stopped, drew his muscles together, and sent his call ahead.

"All right, DePittars."

DePittars hurled himself about with a terrific leap, a great gust of air pouring out of his mouth. All his features were away from the light and so obscured — and he broke for the center of the street at a dead run. He yelled: "Travis!" He stopped dead. He emitted one black curse, and afterward his lank body seemed to break in the middle. Clay Travis remained rooted, but his nerves and his muscles answered the warning of that fractional moment. His broad palm slapped the protruding gun butt and wove it upward and forward. A wisp of wind touched his cheek, and a detonating roar smashed the thin-drawn silence to fragments; and then his own tardy shot roared out deeply and found its fair mark. DePittars's broken cry went wailing along the street and high over the housetops, and DePittars fell with some short effort to keep his feet. He called again, but it was a small and despairing cry that died in his throat.

Of a sudden another gun began beating up the disturbed echoes from a place across Main. Dust rolled in Travis's face as the bullet ploughed its way beside him. A second was higher, wider, and he heard it hit the wood of the adjacent building. After that, he located the marksman in the White Palace alley and went forward on the run, seeing the man's gun muzzle spew out a crimson-purple bloom. His own reply went aside of its mark, yet the slash of the lead along the saloon wall obviously shook the DePittars henchman, for he faded into the depths of the alley and fired no more.

Travis meant to follow but never did. Out there in the center of the street he was halted by a sudden burst of guns all along the walls. One crashing echo and another went bounding upward to the sky. House lights flashed on; house lights winked out. Bodies wove from black aperture to still blacker aperture with a spider-like swiftness; and five of the outlaw's crew, elbow to elbow and bracketed by the glow of the hotel, slowly gave ground. One stumbled and dropped. Doggedly the others closed that gap and kept the deliberate backward pacing. Men's voices were rising in full halloo; the fusillade was catching on. Something had happened to the town. The taste of blood was in its mouth, and now it rose and spoke with a more deafening accent of fury. Standing silent, all the action out of his hands, and nothing needed of him now, Travis felt a profound pity sweep over him for those raggedly retreating four, hemmed in by an increasing wall of townsmen to either side. An end outlaw fell; a moment later the middle man of the remaining trio seemed to be bodily punched off his feet. There was nothing left for the last two then but to break and make a try for the near darkness. And motionless, Travis saw them make the try. One made it; the other lunged to the earth with his fingers touching those shadows that meant safety.

It was over as swiftly as that. The firing fell to a sporadic challenging beyond the courthouse, and that way a whirling, confused group of men rushed. There was a long cry from the distance; the doors of the White Palace came open and were held thus while the golden lamp beams gushed out. Gib Smith flashed across that puddled illumination with Mack Setters behind him. Gib came up, breathing hard, words roughened.

"We've broken their backs, Clay! By God, there's no more DePittars and no more DePittars gang!"

Mack Setters came within arm's length of Travis and said slowly: "I said I'd maybe pay off my debt to you someday soon." And, holding up a gun, he added: "I had my part in this."

"Setters," said Travis, "how much of that little talk you spilled before the fight did you mean?"

"All of it."

"Gillliam pulled the strings?" pressed Travis.

"Yes."

"Then," cried Gib Smith, "let's go get him!"

"No," interrupted Travis. "Say nothing about it. This is my affair."

"I'm through with him now," muttered Setters. "I'll never get inside of the White Palace again, and I'll never dare stay within reach of Gilliam. Travis, I tried to borrow five hundred from him to send the girl out of the country . . . and he wouldn't give it to me."

Travis moved forward, saying: "Come with me." He shouldered through the crowd at the saloon door and went inside. Gilliam was not in sight, but he knew where to find the man. Rounding the counter, he kicked open the inner office door and faced the saloonman. Gilliam stood with his back to a wall, a brooding watchfulness etching his florid cheeks. Part of the crowd started to come in, but Travis motioned those urgent ones back, and shut the door in their faces.

"Gilliam," he said, "these things you'll do. Tell Derwent in the morning to resign. And pay this man the five hundred he wants . . . now."

Gilliam's hard face seemed to set. The silence went on. Travis repeated patiently: "Now, Gilliam." And Gilliam walked to his safe and knelt beside it. When he rose, he threw five folded bills on the table, and he said contemptuously: "It's you I'm buyin' from now on, Travis?"

"Open the door," called Gib Smith, "and tell the crowd what you know about this monkey, Clay."

"No," said Clay. "If Gilliam goes, another crook would take his place. I'd as soon have you to watch as any other,

46

Tom. And I'll watch you. I'm going to be next sheriff of this county, and you won't be buying me. You've lost your gang. Maybe you'll get another . . . but I'll break it up. Maybe you'll try again for me, for no crook ever learns better. But I'll know where the try comes from, and that will make it interesting. Remember it, Tom, next time you get ambitious."

Gilliam had nothing to say, nor was Travis waiting for a reply. He moved to the side door with the sense of haste in him, and he went down Hogan's alley into Custer Street and across to the Rambeau house. Rambeau was there on the porch, a straining anxiety on his cheeks; and Gail stood at the top of the steps, straight and silent and queerly rigid. When she saw him, she said, slowly: "I have kept your supper hot for you, Clay." But the next moment she walked down to him and put her hands against his chest, and he felt the trembling of her body.

"What's this?" he murmured, puzzled by the laconic words.

"I'm training myself to be a peace officer's wife," said Gail. "And I guess I might as well start now. There'll be no crying, Clay."

"Never think of fear," said Clay quietly. "What's written is written."

Rambeau, turning through the doorway, called over his shoulder. "Still, it's comfortin' to know that story's closed. Supper's waitin'."

THE KID FROM RIVER RED

I

"STAND AND DELIVER"

The stage road came out of the open and smoky south as straight as a string, dipped across a small depression and strained toward a pass between the northern buttes. Right where the wagon ruts cut into the depression lay the youth from River Red, gray clothes blending with the sandy soil and some of that soil heaped over him to make the concealment more effective. He had a shotgun cuddled to his side, a floppy coat, a bandanna pulled up over his face, and a drab hat jammed over his ears. Between the rim of the hat and the edge of the bandanna nothing was revealed but the bright, eager flash of agate-blue eyes; and these eyes were at present immovably fixed on a train of dust kicked up yonder by an advancing stage.

In all the length and breadth of the desert no worse a place could have been found for a hold-up. There wasn't a tree or a butte or a rock within three miles, and, though a circling line of bald ridges ran east and north of him, about twenty minutes off these made a perfect view for anybody who might be watching the youth's antics. To make the situation more dangerous, he had left his horse in the only roundabout arroyo deep enough to conceal the animal, and this was fully eight hundred yards removed. But all great artists work with original ideas, and the youth from River Red had embarked on an outlaw's life with a most definite belief in his own toughness and ability. He was scarcely sixteen and so far had a clear record — except for, perhaps, the occasional appropriation of a maverick, which in this land and time was less than no crime at all. Briefly, he awaited the stage here because nobody would ever think of such a thing.

Meanwhile, the stage, doing a good twelve miles an hour, rolled forward. Presently the outline of it became distinct, and the youth saw there was but a single man, the driver, sitting on the box; and, when he noted this, a grunt escaped him to indicate both relief and disappointment. One man was easier to handle than two, but an unguarded stage meant skinny rewards. Looking about him, eyes almost violet with excitement and intensity, he inspected the hills to his left and rear. Also, he mentally measured the distance to his horse and again figured the time it would take him to run that far. These things checked, he turned back to the immediate business in hand. The stage rolled on, great flares of dust spouting up into the sun-scorched sky. The clank of chains became audible, also the combined groaning of wheels and singletrees. Sinking a little lower, the youth nursed the shotgun forward and brought his knees beneath him. He cleared his throat, muttered something to himself, and flicked a palm underneath the hat brim to halt the streaming sweat that bit into his eye. When the stage was so close at hand that he saw the driver's face, staring directly between the near animal's ears, he leaped from the depression, charged aside, and swung the shotgun against the driver's body.

"Draw up!" he yelled, voice cracking slightly. And when he heard it, he cursed and yelled again. "Draw up!"

The driver, old Lew Lannigan, had been handling ribbons for thirty years, and it was not in any sense a new story to him. He had no intention of displaying resistance, for he considered it no part of his duty to argue with outlaws. But what did send his hand more swiftly than usual to the brake rod was the tremor of excitement in the road agent's command. Having seen the business end of a gun a great many times, Lew Lannigan well understood how dangerous a thing it was in the fingers of a nervous one. Therefore, his promptness in jamming on the brakes. The stage curved into the depression, sprang violently up from compressed springs, and halted dead abreast the youth from River Red. It was a nice maneuver. The driver was in a poor position to fire even if he chose, and the passengers of the stage were under full control. A woman inside screamed, and another woman said: "Donna, stop that squealin'. Haven't you ever been held up before? Think nothing about it."

"Keep your mittens elevated," said the youth definitely. "Passengers step out."

The coach door opened, and a woman — young and handsome and smiling slightly — stepped to the ground. Following her came another woman, no more than a girl and not smiling at all; she had the oval, dusk-tinted face of part-Mexican blood and dark, liquid eyes that watched the youth in evident fright. The youth was for some unaccountable reason impelled to reassure the girl. "No fear," he said with a broad condescension. "I never hurt a lady in my life. I prey only on corporations. Stand fast just a minute and it will soon be done. Mister Driver, reach down with one hand and throw off the express box. No monkey business . . . throw it clean out here."

The driver shifted his tobacco and obeyed, swinging the box out from beneath his seat and landing it directly at the feet of the youth. "Yore trouble is goin' to be poorly repaid, fella. Nothin' much in that box today."

"Too bad," grunted the youth calmly. "But the experience is worth as much as the money to me."

"I'll estimate you'll get plenty experience," agreed the driver. "Robbin' a stage ain't half the fun. Other half comes when a posse fogs you around the landscape. Whut possessed you to tackle a stage out here?"

"Never expected me to pop up from the ground, did you?" asked the youth, quite apparently enjoying his triumph.

"It's an unlikely spot," said the driver, and let his eyes roam across the hills.

"That's why I did it here," explained the youth. "My style's to hit 'em where they ain't. You'll hear more of me."

"Speakin' with due respect," grunted the driver, "you better cut the palaver and send us on our way. Should a bunch of riders pop out of the pass yonder, you'd be in a pickle."

The youth bowed to the ladies. "You are at liberty to proceed," he said quite formally.

"Thank you for being so kind," said the older of the two. She had hazel eyes that seemed to smile independently of her lips. "I shall remember so gallant a bandit." With that, she entered the coach. But the younger one, whose Mexican blood cast so pleasant a glow over her face, had regained her composure. She stared severely at the youth, saying — "Señor, you frighten me." — and hurried into the vehicle as if frightened by her own boldness.

"Didn't mean to hurt you one bit," asserted the youth, taking a step nearer.

The driver's ironic voice came down. "Let's cut out the lollygaggin'. I got a long trip to San Juan."

The youth sprang back, gun stiffening on the driver. For one brief instant he had allowed his attention to wander, and the thought of what might have happened to him brought a pale flare of anger to his bright eyes. "Don't try nothin' on me, Mister Driver!" he ground out. "I'm not the man to monkey with. Get goin' . . . and go fast."

"Ain't I scared?" grunted the driver under his breath. Releasing his brake, he set the horses in motion and drew out of the depression. Twenty feet off he turned to yell. "Leave that box beside the road where I can pick it up on my way back trip. You won't need it." Then the stage retreated with banners of dust whipping high behind it.

After a moment's watchfulness, the youth unbuckled the straps of the express box, shot away the lock, and threw back the lid. There was nothing at all in the bottom of the box, but a kind of corner compartment held a promise. Opening this, the youth found a packet of papers about as thick as his fist, and, when he riffled through it, a gaudy assortment of purple and yellow printing met his eyes. But as young as he was, he knew these things were worthless to him. Though each sheet represented money, he knew that it was money in some mysterious form that only bankers knew much about. To him it was a worthless haul and his first introduction to an important fact concerning outlawry: money had a manner of assuming many useless shapes.

The youth accepted the turn of fortune philosophically. "Oh, well. Better luck next time. But I held up a stage, didn't I? I got experience. Now I better drift."

Turning, he ran along the depression as it curved and deepened across the desert. When he came to his horse, he mounted, left the arroyo, and pointed for the eastern ridge. Half an hour later he was well sheltered on the heights, watching the trail behind. Nothing moved off there.

"They better stay clear of me," he muttered, "or I'll run 'em bowlegged."

So observing, he got down and unwound a blanket roll tied behind the saddle. In it was a change of clothes that he proceeded to swap for the old ones — new hat, coat, and pants. The discarded garments he rolled in a tight bundle, added the bandanna, and — after some thought — the packet of non-negotiable securities. Any number of rocks offered him a hiding place, and he buried the bundle in a regular cairn. This deed performed, he again got to the saddle and rode at a rapid gait through one ravine and another for perhaps eight miles, or until he arrived at a trail due east and west. This he took, traveling now a little more leisurely. And about the middle of the afternoon he came to San Juan, just a blue-eyed and slightly gawky youngster as the town had seen many thousand times. If his glance was sharper than to be expected in one of his age, or if his features held a preternaturally pinched and poker-faced gravity, it was not really extraordinary. In the hot and fecund Southwest, boyhood was often a brief affair, and manhood came too frequently with a cruel suddenness. Still many seasons shy of majority, the youth from River Red could truthfully say he had neither home nor parents, and that he had done the full work of a man since twelve. Outlawry was for him a release from drudgery and a distorted revival of that play impulse that had been practically crushed out of him.

His entry was somewhat hesitant and wary, but, after he had drawn up at a saloon hitch rack and dismounted, and after finding himself to be no target of accusing eyes, a measure of swagger came to him. He raked San Juan's single street with a regard that was both alert and patronizing, as befitted one who had boldly invaded the camp of the enemy. He regarded the stagecoach standing by the stable, the drowsing Mexicans, the few frame dwellings mixed with the inevitable adobe structures. Having thus conducted his tactical reconnaissance, he entered the saloon — immediately to find the stage driver there. Lew Lannigan was explaining the hold-up to an interested group in laconic phrases.

"In a place, I'm sayin', nobody but a durn fool would ever

think of holdin' me up. He'd never got out of it alive had a party come from the pass unexpected. Well, I braked down sudden. You bet I did. I'm paid to handle a ribbon, not to guard no express box. Moreover, that road agent was nervous. Plumb nervous. I saw his hands shakin'. That's what like to scared me stiff. Never can tell what a nervous fella will do."

The youth from River Red breasted the bar and motioned for a drink. A red color stained his neck, and his ears began to burn. Nervous? Like hell he was. Drinking down his potion like a veteran, he felt a great urge to put that old, leather-faced buzzard right on the subject. Killing the desire, he brooded darkly. Next time he held up a stage he'd get that fool off the box. Make him dance. And say: *"Nervous, was I? Never make allusions about your betters, see? I stood within five feet of you in San Juan and heard the brag you made. Be careful, mister, and don't do it again. You keep your mouth shut and don't monkey with the hand of doom."* That's all he'd say.

Having completed his narration, old Lew Lannigan moved to the bar for a drink. His eyes fell casually on the youth, focused, and remained intently still for a moment. Presently he swung to the bartender. "Where's Buck Duryea?"

"The sheriff?" countered the bartender, putting a slight edge of sarcasm on the words. "Why, now, he's off chasin' Dusty Bill some more."

"I got to tell him about this affair," said Lew Lannigan.

"You think that it was one of Dusty Bill's men that held you up?" inquired a spectator.

"Naw," grunted Lew Lannigan. "Dusty Bill or any of his men would know better than to pull it like that. And Dusty Bill would know blamed well I didn't have any money in the box today. His source of information would keep him from pullin' a johnny on an empty stage. Moreover, did you ever hear tell of any man in Dusty's crowd being nervous?"

The youth from River Red pricked up his ears at the mention of Dusty Bill's name — Dusty, the scourge of the land, the outlaw of outlaws.

Lannigan said: "Well, here's more grief for Buck Duryea."

"He'll pay no heed to you," declared the barkeep. "All he's worryin' about is chasin' Dusty Bill."

"That's what he was elected for . . . and that alone," said Lew Lannigan.

"He'll never fulfill the election promise," replied the barkeep, still ironic.

Lew Lannigan shook his head. "He'll come as close to doin' it as any man in the country."

"Which ain't very damn' close," maintained the barkeep. "I'm no friend of Dusty's, but I'll assert he's just about six too many fur anybody around San Juan. Buck Duryea's a good guy. Sure he is. But good guys die sudden when they monkey with Dusty Bill."

"Well, if I was the road agent that held up Lew Lannigan," added another bystander, "I believe I'd breeze outta the country. Dusty's men won't stand fur any competition in the outlaw trade. It's a closed market . . . and all his'n."

The youth from River Red toyed thoughtfully with his glass and kept his attention subdued at the bar; once he essayed a quick look about him and found Lew Lannigan's glance on him, a slightly speculative glance. But it was soon diverted elsewhere. Lannigan poked a bystander in the ribs and muttered: "Will you observe who is payin' San Juan a visit. Teeter Fink, no less, and ain't he got brass?"

The youth turned. A grotesque, scarecrow figure darkened the saloon doorway, slouching silently there a brief interval. His clothes were ragged and in keeping with a flat, gangling body surmounted by a bearded face. Out of that tangle of whiskers sparkled a pair of the deepest, darkest, most inquisitive eyes the youth had ever seen. At one sweep those eyes absorbed the saloon interior, its contents, and its significance. Then Teeter Fink passed on. Lew Lannigan paced to the door, and from this point of view reported the man's progress.

"He's gone to Magoon's store."

"That's just where you'd expect him to go," grunted the barkeep. "But whut brings him to town? Answer me that?"

"Plain enough," said Lew Lannigan. "Dusty Bill wants to know something, and he's sent Teeter Fink to find out. Ain't I said Dusty's got the best information-getting system in this country?"

"Too bad the sheriff ain't here to ask Teeter where Dusty Bill's hiding," was the barkeep's malicious observation.

Lew Lannigan turned to look in the opposite direction. He grinned slightly. "Oh, I dunno. Here comes the sheriff now."

"Judas Priest!" breathed the barkeep. "Whut'll happen when he sees Teeter Fink?"

The youth from River Red left the bar and went outside, casually passing Lew Lannigan and pausing at the edge of the saloon porch. A cavalcade filed in from the east, half a dozen drooping, dusty men with the glare of the westering sun cutting bronzed features into bold lines. Studying the leading horseman, the youth from River Red instinctively knew him to be the sheriff, Buck Duryea. The mark of authority was too plain to be missed. Duryea was tall, slim, and surprisingly young for his job. Cast in much the same mold as the average Western rider, there was at the same time a subtle difference in his bearing. The face of the man was firmer, more watchful, and touched with care. Above a bold chin and an equally bold nose rested a pair of gray, searching eyes; and, as he came abreast the saloon and turned his head toward the porch, those eyes fell on the youth. It was an odd feeling that shot through the youth then. Instantly he went on the defensive; instantly he summoned the full poker mask to repel the cool, careful scrutiny the sheriff gave him. But it lasted only a moment and was ended by a courteous bow on the sheriff's part. Not understanding just why, the youth from River Red bowed back. Afterward, the cavalcade passed on to halt in front of another building and to dismount there. The sheriff went inside, followed by his men.

The youth from River Red tapered off a cigarette. *Not a bad gent,* he admitted reluctantly to himself. *A man could like him. Kinda tough to consider him and me will probably battle it out someday. Can't let sentiment interfere.* Posted there, the youth waited and watched for developments, observing that other men, some of them seeming pretty responsible figures, followed the sheriff into the building.

II

"DUSTY BILL"

Inside the sheriff's quarters of the San Juan courthouse, Buck Duryea settled to a chair and built himself a cigarette. The other members of the posse assumed their several attitudes of relaxation, patently weary and pessimistic. Lon Young, the sheriff's chief deputy, looked at Duryea with an owlish disfavor. "Well," he grunted, "there's the end of another wild goose chase. By thunder, I'm ridden down to one big callus!"

"Didn't expect Dusty and his boys to be on the spot waitin' for us, did yuh?" drawled Buck Duryea.

"We're doin' a lot of runnin' around for no good purpose," said Lon Young.

"That's percentage," offered Duryea. "We'll have to follow

twenty cold trails to get a warm one."

"Seems a fool caper to me to hike off on every floozy whisper we get," objected Lon Young, and looked around him for support. But the rest of the crowd was silent, and Young's rather thin mouth narrowed increasingly. He was a sorrel-colored man, lean as a lath, and naturally taciturn.

"Never can tell which one of these whispers is the right one," was Duryea's patient rejoinder.

"I doubt 'em all," said the deputy.

"Sure," agreed Duryea. "You'd doubt your own parentage, Lon."

The deputy was about to snap out some testy reply when other men began to file into the office — older and more deliberate men. One of them, a rugged and middle-aged character with a dogged chin, closed the door and took a chair one of the posse members rose to offer him. Buck Duryea cast away the cigarette and squared around. "Not this time, Dane. Cold trail again."

Henry Dane laced his fingers across a substantial paunch and considered the information gravely. This was his habit, to ponder and to debate internally. In others it would have aroused resentment, but Henry Dane was too great a figure in the land to trifle with. In some small measure of truth it had once been said of this man that a tenth of all the shoes in America were made of leather off his cows; therefore, the West opined that, if pondering was responsible for his material prosperity, it might be well for people to indulge the habit.

"We'll never get him," said Lon Young. "I'm tellin' you that."

"You boys discouraged?" queried Dane quietly.

Sheriff Buck Duryea broke in. "Lon is speakin' for himself. He's always discouraged on an empty stomach. I have said before and I will repeat now that I was elected on the single platform of gettin' Dusty Bill. I'll live to see it through, or I'll die tryin'. But it will take time. I'm going at this my own good way."

"Proper," approved Dane. "That's why the cattlemen of the county picked on you, Buck. You don't wilt easy. Now listen. The Association held a meetin' at my ranch yesterday and increased the reward on Dusty to ten thousand dollars. Also to five each on the heads of his followers . . . Baldy Zantis, Sam Ellen, Tom DeStang, and Colorado Clarney. That's all of 'em, ain't it?"

"All he has left of his gang," agreed Buck Duryea. "He's pared 'em down to the best and most trusted fighters."

"Lot of money on those fellows," grunted the deputy.

"Maybe," said the cattleman, "but it ain't one-fiftieth of the harm Dusty Bill's done to the name of the state and to the prosperity of this county in particular. Dusty's outlived the old, hell-roarin' times, and he don't seem to realize it. When he goes down, we'll be enterin' a new age, but, until he goes down, San Juan's still what the rest of the country is pleased to call us . . . the land of shotgun law. Now, Buck, the Association agreed to do this if you approved . . . to establish a posse of ten men at each of about four settlements so that no matter where you may be on the chase, you can get reinforcements in a hurry."

Buck Duryea thought of it a little while and finally shook his head. "That'd be too many riders clutterin' the landscape. It ain't more men I need, Dane. Dusty can ride through a hundred as easy as he can dodge the six I've got here. I've considered this a long time, and the thing's clear to me. I'll keep ridin' and keep my ear to the ground. Sooner or later there'll be a break, and, when it comes, I'll move into action."

"We'll be ridin' forever," stated Lon Young.

"I don't think so," replied Buck Duryea. "Dusty Bill's a

cagey, clever devil, and he figures his moves mighty careful. But there is this kink in his nature . . . when he's pressed about so far, he loses his temper and all his caution. He bets reckless and strikes back like a crazy man. That's what I'm waiting for now. And," continued Duryea, casting a speculative glance around the room, "I have a hunch we won't have so long to wait."

"What makes you think so?" demanded Lon Young, suddenly interested. But Duryea only shook his head.

Henry Dane frowned a little. "There's one danger you shouldn't overlook, Buck. With all this dashin' about, from one place to another, you may be drawn off guard yourself and fall into a trap. And I'm sayin,' if Dusty Bill ever does pull you into a trap, it'll be a wicked one. That's the kind he sets. Consider it well. Dusty Bill has no compunctions about linin' you up for slaughter."

"Correct," agreed Buck Duryea. "I'm watchin' my step. It'd be just like him to make some hell-roarin' play to wipe me and the boys off the map at one move."

Henry Dane changed the subject abruptly. "You know the stage was held up today? And that Teeter Fink's in town?"

Buck Duryea straightened alertly. "The mornin' stage? Well, I better look into that."

"Lew Lannigan's got the dope," said Dane. "But what interests me is Teeter Fink, breezin' around here. He's got a damned inquisitive pair of eyes and plenty sharp ears . . . and he is Dusty Bill's spy, body and britches."

"I'm leavin' him alone," said Buck Duryea quietly. "Just between us, I consider Teeter Fink to be one of Dusty's weak points. Teeter's goin' to give that gang away one of these days. Leave that to me, Dane."

"Good enough," said Dane, and rose.

The meeting dissolved, and men strolled out to the street.

Buck Duryea stayed behind a few minutes to consider thoughtfully the flat surface of his desk. There was a map of the county spread on it, a map across which lines had been lightly traced with a pencil. Looking at these, Duryea shook his head.

"Won't do much good to try to plan anything definite. Dusty jumps around too much. I'll just have to keep moving and wait for the break. He's a gambler . . . and so am I." With that, he left the office.

Lew Lannigan saw him and crossed the street immediately.

"I heard about the hold-up, Lew," said Duryea. "Lose much?"

"It was an empty express box," explained Lannigan. "But what gets me is where he pulled the job . . . just two miles short of the pass and plumb in the open. And him nervous to boot."

"That lets out Dusty's bunch," reflected Duryea. "None of that gang knows what nerves are. Who's the kid roamin' towards Magoon's store?"

The stage driver turned to find the youth from River Red moving casually along the far sidewalk. "Him? Dunno. Thought I sorter reco'nized him once, but I guess I don't. Some new punk . . . ."

There was a sudden yell of alarm and a warning, followed by the sound of pounding hoofs. Swinging about, the sheriff saw trouble. A team hitched to a light rig had backed away from a hitch rack near Magoon's and was now breaking into a plunging run. For one moment the horses were within control; the next moment the effort of a man to intercept them added the extra measure of fear. They broke madly, straining away from each other, rig careening from side to side. A greater shouting rose, and a woman screamed. Leaping forward, Buck Duryea saw this woman trip in her effort to cross the street and fall directly in the path of the oncoming brutes.

As the sheriff ran, his arm went toward his gun. But the impulse was defeated before it got under way, for the townsmen lining the far building wall were in a direct line with any shot he might make. Turning slightly, he aimed for the girl, now half risen. A slim figure came into one corner of his vision — it was the youth from River Red — and dropped to a knee. Almost simultaneous with that move a single gunshot crashed like a dynamite explosion through the town, and the off horse of the team sagged. Buck Duryea halted in his stride, caught up the girl, and pushed her aside. Dust rose in great yellow sheets, and the remaining horse, brought to a halt by the anchoring weight of the dead one, fought with an unreasoning fury in almost the exact spot where the girl had been — bucking against the harness and kicking the rig to splinters. The men of the town ran forward, and a tide of excited, contradictory talk rose.

Buck Duryea had shoved the girl against the saloon porch, but he caught up with her again and held out an arm to keep her from falling. "Take it easy, Donna," he said. "You're all right. Excitement's finished."

The girl lifted her face, all the pert prettiness gone out of it. "*Señor* Buck . . . I fell! Thank you . . . thank you!"

"Sure," soothed the sheriff. "But don't thank me. Thank this lad that got in a good shot."

The youth from River Red stood beside the porch, attempting to assume a nonchalance that only accented the awkward self-consciousness about him. "Shucks," he grunted, "that wasn't nothin'. I could make that shot ten times out of ten."

The girl looked at him with wide, deeply dark eyes and made a small curtsy. "You are ver' brave, *señor*. It is to you I owe my life."

"Nothin' to it," said the youth, increasingly embarrassed.

62

The girl's brows arched a little, and her glance seemed to dig into him more. "My name," she said, after a pause, "is Donna Chavez." Then she turned and hurried away.

Buck Duryea reached for his cigarette papers, eyeing the youth. "That was quick thinkin', old fellow. And a damned good shot. You don't look so ancient, but you certainly carry an old head on your shoulders."

"It ain't age that counts," said the youth with an air of tolerant wisdom. "It's experience. Experience is the thing. I've had lots of it."

"Good enough," drawled the sheriff. "Don't believe I've seen you before. New here?"

"Yeah. I'm from River Red."

"That would make you the River Red Kid," considered the sheriff, well knowing that such a name, given under such circumstances, had all the effect of a medal. The youth pursed his lips and struggled to maintain his manner of grave assurance.

"I reckon," he admitted. "One name's as good as another when a feller's traveled around considerable, like me."

"Sure," approved the sheriff. "Come in today, I suppose. Strange that I didn't happen to meet you on the road."

"I come straight from the east," said the youth swiftly.

Duryea nodded and turned away. "If there's anything I can do for you," he called back, "be sure and let me know. One good turn deserves another."

The River Red Kid muttered something that Buck Duryea didn't quite catch. For that matter he dismissed the youth completely from his thoughts almost on the moment. Going along the walk, his eyes narrowed on the doorway of Magoon's store, inside of which Teeter Fink and Magoon were undoubtedly hatching up some sort of hell. He had nothing on Fink, but, nevertheless, the bushy-bearded man carried the secrets of Dusty Bill's bunch in his head and was everlastingly faithful in his performance of that outlaw's orders. Something of more than average importance had brought Fink here today. Turning that belief thoughtfully over in his mind, Buck Duryea passed into the store to catch Fink and Magoon deeply engrossed in a subdued conversation that came to an abrupt halt. Teeter Fink swung around defensively and stared at the sheriff with an open defiance.

"Nice day, Teeter," observed the sheriff. "Come from your mill?"

"I did, if it's any of your business," grunted Fink.

"Seen Dusty lately?"

"I'd be tellin', wouldn't I?" jeered Fink. "Don't try to spy around me."

"But you've seen him in the last day or two," pressed the sheriff casually.

"What of it?" growled Fink.

"Nothing much," drawled the sheriff. "But, when you see him again, you tell him I heard of his little boast to the effect he was goin' to shoot me in the back like a dog. The inference bein' I'd be runnin' away from him at the time. Also tell him the statement is some wide of the actual truth."

"*You* tell him," snapped Fink, and deliberately placed his back to the sheriff.

Magoon, the storekeeper, looked on with a heavy-lidded passiveness. Buck Duryea turned slowly and walked into the hot afternoon's sunshine with a dissatisfaction boiling up in him. *Story there,* he reflected moodily, *if I could just get it. Dusty's told him to come in, for some good and sufficient reason. What's the reason? Something's in the air and has been for the last forty-eight hours. If I don't look sharp. . . .*

"What are you scowling at, Buck?"

He lifted his head to find a rather tall and pleasant-faced

girl standing directly in his path — that same girl who had smiled through the stage hold-up. Buck Duryea reached for his hat, the gravity on his cheeks relaxing somewhat. "Hello, Anne. Thought you were visitin' at Fort Smith?"

"Came back," said she, equally laconic. "Got lonesome."

"For me, I suppose?" countered Buck Duryea, grinning.

"Might be some truth in that, Mister Duryea."

"If that's a hint," said Buck, "stay around a while and let me entertain you. Where's your adopted orphan child?"

"Donna? In the house recovering from the shock of that wreck. Poor girl, that's the second scare she got today."

"As how?" queried the sheriff.

"Haven't you heard? She and I were in the stage that got held up. Donna thought she was going to be captured. But really the road agent was nice about it. Bowed and scraped. He must have been a philosopher for when Lannigan told him the express box was empty, what do you suppose he did? He said it didn't matter much because the experience was more important. Can you feature anything more funny?"

Buck Duryea's attention, which had been more on the appearance of Anne's clear, slim face than on her words, suddenly came to a definite focus. "He said what?"

"That experience counted most," repeated Anne. "Why?"

"I've heard that remark from another source real recent," said Buck Duryea, softly alert. "Something to look into. A man's mouth often gives him away, Anne."

"You're so up to your ears in trouble," said the girl, "that you don't hear half what I'm saying. Buck, do you want to know what really brought me back from Fort Smith? Listen. I heard a very strange and disturbing thing over there. It's such a creepy, horrible thing that I couldn't sleep last night. Everybody knows it . . . everybody's whispering about it. Buck . . . you and your men are to be trapped, lined up, and shot down! That's why I'm back . . . to warn you."

"Sounds like a typical Dusty Bill scheme," opined Buck Duryea.

"Don't take it so lightly!" exclaimed the girl. "It's spoken of as if the outlaws had the trap all set and ready for you! I asked questions. Naturally, nobody told me any more. But I came back in a hurry because I gathered this killing was to be done within a day or two. Buck, you've got to watch yourself!"

"I'll try, Anne," agreed Buck, and swung off in the direction of the courthouse. A man — one of his posse members — came idly down the street, and Buck Duryea stopped him and issued a quiet order. "See that kid lounging by the saloon porch, Alki? The one with the long nose and the yellow hair? He said he came into town by way of the eastern trail. Now you lope back on that trail about ten miles and inquire of the settlers along the road if they saw a boy of his proportions pass by."

"Okay," said the posseman, and strolled off.

Going into the office, Buck Duryea dragged a chair by the window and sat down. In a little while he saw Teeter Fink ride by, outbound from town. Almost directly afterward the River Red Kid got to his horse and likewise left the street.

Just a youngster, grunted the sheriff to himself, *and plenty of stuff in him to make a good citizen. Can't let a boy like that go bad . . . it ain't right. What's his part in this business, anyway? Something's smoking up, and I've got a hunch it won't be long now.*

III

"THE TRAP"

The River Red Kid had loitered on the saloon porch with a purpose, which was to keep track of Teeter Fink. And when the latter left San Juan, the Kid followed at a discreet interval. But directly after leaving the town behind, the Kid changed tactics and rode into the hills to the south. At the end of ten minutes he was quite buried in the rolling ridges and ravines. From one high point he saw Fink curving down the main north and south stage road, and, varying his course to conform, he presently fell into the stage road a little beyond the pass. By and by he heard the sharp tattoo of Fink's fast-traveling pony, and instantly the sharp, blue eyes began to freshen with excitement. He knew the danger of this sort of meeting, but even so he dared not risk turning about to confront Fink and arouse the other's suspicion. So he idled onward, slouched in the saddle and making his ears do double duty for him. Fink had slackened speed, once appearing to halt entirely. A little later the outlaw's henchman swept forward at an impatient pace, came abreast of the Kid, and reined in. Fink's piercing, brilliant, black eyes seemed to stab the youth.

"What you doin' here?"

"Waitin' for you," said the Kid evenly.

"Yeah?" grunted Fink, openly hostile. "Whut for?"

"I want to join Dusty Bill's gang," was the Kid's astonishingly calm proposal.

Fink's eyes narrowed to slim apertures of harsh light. "Whut makes you think I know anything about Dusty Bill?"

"Heard it said in the saloon," said the Kid. "I'm a great hand to pick up things."

"Yore just a punk," stated Fink, "and you got a god-awful

nerve bracin' me thisaway. Don't you know what happens to folks that get too cur'ous?"

"You got me wrong. I'm not curious. I want to join Dusty's gang, and I want you to let me see him. I ain't no punk, either. I been places, and I done things."

All this while they were riding side by side into the open desert. Teeter Fink was probing the Kid with a constant, aggressive inspection. Suddenly he laughed sardonically. "So you think I'd fall for that guff? Go on back to Buck Duryea and tell him it's a poor play. Sendin' kids out to trap folks like Dusty . . . if that ain't a hell of a note. Now you beat it!"

"Don't believe me, uh?" asked the Kid. "Well, look ahead on the ground there."

They were, by this time, approaching the depression where the stage had been held up, and the River Red Kid's pointing finger indicated the abandoned express box. "I did that," he added.

"You?" boomed Teeter Fink. "How many more damn' lies you goin' to tell me?"

"Want proof?" challenged the Kid. "Turn off to the hills. I'll show you I did it."

Fink halted and faced the Kid. "What kind of proof?" he wanted to know.

"What I took out of the box," said the Kid.

A cold, shaft-like flash of light emerged from the imbedded eyes of the go-between. Suddenly he nodded. "All right. You show me."

They set off beside the arroyo, followed its ragged course, and tackled the foothills. The River Red Kid confidently led the way up a widening ravine, turned through one lesser alley and another, and at last halted. Dismounting, he approached a pile of rock. But, just short of it, he swung around to face Fink and very shrewdly said his say. "You move over so I can keep you in sight better. I know what you came up here for . . . to get anything valuable I might have and leave me flat."

A change came over Fink's face. He stiffened, relaxed, and prodded his pony a few yards aside. The youth, still maintaining a watch on the go-between, rolled the rocks aside and retrieved his bundle of clothes. Opening the bundle, he took out the packet of securities and held them up for Fink to see. "That's what I got. But they're no good for fellows like us."

"No money?" queried Fink, visibly disappointed.

"Nope. But it shows you I held up the stage, don't it? I'm no spy of Duryea's. I want to join Dusty's gang. You goin' to take me to him?"

Fink apparently had already made up his mind. "You come with me," he said. "I ain't promisin' you anything, see? But yore too damn' inquisitive to be floatin' around the landscape like this. Ride right beside me."

The Kid left the clothes lying there but tucked the securities in his pocket. Mounting, he ranged beside Fink, and so they passed on along the rugged spine of the hills, saying nothing at all. It was sundown, with the last, long shafts of the sun exploding riotously in the sky. Then twilight came and held on for its brief period of calm, empurpling beauty. Fink began to cast his eyes more alertly behind and beside him as they fell into the deeper contortions of the hills; his manner became more guarded, more constrained. At dusk they came around a bald butte and faced a bowl-like clearing within which sat a mill beside a creek, a rambling house, and a few outsheds. Nothing stirred here; no kind of life was evident; no beam of lamplight broke the graying fog. Fink began to sing a loud, unmelodious song about a girl named Annie Lee, but after the first dozen words ceased. Coming to the front of the house, he got down and ordered the Kid to go in ahead of him.

"And be damn' careful in yore acts," he warned. "Do just what I tell you to do . . . no more, no less."

The River Red Kid passed into a dark room, stale with tobacco smell and still containing the stifling air of the hot day past. Fink passed him, lit a lamp on the table, and walked to another room, closing the door behind. Another and more remote door banged shut, and somewhere was the faint, indistinguishable murmur of a voice. After that, he heard boots pass quickly across the floor, and in a little while horsemen — two or three of them — rode out of the clearing in evident haste. Through all of this the River Red Kid remained silent and steady. Once he shifted so as to put his back to the wall, and his eyes, again deepening to violet, scanned every crack and cranny of the place. Sweat began to trickle down his forehead to indicate the ordeal he was passing through. For he was no fool, and he understood what might well enough happen to him at the very turn of a word or lift of an eye. But, stolidly clinging to his established and definite purpose, he waited out the situation.

A door opened, and a stranger came through with a queer, cat-like suppleness of stride. He was not much taller than the River Red Kid but obviously matured and seasoned. His face had a strange lightness about it — lacking the usual deep tan and the usual weather lines; at each lip corner the curve of his mouth ran slightly upward to pull the flesh slightly off the teeth and so give him the aspect of continually smiling. His eyes, as well as the River Red Kid could determine, were a shade of pale slate and oddly large and unwinking. In fact, he seemed as he stood there on the balls of his feet to be lacking the usual muscular tremor and restlessness of the average man. The Kid quelled a twinge of uneasiness and held the glance, knowing he had somehow stumbled upon a member of Dusty Bill's gang. One corner of his mind wondered what Buck Duryea would think if he knew the proximity of the outfit.

"So you want to join up, kid?" said the stranger in a slurring, husky voice.

"My intention," said the Kid stoutly.

"Had the idea for some time?"

"Oh, for a matter of months. Had to get a little experience, y'understand. So I held up the stage. Nothin' to it."

"Sometimes not," mused the stranger, more definitely smiling. "Think you can do this Dusty Bill some good by joinin' him, huh?"

"Listen," admonished the Kid, "I can ride anything that's got hair, drill the carnation out of a milk can at ninety feet, track like an Indian. I'm not dumb. I've had experience."

"Ever see Dusty Bill?" drawled the stranger.

"No, but I will," stated the Kid. "When I make up my mind to do a thing, I don't let go. I ain't a man to monkey with."

"As I observe," said the stranger softly. "Well, boy, you've got your wish and you've plumb arrived at your destination. I'm Dusty Bill."

The River Red Kid's eyes widened, and his stare grew pronounced. Unconsciously, a trace of disappointment appeared, and Dusty Bill, never a man to miss the quick changes of expression on faces opposed to him, caught it.

"Well?" he challenged.

"I thought you was bigger," blurted out the Kid, and could have bitten off his tongue.

But Dusty Bill grinned, a peculiarly unsentimental and heatless grin. "They make outlaws small these days, kid. Like you, for instance. Can't pack a lot of weight around in this game. Think you could do me good, huh?"

"I'm not a man to monkey with," declared the Kid. "In

some things I'm right smart. I found you, didn't I? Who else could have done that?"

"Ever kill a man?"

"No-o," admitted the Kid, and for once his air of worldly tolerance fell from him. He had never killed a man. That was the weak point in his armor, and he hoped, in a spasm of half fright, that Dusty Bill wouldn't pursue the thought. There was a still deeper humiliation to bear — he didn't like to kill and his toes curled at the very thought of it. But Dusty Bill cleared his throat and spoke with a change of tone. "All right, I'll take you on."

"Yeah . . . you will?" cried the Kid. "By gosh, that's swell!" Then he pulled himself back to the properly non-committal attitude of a hard man. "We'll get along all right," he finished.

"Now here's my chore for you," proceeded Dusty Bill. "Go back to San Juan. Stay there till I want you. Keep your eyes open, and see what the sheriff does, but don't leave town. I'm depending on you, understand? Even if a stray cat crosses the street, you make a note of it. You'll be my agent in town, clear?"

"Count on me," said the Kid, stiffening his spine. "But how'll I get in touch with you?"

"Leave that to me," replied Dusty Bill. "Get goin' now. And, by the way, I think you better kill a man before I see you again. That'll assure me of your intentions."

He put out his hand, and the Kid took it, to discover instantly that this small, whip-like man had muscles made of woven wire. The pressure of that grip bit into his fingers and numbed them, and a cold, creeping feeling went through his body. At the first opportunity the Kid pulled his hand away and stood a moment, uncertain and touched with an actual dread. The lamplight illumined Dusty Bill's face, a face that suddenly was wolfish in its cruelty; the smile was only a thin pressure of lips. The apparent friendliness of Dusty Bill's eyes had become but a freakish result of coloring, and the dead, flat stare continuing through the strained moments took on the venomous, glass-bright quality of a reptile.

"Get goin', kid," breathed Dusty Bill.

"Yeah, see you later," muttered the Kid and stumbled out the door, glad to be in the open again. His breath came small and fast, and he put the spurs into his pony, prompted by an impulse he could not at the moment fight away from. Leaving the clearing, he rose along a gentle grade, turned the face of a butte, and lost the lights of the house; as he did so, he seemed to fall apart. His throat hurt, and there was an ache in his lungs. Breathing deep of the crisp night air, he became aware of the freedom about him and the cheerful light of the full moon above. It was mighty pleasant to be securely in the saddle and riding again.

"But to kill a man," he muttered. "Good gosh, how'm I goin' to do that? That's . . . why, that's *murder!*"

A full mile along the ridge he heard the advance of a rider still unseen, and he promptly put himself off the trail and in the shelter of rocks. The rider came on at a steady gait, passed abreast, and disappeared in the direction of Dusty Bill's hideout. After a long wait, the River Red Kid regained the road and settled to a full gallop, fresh wonder in his mind. The moon had touched that man's face briefly and betrayed it. It was one of Buck Duryea's deputies and the name, if he remembered the saloon talk right, was Lon Young.

"What's he doin' with Dusty Bill?" pondered the Kid. "Great Smokes, he *ain't* doublecrossin' Buck Duryea?"

After repeating the first few lines of the song about little Annie Lee, Lon Young passed into the bowl and dismounted at the house porch. Entering, he found not only Dusty Bill, but Teeter Fink and the other four who constituted the gang. All of them were lounged about a table, drinking.

"Early," said Dusty Bill. "Meet the kid?"

"What kid?"

Dusty Bill grinned. "He must be good. Evidently faded right from sight. Why, a little, long-nosed, agate-eyed babe who tried to join me. I give him credit for nerve. Said he'd held up the stage."

"Never saw him," said Young, and showed sudden worry. "Wonder if he camped out and saw me come here. Judas Priest, Dusty, why did you let him go?"

"Aw, he's harmless. I told him he was a member and to go back and watch San Juan. You'll probably see him posted around town when you get back, lookin' wise as a bench full of judges. Takes life pretty serious."

But the deputy shook his head and in this was supported by Teeter Fink who spoke doubtfully. "Never should have let him go, Dusty. Bad business. Can't tell what a whelp like that will do. If he's got brass enough to sugar his way in here, he's got brass enough to betray you. Remember, there's a round total of thirty thousand dollars on the heads of you five men."

"Betray?" replied Dusty Bill. "What'll he betray? I'm here, but I'll be gone in an hour, and nobody's fast enough to find me. What's on Buck Duryea's mind, Lon?"

The deputy said: "He doesn't think you're this close, Dusty. He ain't got any idea you're within fifty miles. He's playin' a waitin' game and followin' all rumors."

Dusty Bill's thin mouth twisted. "That's fine. We'll give him another rumor to follow. Lon, you go back, and in the mornin' whisper to him that you've got it on good authority I'm passin' out of the hills and will strike Fort Smith in the middle of the afternoon. That will get him and his posse out of San Juan for a while."

"Then what?" asked the deputy.

"Then, when he gets to Fort Smith, we won't be there," grinned Dusty Bill. "But by dark of tomorrow Mister Buck Duryea, who was sworn to office on the single promise of gettin' me, will be dead and so will the bright boys followin' him. As for you, Lon, you ride to Fort Smith with him and also ride back to San Juan with him."

"Where you goin' to frame this play?"

"I'll take care of that," replied the outlaw.

The deputy showed a trace of nervousness. "Yeah, but how about me? If you're goin' to ambush him, how about me right in the middle of that party?"

Dusty Bill rose and pulled up his belt. "What you don't know won't hurt you, Lon. But you're safe. If it'll satisfy you any, do this . . . when you come back from San Juan with Buck's party, lag behind a little bit and go to the saloon for a drink."

"You're goin' to . . . ?"

"I'm goin' to catch him where he wouldn't dream I'd be," interrupted Dusty Bill, the words crawling out of his throat. "I'm goin' to put a bullet in the back of his skull as warnin' to this county that nobody's big enough to dog my heels. I've said I'd leave him dead in the dust, and I will. Come on, boys, we've dallied here long enough."

IV

"THE TRAP SPRINGS"

Standing in the bright sunshine of another hot San Juan morning, Sheriff Buck Duryea listened carefully to his chief deputy's tale.

"I've got this thing straight," said Lon Young earnestly. "Last night I had an idea in my bonnet. So I rode to the east. There's a Mexican farmer over yonder whose name I can't mention. He's a solid friend of mine. He said one of Dusty's men rode in for somethin' to eat . . . Baldy Zantis, it was. Zantis was out on scout, and he knew this Mexican pretty well. Sort of friendly to him, and in the course of the talk he let somethin' drop about the bunch bein' in Fort Smith today around noon. Then Zantis rode off. The Mexican told me in strict confidence."

"Sounds odd," observed the sheriff, "that Zantis would tell the Mexican and still more odd that the Mexican would tell you."

"Didn't I say the Mexican and Zantis were friends?" queried Lon Young. "And you know Dusty Bill's gang is ace high with 'most all Mexicans around here. He's been good to 'em. None of that race has ever given Dusty away yet. In this case, I did a favor for this Mex once and that's why he told me."

The sheriff studied the distance with half-closed eyes. "What's in Fort Smith?"

"A bank."

"Possible."

"Or, if not that," added Lon Young, "maybe he's making a shift of location and wants to stock up on grub."

"Also possible," agreed Buck Duryea. "Sounds fishy to me."

"You want rumors. Here's one for you," was the deputy's next remark, colder and more impatient.

"That's all it is," said Duryea. "But we'll act on it. Get the boys rounded up, will you?"

Lon Young ambled away. The sheriff walked into the stable, saddled his pony, and led it around to the office. As he did so, his thoughts were interrupted by sight of the River Red Kid, strolling down from the direction of Magoon's. In itself, the act meant nothing. But the Kid carried himself with an air of suppressed importance. There was a slight swagger in his walk, and his eyes kept roving restlessly from one part of the town to the other. At the saloon door, he cast away his cigarette, stared a long while at some object beyond the limit of the street, and passed inside.

Buck Duryea considered all this gravely. *Acts like he's got a bug in his bonnet. Damn' little fool. He never came in from the east trail yesterday, either. Sure as apples are green he held up that stage. Give himself plumb away with his talk about experience. Just another kid considerin' the glory of an outlaw's life . . . led on prob'ly by all the lyin' tales he's heard about Dusty Bill. There's the rotten part about outlawry. It influences kids to do the same . . . it turns the heads of good citizens. Wish I could do something with that boy. He's got the makin's of a man.*

Suddenly the sheriff, moved by one of those kindly impulses that so frequently possessed him, walked across the street and entered the saloon. As he approached the bar, he found the Kid taking a drink.

"Nice mornin'," said the sheriff, reaching for a cigar.

"Yeah," agreed the Kid. The blue eyes met the sheriff's gray glance and slid away. As young as he was, Buck Duryea could read a man's face, and he saw something like confusion on the countenance of the boy. And, as he observed this, he felt a deeper certainty of the boy's intrinsic worth. Hard or worthless characters never knew the stirrings of conscience. "Have a drink?" urged the Kid.

"Thanks, no," said the sheriff, and spoke as if he were addressing an equal. "I've got some business on tap, and it won't do to get blurred up with whiskey."

The Kid nodded and started for the door. The sheriff moved out to the porch with him and halted to touch off his cigar. Casually enough, he asked a question.

"Had any experience on the trail?"

"Some," said the Kid. "I can read sign. An Apache taught me."

"That's fine," approved the sheriff. His tone grew more confidential. "I'm mighty glad to hear it. If you stay around San Juan, I'll be using you in my posse. It's a tough country, and I'm always needin' good, stout men, like you."

"Me?" said the Kid, showing astonishment.

"That's right," agreed Buck Duryea. "I don't often make a mistake in judgment." He paused for a moment to let the phrase sink in. Cigar smoke curled about his calm face. "You see," he went on, in the same level, fraternizing manner, "it takes a tougher, harder, stiffer specimen of a man to keep the law than to break it. Ever think of that? Consider it. Any fool can go out and push over a stage or steal a few cows. Nothing to it. But to be honest and fight off the crooks . . . there's where the test of a fellow's nerve comes in. Next time I ride, I'll be swearin' you in, too."

The Kid said nothing. He held his cigarette tightly between his fingers and stared at the sheriff with a long, wondering glance. The members of the posse had collected at the stable and now came riding forward. Buck Duryea left the porch and started across to reach his horse. Halting and turning, he threw a casual afterthought back to the youth. "Ever notice our graveyard? There's a line down the middle of it. Decent

78

folks to one side, crooks to the other. You'll observe the honest folks have tombstones to mark their memories. The crooks have nothin' but a board headpiece that soon enough will rot into the growin' weeds. A crook's a fool to play the easy game, for it always ends up the same way. Well, see you later."

The River Red Kid watched the posse go, his attention riveted on the tall and easy figure of the sheriff leading off; and, as long as Buck Duryea remained in sight, the Kid never stirred from his place on the porch. But when the curve of the trail swallowed the outfit, the Kid threw away his cigarette and ambled along as far as a bench in front of the saddle shop. Here he sat down.

Not a bad gent, he admitted to himself. *Nossir, he talks to a fella like he meant it. I could like a guy like that. Ain't I in a funny fix now?*

The street moved with men and women bound on their various chores, and it occurred to him he was not obeying Dusty Bill's injunction to keep a sharp eye on all that transpired. Tipping his hat farther forward against the sun, he watched the scene unroll. A wagon came in; the stage departed; noon arrived; and, as he rose, strangely suspended between happiness and uneasiness, the Mexican girl, Donna, walked gracefully from a far house and came directly toward him. The Kid whipped off his hat, a flush of color staining his cheeks a deeper shade.

"*Señor,*" said Donna, "you will have dinner with us? Come."

"Me?" said the Kid. "Me?"

"Of a truth," agreed the girl and beckoned. The Kid, feeling the eyes of the world upon him, stepped awkwardly beside her and followed her into the house. Down a semi-dark hall he saw the other woman waiting — that one who had been with the Mexican girl on the stage. Not knowing just how it was all managed, he presently found himself sitting at a table with these two.

"It was nice of you to come," said the tall woman.

"Ma'am, that's a generous statement, but the truth is nowise in it. Folks like you are sure kind to endure a fellow like me. Why, I never sat at a table with a white cloth on it in my life."

"Señor," said Donna, sitting very prim across from him, "what is a tablecloth? You save my life."

"Shucks," muttered the Kid, and for the moment was utterly at a loss. But the small services of the meal saved the day for him, and the tall, serene lady spoke pleasantly of things the Kid only half heard. Before he quite realized it, the dinner was done, and he stood again at the door. And the Mexican girl's eyes, round and glowing, were looking up at him.

"Señor, there is a dance tomorrow night."

"Would you go with a fellow like me?"

"With all my heart," said Donna.

"By thunder, I'll be here!" exclaimed the Kid, and walked down the street in a haze of wonder. In the saloon he found the hands of the clock at two. It seemed incredible. Returning to the street again, he sat on the edge of the porch and marveled. *And I ate too much, that's what I did! Never missed a thing they passed me. And I talked. What'd I talk about? Lord, I wish I recalled. I bet I told 'em about my life since I was a pup of four. Lord, what kind of a fellow am I, anyhow? But they was kind . . . mighty kind to me that ain't known such a thing. Never knew folks was like that.*

Critically, he surveyed himself in the light of tomorrow's dance. He needed better clothes and a coat that wasn't so full of wrinkles, and, as his hand ran along the coat, it suddenly stopped at the bulge made by the packet of securities hidden

80

within the pocket. On the instant, the feeling of pride went out of him.

I knew I'd wake and find it a pipe dream, he thought. The bright flare of enthusiasm died from his eyes, and, humped against the porch pillar, he battled with reflections that jeered at him, accused him. So he sat, while the droning afternoon went along, and the sun fell into the west. When he at last roused himself from the spell, San Juan was astir, and the supper triangle was ringing in front of the restaurant.

Well, grunted the kid to himself, *what'm I goin' to do? Can't be two things at once. Can't dance with a nice girl and be in the wild bunch, too.* A pair of riders drew in from the hills and that reminded the kid of Sheriff Buck Duryea — and the sheriff's words exploded in his mind, at last significant. *"Easy to hold up a stage,"* that's what he'd said. *But hard to go right. How in thunder could a fellow like me, what never was an outlaw, know about such things? Well, I guess I'm cooked. Better ride from town and forget it.*

Automatically, he turned to the hotel and went over for supper. As he tackled his soup, he was deeply submerged in melancholy, but, when he had reached his pie, the normal optimism of youth had reasserted itself, and out of that optimism came an idea that sent him to the street with his blue eyes sharply bright again. It was going on dusk, and over San Juan lay a stillness and the smell of dust and sage. Pausing on the hotel porch, he built a cigarette and calculated his chances. *Nobody knows I held up that stage. Now, look. Here's this package in my pocket. Supposin' I get it back to the bank. That clears me. I won't steal no more. Nobody knows . . . except Dusty Bill, and his word don't count.*

The bank, he observed, was down toward Magoon's store, on the hill side of town. Doubtless there was a window he could break and through which he could pitch the packet of securities. And here was dark, deepening over and through the town like layers of soft, felt cloth. Of a sudden, lights sprang out of buildings and from the saloon came the twang of a guitar. The River Red Kid threw away his cigarette, mind made up. *I'll have to play it square. Can't go on any of the sheriff's posses and chase Dusty Bill. Wouldn't be right. But I can mind my own business and be honest.*

With the decision quite crystallized, all things seemed brighter. The very air had a wine-like vigor in it, and immediately a vast impatience possessed him to make restitution. By now the shadows of the porch had completely absorbed him. Men tramped along the boardwalk, murmuring amongst themselves, cigar tips creating points of light. The Kid waited another moment, then lifted himself over the porch and railing, and faded down an alley between buildings to the rear of town. Treading lightly, he passed the full length of San Juan, turned a corner, and flanked Magoon's store. This brought him to the hill side; and with infinite caution he crept as far as the side of the bank structure and waited.

There was a window, out of which gleamed a dismal, cross-hatched lamp glow. Adjoining it was a door. On the point of pressing in the glass of the window he conceived the idea of trying the door. It was, of course, locked, but his exploring hands ran along the bottom and found a small crevice. This was much better business than breaking glass and risking discovery; so he took the packet from his pocket, ripped it apart, and fed the individual slips of paper through the crevice.

When he stood up, he sighed profoundly, like one who had held a long, accumulating breath. *It don't make me exactly honest yet,* he reflected candidly, *but, by thunder, it's a beginnin'. Now I better get out of here before I'm found.*

Instead of retracing his path, he elected to sidle forward and come into the street at the open end, thus making a circle.

Onward, a distance of fifty yards — the bright moon aiding him considerably — he came to a gap in the building line. At this point he stood directly behind the saloon. Beyond that was an open area, closed off from the street by a high wall, and at the far side of the area another building terminated San Juan's southern row of structures. This open space seemed to be a kind of town pasturage, for in it was a straw stack, a few abandoned wagons, and a lone horse, grazing. Pausing there, he suddenly fell on his stomach. A man moved out of the hills on a dead run and gained the shelter of the straw stack; a moment later he left the straw stack and placed himself against the boards. As he did so, the Kid's wide eyes discovered what he had previously missed — four other men hidden against that wall.

His first impulse was to retreat. Before he could move around, one of the men seemed to grow restless and backed away from the wall. Advancing toward the saloon's rear, he came within fifty feet of the Kid, stopped, turned, and started back. The Kid's muscles suddenly turned to layers of ice, for the moonlight had revealed the pointed, set cheeks of Dusty Bill.

Dusty Bill was against the wall again. The Kid, taking this advantage, crawfished a full forty feet along the saloon's end, reached an opening between buildings, and rose to scuttle down it, thus coming to the street again. One glance reassured him, and he stepped on the walk.

He's in town. Him and his gang. Some hell's about to bust loose, and I'm supposed to be in it. By thunder, I'm ridin' out!

His horse was in the stable, and that way he turned, moving across the street. By now his senses were on the race, and all the sights and sounds of San Juan fed through him in a constant stream. Exactly in the middle of the street he halted and swung about, facing to the east. Out there on the margin of town was the distinct crunch of a cavalcade coming on; and, as he heard it, the whole forthcoming scene became clear and cold and terrifying in his mind. That was Buck Duryea returning. Buck would pass the board fence and become a target. Buck would die — that was the meaning of Dusty Bill's being in San Juan tonight. Even then, he saw the sheriff appear from the shadows, riding away and unconcerned at the head of the posse, and only a few yards from the fence.

In that terrific, racking interval, the River Red Kid became what he was ever afterward to be. And in that interval the volcanic force of warring loyalties was not in his heart. He was proud of his word because he knew a man had no greater possession — and his word had been given to Dusty Bill. Yet, even as he felt the force of it, the calm and kindly figure of Buck Duryea strengthened before him. For, after all, at sixteen the Kid was still a worshipper of heroes, and through the strange irony of events Duryea had become that to him — Duryea, the man of the law whose few words and quiet sympathy had performed this alchemy. The Kid had not wanted it so in the beginning; he had sought out Dusty Bill with the glamour of Dusty's name moving him. But it was given to a greater man than Dusty surely and inevitably to make a follower of this youth.

All this was but a brief moment's transaction in the Kid's mind. The battle had been waged and won without his conscious will; and the decision made equally without deliberation. The Kid responded to the strongest pull. Reaching for his gun, he broke into a shambling run down the street, abreast the board fence, straight toward Buck Duryea.

"Watch out . . . a trap . . . Dusty . . . behind that fence . . . !"

That was all. There was a roar and a crashing as of the heavens falling in. The Kid staggered, spun backward, and

84

fell to the dust. But from his position he saw Buck Duryea, straight and sure in the saddle, charging the board fence and the posse spreading beside him. A single rider broke out of the posse and galloped toward the saloon — Lon Young, crying at the top of his voice: "Me . . . me . . . Dusty!" And then above the fury his cry rose to a scream, and he pitched from the saddle, whirling over and over on the street.

There was a splintering and ripping of boards. The posse jammed against it; horses pitched wildly and tried to fight closer. But Buck Duryea, towering above the fence, was slanting his fire downward, ever downward while the purple-crimson muzzle light flickered through the shadows. Another member of the posse drew off, plunged his horse into the fence, and broke one of the sustaining posts; the line of boards sagged, and the concerted rush of the sheriff's party did the rest. Dust rose in heavy eddies around the River Red Kid, and he heard, through his pain, the echo of firing diminish and presently die. After the whirlpool of conflict was an overwhelming stillness, broken only by the rush of horses, breathing hard, and the low mutter of the possemen beyond the broken fence. Then, as swiftly as the street had cleared, it filled again, and San Juan raced toward the scene.

The Kid heard broken phrases all around him.

"That's the end of Dusty. . . ."

"Never was a fight like this in the history of the country!"

"Duryea, you kept your promise!"

The Kid felt a hand on his shoulder. Buck Duryea dropped beside him, straight and deep lines across his forehead. "They get you, Kid? Where?"

"It ain't fatal," mumbled the Kid. "Somewhere up along my shoulder. It just hurts, that's all."

"Old-timer," said Buck Duryea, a queer set to his cheeks, "you'll be my right hand man when you get well."

"Listen," said the Kid, "I ain't what yuh think. . . ."

"Shut up," said Buck Duryea. "Dusty's dead and so are the rest of his gang. He was the one that held up the stage, Kid. He was the one."

"Yuh'd do that for me?" groaned the Kid.

"Better to make one good citizen than an outlaw," said Buck Duryea softly. "You've got everything a good man needs, my boy."

"Hell," said the Kid. "It ain't goin' to be so hard as I thought. Sheriff, don't you never worry about me no more."

There was a swirl of skirts near him and a small hand pressing against his head. Donna Chavez's agitated question was like a shock. "*Señor* Buck, is he hurt?"

"Not too bad," said the sheriff. "I'll carry him to the house. You can take care of him, Donna. Better do it well. He's my right hand man now."

"Me!" cried Donna. "I will take care of him. For a long time!"

"Can you imagine," muttered the youth and ground his teeth together when Buck Duryea lifted him from the ground. But above the patio was the exultation of a risen spirit, the blaze of a tremendous emotion. *Me . . . a no-account like me? By thunder, I won't make liars outta fine folks! Never, never in this world!*

HOUR OF FURY

I

"A MAN ARRIVES"

The main street of Dug Gulch ran to the very brow of the hill, and the slopes of that pine-swept hill descended gradually a thousand feet to the prairie — to cattle land, running without a flaw into the mists of a tawny and purple-shot horizon.

Coming up the long trail, Dan Smith attained the street and halted there a little while to give his leggy claybank a breather. His glance went back to those distant flats along which he had ridden for five days without a break. The mica glint of dust was refracted from his clothes, and in his eyes, a vivid cobalt against the bronzed breadth of a passive face, lay the weariness of travel and of thought.

It was betrayal, however, for a man to inspect his back trail too closely, and so presently this Dan Smith turned the claybank along the rutted street leading into Dug Gulch. Without appearing to look at all, he saw everything. The town was another mining camp in the pine hills, another double row of raw-wood buildings, flimsily thrown up to seize the profits of those men who were gutting the emerald ravines for gold. He passed assay office, courthouse, store, and saloon, all elbow to elbow. High up on a larger structure ran a vermilion sign: **Benezet's Hotel**. Out of a blacksmith's shop, anvil echoes sailed with a rending clangor. A row of private houses ran on, butting against the virgin pines, and somewhere in the greenery beyond there arose a halloo and clack of miners working.

Dan Smith cut across the street to a stable and dismounted in the cool half dark. A roustabout rose from a bale of hay.

"Be careful with the water," said Dan Smith, his voice effortlessly gentle. "Hay now and oats later."

He turned out then, carrying his saddlebags, but stopped before the street, and put his broad back to the stable wall. This was strange soil, and the self-protective instincts of a lifetime could not be broken.

Paused there, he made a high, flat shape against the last of the day's sun, a big-boned man possessed by a stolid calm. But his eyes, slightly sad and faintly bitter, raked store and alley and window of this camp in the manner of one who was following an oft-repeated custom.

Crossing the street afterward, he fell into the straggling stream of citizens, drifted as far as the saloon, and there entered. At the bar he asked for his customary drink.

The bartender was a big, blond fellow whose cheeks faintly shone with perspiration. He said nothing as he set up bottle and glass, but his attention remained on Dan Smith for one suspiciously casual moment and slid away. It was a perfect indifference, yet the long-nursed resentment deepened in Dan Smith as he drank and paid for his whiskey. A man's history was like a label to be seen by the world, as permanent as a scar. That was the way of it. The barkeep had judged him, and something would follow that judgment. Once again out in the flow of the crowd, he allowed himself to be carried as far as the hotel.

The game never changes, he mused. *Why did I think I could change it?*

In the hotel he registered and was told the number of his room. He went up the stairs — slowly, because his weariness was half in his muscles and half in his heart — and followed a dim, musty hall almost to its end. His room was pretty rough, being nothing but four thin walls enclosing a bed and a chair and a bureau. All the sultriness of the day was compressed in it; noise and street dust flowed through the open window. With the hopes of getting some small cross-draught, Dan Smith let the door stand wide, dropped his saddlebags to the chair, and laid himself full length on the bed.

Dug Gulch — two hundred and eight miles from Fort Rock. There was no escaping the past. Five days could not erase it, and now that he had closed his eyes, the image of Fort Rock's street, turned mad and bloody, spread across his inner vision. All motion and all sound returned, more vivid than originally. Ned Canrinus was walking around the corner of the bank. He was saying: "This is the end of it." Then he began firing.

White strips of dust rose out of the hot earth, and another man, rage boiling in his gullet, made a deliberate broad jump through the saloon doors, joining Canrinus. A third gunman opened savagely from behind. Even now, Dan Smith felt the heavy recoil of his own Forty-Four, heard the sound of this gun play crushing against the town walls.

Canrinus fell screaming, and died. The partner beside him became a squalling victim in the deep dust. And that third man, in the rear, quit firing and raced diagonally across Gurdane's vacant lot. Turning, Dan Smith had pinned him mortally to the spot, and afterward the silence was heavier than anything in his memory, broken only by a voice that was his own. He had said: "That's right . . . this is the end of it."

An old buffalo gun began to boom at the far end of the street as he walked into the stable. In all Fort Rock, no other soul was visible at the moment. Dan Smith got on his horse and left the town behind. The buffalo gun was the last sound in his ears. Behind it, he knew, was Marshal Drain, furiously fighting three men dead in the silk-yellow dust.

"Was the name Smith?" said a slow, still voice.

Dan Smith opened his eyes. Three men filled his doorway, the foremost nearly broad enough to fill it alone. He was fat and blond and pink of face, and a wicked wisdom of the world flattened the color of his small, unrevealing eyes.

Dan Smith sat up on the edge of the bed. This, he realized, was the aftermath of the barkeep's glance. But Dan only nodded and reached in his pocket for the makings of a cigarette.

"I'm Benezet," said the fat one, and moved on and sat in the chair, releasing his weight to it by cautious degrees.

The other two stood fast by the door.

"Your horse," Benezet went on, in a thready, indifferent tone, "is a beauty. I notice the brand is U Bar, which is Morgan Mountain way. I'm familiar with that territory. Never heard of a Dan Smith being there."

Dan Smith's regard remained inscrutably on the cigarette being formed in his tough fingers. He said, equally indifferent: "My own horse was in bad shape. I came through Morgan Mountain and traded for the claybank."

"What was this other horse's brand?"

"T Y," Dan Smith said gently.

"I know Tom Yount. Never heard of a Dan Smith workin' there."

"Still traveling," Dan Smith murmured. "Another tired horse swapped at the Yount ranch."

Benezet said very softly: "What was the brand of the horse you started with, wherever you started?"

"We won't put that on record, friend."

Benezet looked like some heathen god. All his emotions were hidden behind the sluggish fat. He had a blue handkerchief in his fist, and this he rubbed across his forehead, erasing moisture. "You wear no gun, which lays you wide open to wonder."

"Why wear an overcoat when it doesn't rain?"

"Rain always comes when you got no coat handy." Benezet rolled his head at the door and murmured, "All right, boys."

The two silent men came in, one reaching for Dan Smith's coat lapels and pulling them aside.

"No shoulder holster," said Dan Smith, unresisting.

The second man, searching the saddlebags, turned on Benezet. "A razor and shaving mug, and a box of Forty-Four shells, and a Forty-Four."

"So," Benezet said, merely breathing it. He sat there loosely, legs apart, seeming to suffer from the room's warmth. The fat fist continued to hold the blue handkerchief. "I could trace your trail," he said.

"Be sure that you want to," said Dan Smith.

"It might be worth the trouble."

Dan Smith stood up, whereat the two exploring men wheeled alertly. But he remained still, looking down at Benezet's bland, suspicious face. His own blunt features were darker and more turbulent than they had been.

"This game," he said somberly, "never has a different end. I never met you before, but I could lay your story out in ten words. It wouldn't be advisable for you to follow my trail back. What's behind me is over. I closed the door. Don't open it."

Benezet's cheeks never changed, yet the light of his eyes seemed to be of laughter. He pushed himself upright. "Let a man talk," he said. "Always let a man talk. I get you, Smith. More than one sort of man comes up here. It's to my profit to know which is which."

One of the silent henchmen looked a little troubled and spoke. "He might be carrying a star some other place in his clothes."

"Star?" said Dan Smith.

Benezet's little eyes touched his man. He said in a voice as smooth and frigid as ice: "You fool!"

That phrase rapped the sultry silence. It struck the fellow who had been addressed as if it had been a whiplash. All his nerves seemed to recoil.

Benezet rolled his vast shoulders and rocked through the door, blue bandanna dragging from his hand. The others followed. Still in his tracks, Dan Smith listened to the creaking of warped boards, the groaning along the stairway.

"Star?" he said again, and scowled faintly.

The stairs stopped protesting, and then started again. Somebody was advancing slowly, unevenly down the hall, making a great labor out of walking.

Dan Smith turned to the window and pushed the dirt-gray curtains aside on the impulse of a sudden curiosity. Below, Benezet propelled his big bulk saloonward, his two henchmen behind. The blue bandanna hanging from the fat man's fist was ridiculous, but there was nothing ridiculous in the way the flowing stream of miners moved aside to give his gross bulk a right of way.

Dan Smith leaned back from the window and wheeled, feeling more and more irritated. A man wretchedly deformed supported himself by the frame of the doorway, one useless foot hanging six inches from the floor. He was hatless, and his hair, black as jet and coarse as horsehair, matted a heavy skull. Two friendless, cheerless eyes peered sullenly.

"Got anything to give me?" he grunted.

"Why climb the stairs when you could have met me below?" Dan Smith asked.

"A beggar's supposed to do something for what he gets."

Dan Smith found a dollar in his pocket and walked to the cripple. The eyes of the deformed one narrowed on the money, and he took it without comment or thanks. Swaying slightly on his one good foot, he stared at Dan Smith, actual hatred burning in the queer glance. He started away, and then he turned back.

"Next time I ask, throw it on the floor, like the rest do," he said.

"What's your name, friend?"

"A man like me don't need a name." The cripple's brutal lips receded from strong, white teeth. "This camp's busted better men than you, mister. You've been visited by Benezet. It ain't no compliment."

Dan Smith said: "When did the last sheriff or deputy visit this camp?"

The cripple only laughed, a soundless laugh that drew his pitiful cheeks into odd knots. After that he labored down the hall.

Dan Smith drew a deep gust of cigarette smoke into his lungs, expelled it, and for want of something to occupy his strange restlessness, he removed his coat, rolled up his sleeves, and went to the wash basin. There was never any change in the game. It was something timeless, and the end was as fixed as the hours. All long trails led to this.

But the star business is something extra, he thought. *What would that be?* Alert to the question, he sat on the bed, building a new smoke while his mind cut keenly back and forward. *I expect him to consider me an outlaw,* he mused. *That's the natural thing. But if he thinks I'm an officer — what's he afraid of?*

A man ran up the stairs and advanced quickly, pausing and knocking at a door directly across the hall. What Smith saw then was little more than a strained profile and a set of small shoulders on an immaculately dressed body. A woman's voice, eagerly lifting, said: "Wait!"

Directly afterward the door opened, and she stood slim

and smiling against the fading daylight from her room. At once pulled out of his thinking, Dan Smith let his attention remain on her. It wasn't often a man saw a woman alive and eager like that, a woman wrapped up as she seemed to be in the dapper figure waiting at the door. There was a gallant tilt to her head, a supple vigor to her body.

"Come in, Clare," she said.

The man's tone was half impatient. "Only a moment. I have a case to try."

There was something more, but the door closed behind them, and their voices began to blend, to interrupt, and to grow more peremptory.

Dan Smith got up, striding the room with a caged restlessness. One phrase from the girl clearly penetrated the panels of the door, somehow desperate.

"But you've got to get yourself out of this mess!"

That was all. The door opened again, and the man closed it strongly behind, and hurried down the hall. What Dan Smith heard next was the one sound to hurt and enrage him beyond all others. The girl was crying, quietly crying.

Damn, thought Dan Smith. *Is there nothing but trouble in the world?*

He dropped the cigarette and laid his pointed rider's heel on it. He made one more indecisive turn of the room and stopped at his own doorway, the blue of his eyes going dark and deep from the sound of grief. All his quiescent sympathies rose, wiping out weariness, stirring a swift partisan anger. It was like a challenge, that cry. He thought: *It's always like this. I never know when to quit.*

He took half a dozen paces toward the girl's door. His knuckles fell lightly on the panel, and he heard the crying stop, and her steps come nearer. The door opened. He saw a blaze of hope lighten all the firm, fine features for a moment, and then utterly die. A profound regret went through him. But he stood there, tall and wistfully grave, a young man hungrily whipped to bone and sinew, a quiet sympathy in his look.

"Most of the grief in this world comes from what people do to each other," he said gently. "But it isn't worth tears. Nothing's worth tears."

II

"AN ANCIENT DEMAND"

She was watching him, the clear and definite surface of her face terribly sad. But he knew that the cloud of her troubles lay between them, and he spoke again in the same quiet, melody-making voice: "What sort of help do you need?"

The question broke through her preoccupation. He felt the full effect of that taut and grieving glance, and his admiration grew at the sight of her small shoulders so resolutely squared. The light was fast going from the windows of her room, its reflection stealing from the corn-yellow surfaces of her hair, its shadows more somberly pooling across the straight brow.

A small breath disturbed the silence. "What kind of help could you be to me?"

"Anything you need destroyed or broken or torn up," he said, his gentle tone faintly bitter. "What else can a man do? When a woman cries, she may be happy or she may be sad. If it is sadness, something has got beyond her."

She said, curious: "You are the only man . . . do you know this town?"

"No."

"Do you know my name, or anything about me?"

"Nothing."

"My name," she said, "is April Surratt. And if you knew this town, you wouldn't offer help. You wouldn't dare."

"You misunderstand men," he said. "Plenty of them will pull away from the pack."

She remained quiet a little while, growing dimmer and dimmer before his eyes.

The stairs began to whine under the pressure of an approaching body. April Surratt retreated into her room.

"The pack?" she asked. "Then you know this town?"

"The game never changes, one town or another."

"It will do you no good to be seen speaking to me." And she shut the door.

Dan Smith returned to his room and lit the lamp. He stood for a moment before the bureau's leprous-spotted mirror. What reflected dimly back only increased the irritation stirring in him like a toxin. That face was old and preoccupied, and all the cheerfulness, all the careless laughter of another day, was gone. At twenty-five, part of him was dead. The reckless desires of life lay flat and thin and starved in their remote places.

Dan Smith turned and circled the cramped room. He laid out on the bureau the few articles from the saddlebags, neatly, as was his habit; and for a moment he held the dull, wooden-butted gun, and felt its solid reassurance. Then, astir with anger, he dropped it.

That's what I'm trying to get away from, isn't it?

Extinguishing the light, he went down the stairs and into a street awash with the shadows flowing like water off the higher hills. The walks were crowded. One by one, the store lights began to shine, through pane and doorway, and to lay golden hurdles across the dust.

Two men passed him rather rapidly, and he heard a sullen, cautious phrase drop. "He'll get free. Benezet will see to it."

At the courthouse a considerable group made loose, semi-circular ranks near the entrance. Turning that way, Dan Smith's shrewd thoughts returned to Benezet, and he said inwardly: *Why is he afraid of a star?*

The sudden odor of burnt coke and singed hoof tissue fell on him, and, as he threw a casual look into the murky depths of the blacksmith shop, a man there — a squat and ugly giant covered by a leather apron — suddenly reared from a water tub and stared back. Surprise spread his jaws apart.

He said: "Dane . . . ?"

Dan Smith's head shook imperceptibly. He went on.

But the blacksmith, water running from his face into the bare breadth of his chest, abruptly laughed, a suppressed and deeply amused laugh. He said — "Well, now!" — and plunged his face into the tub once more. And the next moment he stood up and stared into the drifting files of men with a sly humor on his burnt cheeks.

Dan Smith went on, faintly scowling. There was something here. All faces were pointing toward the courthouse door, and he felt that the temper of that assembly was like the heat of a covered fire. Curious, he pushed through and on up the steps into a hall guarded by miners, all the way to an open door. Through that door ran the even-pitched and persuasive voice of a man in argument. That voice, Dan Smith thought, was faintly familiar, and he worked his way uncivilly along until he looked across the rows of a seated courtroom audience. There was no jury — only a bald, bullet-headed man sitting behind a high, pine desk, obviously bored. Below him stood the meticulously dressed fellow whom Dan Smith had seen talking with April Surratt, across the hall at the hotel. A lawyer, then, and coming to the end of an argument.

"What kind of evidence is that?" the fellow said. "It has all been circumstantial. No man directly saw Loma Sam's face. No man saw him actually tampering with the sluice box. When surrounded by this party of amateur detectives, he was leaning against a tree, a hundred yards away from the McNeish claim. There is no proof of robbery. I urge you to dismiss the case."

The judge bobbed his head, the flaring wall lamps detailing his white, compressed mouth across a flinty skin. He said: "Stand up."

A man who was extremely thin and slovenly, slowly unfolded himself from a chair.

"You're discharged, Loma," said the judge.

The attorney said carelessly — "Thank you." — and turned to go out.

There was an absolute lack of sound in the courtroom at that moment, a strangely sultry stillness. It was as definite as that to Dan Smith, and it was no less definite, he saw, to the attorney. For that man stopped and pulled back his little shoulders, flashing a swift glance all along the corners of the room, at once calculating and scornful, placing his will against the speechless hostility of the crowd.

Dan Smith's eyes began to narrow, taking in the details of that thin face with its skeptical half smile. He turned on impulse to the nearest watcher. "What is his name?"

The man's answer was throaty. "Clare Durran."

The show was over. The ex-prisoner, Loma Sam, came rapidly out, looking neither to left nor right, and got to the courthouse steps. Deeply interested in this obscure play that was becoming at each step less obscure, Dan Smith followed.

Loma Sam's forward progress ceased at the steps. He stared down at the massed and saturnine faces, and seemed to shrivel. Placed as he was, Dan Smith could observe that crowd's anger. The man, he thought, was acquitted of robbing a sluice box — but he's as good as dead, and he knows it.

Loma Sam moved his thin arms futilely. He threw his heel around, fear bursting in his eyes. And then a curt, unyielding voice said: "Open up and let this man through!"

Dan Smith's alert glance searched the shadows and fell upon a hulking figure, reared against a pillar of the courthouse front — an implacable figure with a great jaw, the pockmarks on his face visible beneath a hat's brim. Loma Sam's nerves grew perceptibly calmer at the sound of that voice. He straightened and walked boldly on into the crowd.

The iron voice at the pillar rose again. "As long as I'm marshal, there will be no lynching. Understand me!"

A heavy, sibilant undertone spread like a runner of wind through the massed miners.

Then another shape came from the courthouse at a rush, passing Dan Smith. The man stopped halfway down the steps, swaying from side to side, the breath gushing in and out of him.

The rustling discontent quickened through the waiting ranks, and a man called up: "McNeish, never mind. Your friends will take care of Loma."

"Who said that?" challenged the figure by the pillar.

McNeish ceased swaying. He was long and mature, a full-bearded man seized by an unsparing anger. He raised a hand into the twilight, shaking it at the pale, premature stars.

"Everybody knows me," he said. "Everybody knows Bob McNeish. I made discovery in this camp. I saw it grow. I saw the houses spring up. I saw the good men come . . . and I saw the crooks come. Listen. It's got beyond us! I've been in a lot of camps in my life, and there's always been crooks. But the time always came when the crooks died with the wrath of God on them. I caught Loma Sam flatfooted, with his dirty paws scooping dust out of my sluice. Listen, I'm a patient man, but I tell you, this camp's turned rotten! The leeches have got to go, the hooded scoundrels, the shyster lawyers, and the judge that sits behind the court desk and deals out the orders a certain man in this town gives him." McNeish stopped for a full breath of wind and exploded mightily: "You know that man!"

The man at the pillar said coldly: "This is a little rash, McNeish."

Dan Smith turned his engrossed eyes. An angling beam of light struck out of the courthouse to play on the stiff-jawed fellow with the pitted face who had just spoken. On Clare Durran, too, now standing there, pale yet still clinging tenaciously to his faithless, sardonic smile.

"I'm including crooked marshals, Sullivan!" cried McNeish.

"A little rash," the stiff-jawed man repeated tonelessly.

There was a stirring along the ranks below, and Dan Smith's eyes fell back upon the enormous, seal-fat shape of Benezet. Benezet had come through the crowd, and he paused now in the cleared space at the foot of the steps, unhurried and unmoved, looking up at a McNeish gone dourly silent. One bulky fist, holding a blue bandanna, rose indifferently at McNeish, and the sleepy voice fell flat and very clear.

"Don't be disturbed by little things, Bob."

That was all. McNeish was speechless, beyond words and beyond motion — a thwarted and accusing shape in the swirling dusk. The very presence of Benezet was enough. Something cold emanated from the hulk, to flow into the furnace-hot temper of the crowd, to beat back the virulent anger, to kill talk.

Looking relentlessly on, seeing the edges of the crowd stir and dissolve, Dan Smith silently applauded the stark quality of Benezet's courage. Divorced from the terror and brutality that went with it, such courage was admirable. There was something else in these men — in Benezet and Clare Durran and the pockmarked fellow — as unshakable as the hills. Something bitter and conscienceless and unforgiving.

But the rest of the story was clear now, and, as the crowd broke and milled along the light-streaked street, Dan Smith slowly returned to the hotel, all the details of this last scene deep in his mind, scorched into it by a fire heat. The game never changed!

Two barking explosions rushed out of the adjacent pines, bringing him to a stand.

A man near him whirled and cried: "That's it!" And his face, in the light, was a wicked smear of pleasure.

Dan Smith went on, pulse slow and strong, the reckless flicker of an old feeling in him. That would be Loma Sam, dying out there in the dark, at the hands of Bob McNeish's friends. The game never changed, and it was all clear now. Wherever men dug raw gold, there also gathered the parasites — living on sufferance till their power grew greedy and overwhelming.

This was Benezet's town. Those fat hands grasped it unrelentingly. That covert and unreachable mind schemed over it. Dug Gulch's commoner men tramped through the alternate lanes of brilliance and shadow with the sleepless surveillance of Benezet's desires on them. The game never changed. This was a stage in the life of a crook and in the life of a town.

Another stage will come, he said to himself. *Why am I here?*

Somebody strode rapidly up from behind, came abreast, and fell in step. The stiff-jawed marshal's pitted face turned sidewise. He said: "At the next alley, turn into it."

"Power," Dan Smith said gently, "is a light in the far desert, a light leading better men than Benezet to ruin."

"What's that?" the marshal said sharply.

"What's at the other end of the alley?"

"Turn in."

Dan Smith's chuckle was reckless, amused. *Never any difference, never a new way. This is just the second step from the barkeep's look.*

He turned at the alley, went into the deeper dark, with the marshal close behind. He came to the cluttered back lots of Dug Gulch, to the discarded boxes and littered junk and débris.

The marshal said — "Turn right." — and stumbled into loose wire, and swore. Twenty feet onward, he said: "That door."

A single pencil shaft of light identified the door. Dan Smith found the knob and pressed the door back into a bright, smoky room disturbed by the sounds of a barroom directly beyond a partition.

The marshal came rapidly in, slammed the door. He was surly, displeased.

"Here he is."

Nothing surprised Dan Smith. Benezet sat at a table. The thin-mouthed judge sat there. And Clare Durran, too electric to stay placed, idly paced beside a wall. The two who had guarded Benezet when he came to Dan Smith's room also were here, behind the big man's chair, and at once they were stiffly conscious of Smith's appearance.

Benezet's hands were on the table. He rolled them gently, palms up and palms down. "You've had your look, Smith. Do you get it?"

"It's an old story," Dan Smith said mildly.

"What am I?" Benezet challenged, little eyes very bland.

"What McNeish said you were on the courthouse steps."

"So I run the town?" Benezet said indolently. "I milk it dry? I make the law and support men who rob sluice boxes

102

. . . with the help of just these five gentlemen around me?"

"I said it was an old story," Dan Smith pointed out. "Behind these five men are maybe twenty roughs at your beck, and half a dozen gamblers at your saloon tables. There are the operators of your bawdy houses, as well as the barkeep who looked me over when I hit town."

Clare Durran stopped his pacing and stared, the ironical amusement on that half-handsome, hopeless face dying.

Benezet, however, chuckled, which was merely a rumbling disturbance in his chest. "You're shrewd," he admitted. "I knew it the moment I scanned you. I'm familiar with your type, friend Smith. Give me credit for knowing the different kinds of men. You've got a mind beneath that poker face. You're slow moving, but you're set on springs. You can use a gun, friend Smith. That's your number."

"Now," Dan Smith said, "sell me your bill of goods."

Benezet said: "You're coming in with us. Beginning tomorrow, you're night marshal of the Gulch."

They were all still, all watching keenly. Dan Smith lifted his noncommittal eyes to Clare Durran, and saw something there in the taut, faithless countenance that he had not seen before — a weariness, a heavy care. But under inspection it vanished instantly. Benezet shifted his great body and slowly hauled the blue bandanna out of a coat pocket, rolling it between his damp palms. His mountainous shoulders tipped toward Dan Smith.

"Maybe you're not aware of the end of this old story," Dan Smith drawled. "The wild ones feed well on the fat of the town. They get ambitious for the little profit that escapes them, and they bear down harder. But they're deceived about men, Benezet. The time comes when the McNeishes think a little too long . . . and then the wild ones die right where found. There's nothing in this world as wicked as the wrath of a peaceful man gone mad." He shrugged. "I wouldn't care to be night marshal."

The blue bandanna disappeared inside Benezet's tightening fist. "I could go back on your trail, Smith."

"Your first idea was that I might be an officer. That interested me. It set me to wondering. Now you've got me figured for an outlaw, running in front of trouble. Be sure, though, that you want to go back on my trail."

Benezet leaned forward, inscrutable but interested. Talk purred across his pendulous lower lip. "Gunmen are not usually bothered with a conscience. Nor are you the kind to scare easily. Is there something else to the story? It's for me or against me, friend Smith. Think about it."

The sounds of the barroom died unexplainably, but from the street a voice began to call, the message reaching those in the room only indistinctly.

Dan Smith opened the back door and then turned to present a smooth countenance to the men he had just addressed. "Loma Sam is dead, which is a leaf sailing in front of a stronger wind to come. I'll not be changing my mind."

Benezet, obviously, was listening to the disturbance outside. He said almost indifferently: "You may have reason to change it soon."

The others were so many fixed shapes in the saffron lamplight, but, as Dan Smith stepped into the night, he looked again at Clare Durran, and caught again that look of uncertainty and fatigue. He closed the door, stood loose muscled in the blackness, listening to the suddenly full-bodied sounds curving around the building to envelop him. Then he swung back on his original trail and passed through the alley.

Before he reached the street a clear and curt voice said: "McNeish, you're pretty proud."

He came at once to the street, and rose to the hotel porch.

Pausing, he turned, so as to command that part of the street running toward the higher hills. It was strange, but in that brief period Dug Gulch's people had faded into doorway and recess and darkness. The silence held. Six men were posted along in the dust of the street, deliberately spaced from walk to walk. In front of them stood Bob McNeish, his mature, half-gaunt frame transfixed by the light beams from saloon and courthouse. He knew, Dan Smith thought grimly. He knew, but there wasn't any fear on his hard, honest cheeks.

"You're pretty proud," the voice repeated, and ceased there.

One man in the center of the line stirred on his heels, and McNeish at once reached for his own gun.

But he was too late. A solitary blast rushed like a heavy gust of wind along the buildings, and McNeish slowly bowed his head.

Dan Smith whirled on his heel, his mind black with fury. Sightlessly, he struck and knocked aside somebody standing in the hotel's door and went up the stairs.

He thought: *This is what I'm running away from . . . but there's never any use of running.*

All patience was out of him, and he was as he had been that bitter afternoon in Fort Rock — a-simmer with a daring, destructive wrath that overwhelmed reason. It had come to this: a man never escaped the judgment of the gods. Whatever he was, he had to be; even if the trail was a thousand miles long, that judgment would overtake him.

My only usefulness, he thought, *is to destroy.*

He paused abruptly, seeing a thin sheet of light shining beneath his door. Then he reached out and wrenched the door open and came forward.

April Surratt stood in the center of his room, waiting.

III

"THE DRAWN ISSUE"

At sight of him she straightened, shocked by the strangeness of that hard face, by the sleety chill of those cobalt eyes. At her door, a few hours before, he had been a calm, gentle-speaking man. Nothing of that man now remained; he stood before her stormy and reckless and keyed to swiftness. Ease and youth were gone, and gone, too, was the shadow of weariness that she had so clearly seen.

"What is it?" she asked.

But he shook his head, and his muscles relaxed. The fighting flash vanished from the bronzed cheeks. "I wasn't sure who was in this room."

She said: "You see? The town is on your nerves. You have only been here since four o'clock, but you feel it. It has caught you."

He said nothing.

She went on, more rapidly: "You are too young to have that look in your eyes. Do you know what you are now? A man ready to kill."

"Why are you here?"

A little color reached her face, brought there by the directness of the question. But she held his glance. "You were very kind to me. I only wish to repay you. Dan Smith, Dug Gulch is nothing but a whispering gallery! You have been here four hours . . . and every soul in the camp is wondering about you. Everything in your saddlebags is common knowledge. Every turn of your head and every word you speak is witnessed, and probably it will be known in the saloon, before ten o'clock, that I was here in your room."

"An old story," he murmured.

"Is it?" she queried. "You are too young to have such gray, dismal knowledge. Is it an old story that Benezet means to enlist you on his side? That is what I wanted to tell you." Then, prompted to a more woman-like quality, she added: "Just who are you, Dan Smith?"

"Another rider at the end of a trail that leads nowhere."

"An outlaw, as they say? No. You're not an outlaw. It isn't in you."

"I'm on the run," he said.

She shook her head. "But not from any crime."

"April Surratt," he said gently, admiringly, "there's nothing like courage. It covers all the sins."

He looked down at her from his flat and tough-fibered height until she stirred and moved to the door. She opened it a little, scanning the hall. Then she looked around at him, inward agitation turning her cheeks faintly pale.

"I wanted to tell you this . . . if Benezet claims you, you are lost!" And with that, she was gone.

Dan Smith made one moody circle of the room, thinking: *She's sunk in trouble, and she won't ask for help. It's this Clare Durran . . . and a thousand of his sort ain't worth one of her kind.*

Afterward he trimmed the lamp and walked down to a lonely supper.

When he returned to his room, he went directly to bed, to stare sleeplessly at the dark ceiling. A strange quiet had come to Dug Gulch's brawling street; the few voices he heard below were suppressed and curt. It was not difficult to guess why. Loma Sam was dead, and Bob McNeish was dead, and the smell of blood lay on the windless air. The night was tainted, oppressed. The old story was working itself into another familiar stage — that of fury, slowly growing and slowly hardening. *The wild ones never know the limits of men,* he told himself. This was what he had run from, yet here he was.

After ten o'clock the next morning, Dan Smith led his haltered horse across to the blacksmith shop and said: "Have a look at the off rear shoe."

The blacksmith glanced indifferently at Dan Smith, then at his helper lounging in the doorway.

"Lee," he told the helper, "go over to Spall's and get me ten feet of strap iron."

The far echoes of men at work in the outward ravines reached back to make small echoes on the silent, sun-drenched street, and the departing helper's dragging feet lifted whorls of dust. The blacksmith stared at Dan Smith again, now sharp and knowing, and he backed his squat body against the claybank pony and pulled the claybank's leg between his knees. A burly phrase rose from his bare, furry chest: "I lived too long in the Fort Rock country not to spot a certain well-known man when I see him."

Dan Smith studied the burning brightness of the day, and slid his words over a flat shoulder. "What does this girl want of Clare Durran?"

"It's common talk," said the blacksmith. "That girl's all right. Durran's a lawyer from Morgan Mountain, come here to make his pile from a claim. Him and the girl were engaged back there, so he sent for her. The claim was no good, and Benezet saw some use for him as a lawyer. So that's the end of another good man. Ain't it? You ought to know Benezet. But the girl saw what Durran was into, and wouldn't marry him unless he got out. There we are! But how in hell is Durran ever going to get out? There's some who wonder if he's all crooked, or just in bad luck."

The helper straggled back. "Spall's got no strap iron," he said.

"Then try Cope's," the blacksmith said. And when the helper was gone again, he added: "You see? It's pretty rotten. This camp's tough, but Benezet's tougher. He's got his bunch well scattered along the creeks, and they ain't all known to the miners. So Benezet's ears catch everything on the first bounce. There's a lot of dead men back in the brush. I say so. Try to get a straight deal! Benezet's rich from his saloon, and his hotel, and his women, and his claim jumping. Hell! What one good man with a gun could do!" The blacksmith straightened and bent his arm until the tremendous biceps whitened the sooty skin. "Just one man with courage. I'm glad you're here."

"No," said Dan Smith. "I'm not in on this."

"No?" said the blacksmith, and laid his chasm-black eyes on the other man. He chuckled then. "Listen, I know who *you* are."

A shadow drifted across the arch, slowly.

The blacksmith let the claybank's leg drop and said: "These shoes will do for another two weeks."

Dan Smith nodded, his glance following the citizen so casually going by. He took the claybank's halter and recrossed to the livery stable. Then he slowly sauntered through the thick heat toward the green promise of the pines.

A broad trail left Dug Gulch, tracing upward into the higher folds of the forest, with smaller paths drifting away at regular intervals. One of these he took, one that led downward into a shovel-scarred ravine, the gravelly entrails of which lay scattered as far as his vision ran.

Brush rustled above him faintly, then ceased to rustle. He was grimly contemptuous. He knew he was being shadowed, but it didn't matter. All this fell into a pattern so old that he knew every black and scarlet thread from memory.

Another thing absorbed his full attention, and he spoke

half aloud. "I'll have to see Durran, but I'll have to arrange it."

He turned then from the gulch, and rose by another trail, through thick trees, stopping suddenly in a covert glade occupied by half a dozen silent men staring fixedly at him. One of those was the cripple, supporting himself beside a pine.

"I'm sorry, gentlemen."

One man with a beard so full as to conceal all his features, save for two sultry eyes separated by a strong, high-bridged nose, spoke in a voice reverberating suspicion. "Your name is Smith. There's only two sides to this camp. Come in . . . or get out."

"You'll see," said the cripple. "He's another gunslinger. It's all over him. Another killer for Benezet."

"Let it ride," Dan Smith said, and cut around them. Their murmuring reached him through the intervening brush, and one voice, hot and headlong, overtook him even as he fell into the broad trail and came back to the street.

It was noon then, with small parties debouching from the hills and half a crowd observing drink time at the saloon. A stage labored up from the lower levels, raising a high dust. Marshal Sullivan appeared from the courthouse and stood by a pillar, watching that stage. Clare Durran also emerged from the courthouse and walked at his swift stride toward the hotel. Not wanting any dinner, Dan Smith went to the hotel room. Leaving the door open, he stretched out on the bed.

There'll be a little more of this, he thought. *A little more thinking and a little more quiet. Then this street will turn red, and here I'll be. Doing what? It's what I ran away from, wasn't it? I have got to see Clare Durran.*

Flat on his back, he built himself a cigarette, somberly observing as his tensile fingers curled and crimped the brown paper. It was odd: the good Lord gave a man long fingers

110

and cold nerves to steady them against a gun, and then the world hounded that man into using his dark gift till the killer's trade was so plain across him that even a half-witted cripple could recognize it.

People came up the stairs slowly. The murmur of April Surratt's voice began to run along the hall, troubled and pleading. Dan Smith lighted his cigarette and held the match until the pale flame sank into his fingertips and died. Presently April Surratt's door opened, and April Surratt cried wearily: "Where is the end of this?"

"Later, later," cautioned Clare Durran's voice.

The door closed. Clare Durran's steps started away, but halted, and the flimsy hall flooring squealed. Dan Smith studied the ceiling above him, slack and motionless. Clare Durran was behind him, in the doorway, watching him without being watched.

Dan Smith blew the thin smoke from his mouth. "I wanted to see you," he said. "Come in. Close the door."

Durran obeyed. He walked the length of the room into Dan Smith's vision, and turned. Fatigue was written clearly on his mobile features. Seeing him thus off guard, Dan Smith's half-formed judgment became a certainty. Here was an educated man, a man of quick imagination, but there was no toughness in him, no vitality, no resistance. Behind the set and unbelieving mask of amusement nothing solid lived.

"You're pretty keen, Smith," Durran said. "Benezet fears you. Why should I make any bones about it . . . for, if Benezet fears you enough, he'll have you killed. You were right. Behind Benezet are thirty men who will break any law God made, if that man says so. It seems small, compared to the camp? Think about it. Those men can collect, shoulder to shoulder, in five minutes' time. And they can shoot."

"Durran," said Dan Smith, "how did you get into this?"

Clare Durran drew a long breath. "How does a man get into anything?"

"I know," Dan Smith drawled. "Do you want to get out?"

"Be careful there!"

Dan Smith rose in one long, rippling motion. The cigarette smoke curled up across the smoothness of his bronzed cheeks. He looked ruffled and ruggedly aroused.

"You're clever, Durran. Your mind has got a razor's cut. But it's too nimble, and it has done things to you. It's furnished you with excuses for the jackpot you're in. But the excuses are lies, and you know they're lies. Your nerves are shot."

"Careful," Durran droned.

"You fool," Dan Smith said, coldly angry. "How long has that girl got to sit in her room and wait?"

Something in Clare Durran snapped. It didn't show on his face, so long trained to conceal, but the faithless eyes went darker and more barren. He said: "How could I get out? It's impossible! I will never get out . . . and neither will you!"

That was all. He drew a rough breath, and the emotion of the moment, too strong for his indifferent frame, poured blood into his sharp features. Quickly, he passed out of the room.

Dan Smith thought: *That show of nerve on the courthouse steps wasn't real. It was just contempt, backed up by Benezet's power. The man's empty.*

Dan rested there, the arctic blue of his glance cutting through the tobacco haze, all his muscles idle. The courthouse fire bell struck two, three, four. The high heat of the day crowded into the room, insufferable within the four walls.

A considerable party of riders clopped along through the dust outside. Doors opened and closed along the hall. Then it was five, and the brilliance of the light began to dim. The miners, returning from work, disturbed the sluggish quiet.

Dan Smith rose and put on his coat. He lifted the blackened Forty-Four from the bureau top, balancing it in his palm and laying it back.

Some men, he reflected, *are born for peace, and some are born for trouble. What is the use of running away from what's written in the book? If I try to support Durran, all the miners of the gulch will be on my trail. If I throw in with the miners, Durran is dead.*

His alert ears identified heavy bodies climbing the hotel stairs. In the hall, a man's breathing echoed sibilantly. Dan Smith stared at the idle Forty-Four again, and turned his back to it. He stood thus when Benezet halted at his doorway.

Behind Benezet, ridden by violent suspicions, stood Marshal Sullivan. Benezet's face was streaming. He blotted it with the wadded bandanna in his fist, and his small eyes, unchanged and changeless, met those of Dan Smith.

"I didn't have to go back on your trail, friend Smith," he said. "A man from Fort Rock rode in today. So I was mistaken."

"Nothing," Dan Smith said gently, "stands still."

"You are not a peace officer," Benezet pondered, "and not an outlaw. You're a man extremely well known for handling a gun. In Fort Rock the other day, you met and killed three riders who had come to find out if you were as good as your reputation. Your real name, friend Smith, is Dane Starr."

The man who had been Dan Smith, and who now, by Benezet's softly issued words, became Dane Starr, stared somberly at the fat, bland face.

Benezet spoke curiously: "Tell me, why did you run? Canrinus was a rustler and Dane Starr could ride high and easy anywhere he wanted. Why did you run?"

Dane Starr said: "The reputation, Benezet. Once a common thief made me draw. It became known then that I was first. I have had no peace since. There is no peace for a man with that reputation. Trouble camps with him, and all the tough ones come to try their luck . . . as Canrinus did, as others did before him, as others will do again. Nothing but trouble, Benezet. Good men wanting me to settle their griefs for them, and bad ones wishing to take my measure. Certainly, I'm Dane Starr, a name recognized as far as it is heard. What for? For the ability to kill. But I want no more of it. I've closed the door on my past, Benezet. My name is Dan Smith . . . and I don't carry a gun."

"You're through, then," said Benezet. "I won't have you in my camp. You're a hero to the country, and you will be a hero to all those fools picking dust out of the gulches. Not in my camp, Starr!"

"So I ride?"

Benezet said: "The damage is done." He turned about and waddled down the hall, Marshal Sullivan guarding his rear.

Dane Starr remained quiet, feeling none of the room's sulky heat, hearing none of the guttural talk in the street below.

Abruptly it was sundown. The hard light died from the window, and faint purple began to streak the sky. The room turned to shadow.

"So trouble comes again," he said aloud, and stood straight and stolid in his tracks.

A flickering restlessness broke the Indian calm. He turned suddenly and lifted the gun, opening and whirling the cylinder until the blue metal blurred. Then he closed it and placed the weapon inside his waistband.

"The waiting and thinking are over," he said, and paced along the hall, slowly down it.

Somebody came running up the flight of stairs at the rear, and turned at the landing to face him. He stopped, seeing that April Surratt's eyes were bright with fear.

"Dane Starr!" she said. "You are too young to have that

114

reputation! Even in Morgan Mountain men spoke of you. Don't go out on that street!"

"What other way would I go?" he asked gently.

Her shoulders ceased to be straight. She was still. She was watching him. Through the lengthening silence feet tramped and scuffed, and voices sank lower and lower. A man came to the foot of the stairs, lighted the wall lamps, and looked up, curious.

April Surratt whispered: "I know. No other way. It . . . it's so cruel! But it's fine to know one man who's unafraid."

She placed a hand on his chest for a moment, trying to smile as she did so. Then she went on up the stairs.

Dane Starr descended to the lobby, brushing past the man who still paused there. Other citizens hurried in from the porch and filled the lobby, shaken with excitement. When they saw him there, a whetted eagerness came to their faces, and they stepped aside to let him pass out.

He turned and dropped down to the walk — and there stopped. On his left was the alley into which Marshal Sullivan, earlier, had ordered him. On his right were the walls of the building opposite, and eyes were watching out of suddenly lightless windows. In front of him, thirty paces onward, was what he had expected — ten or more masked men loosely strung across the dust, all silent, all turned toward him.

One voice said: "Hello, Starr."

Over by the stable's arch, the cripple leaned against the wall, brutally and eagerly looking on. Dane Starr's thoughts remained on that broken-bodied figure, so crowded with hatred, and the precious moments fled by. The dusk deepened, and sounds withdrew from the street. The very air seemed to have been sucked away.

The even voice said again: "You're a pretty proud man, Starr."

IV

"ARRANGEMENT"

Dane Starr said: "I'm a little more ready than McNeish was. Go ahead." He stood on the balls of his feet, watching that shadowed line for the sudden break, feeling the polar cold go through him. It was always like this at the showdown: the fine warmth of a man's muscles disappeared, and solidity and decent reason. He became something without body, without nerves. Time stood still.

His words fell flatly in the crouched, utter stillness, and the scene before him was indelibly clear to its least detail. Thus aloof and indrawn, one faint thread of contempt ran through his brain. His name evidently meant something, for they delayed that moment. They let the precious instant of surprise go by, and he saw then which man in that hooded line would draw first. He had been warned by an imperceptible bending and stiffening of frame. Somewhere a door slammed, its echo tremendously startling.

Somebody in the hooded line — not the crouched man — said: "How fast are you? Let's see."

It was an ancient trick, intended to draw his attention away. The crouched man erupted at the same moment. His arm dropped, rose. But to Dane Starr, ceaselessly watching, it was like the beating of a brass gong. His cocked nerves let go, and the deep and bitter explosion of the gun was his own.

The hooded man never straightened. He tipped silently forward into the dust, and his hat came off and went rolling away.

One fierce yell of approval came from the hotel. Dane Starr took a broad step aside into the alley, and thus shielded by the corner of the abutting building, he fired on the end of the line that was posted across the street. He saw a second man flinch, seize a porch post, and weakly settle.

Two things then followed in rapid succession. The line opened up on him, slugs ripping away the corner of the wall behind which he stood. And then, unexpectedly, a shotgun stirred this bedlam with a deeper ferocity. There were two vast explosions, and the rattling hail of small shot. The effect was instantaneous. The focused firing on Dane Starr ceased, and the hooded line swept across the street. Benezet's men had suddenly melted into the yonder doorways.

Alert and aroused, Dan Starr heard the blacksmith's pleased shout of triumph. Then a voice — Benezet's smooth, indifferent voice launched from unknown shadows — entered the pulsing calm.

"No more firing. Pull up, Starr, pull up."

Dane Starr thought, suspiciously: *Why don't they go through with it?*

Abruptly the cripple yelled his brutal disappointment, and plunged across the street at a staggering run, bound straight for Dane Starr's shelter. He cried: "Get him . . . get him!" His head lay back on his crooked shoulders, and his savage face showed a remorseless bitterness in the intermittent lights.

But he broke the deadlock. Men poured from the hotel lobby, and one of them reached the cripple and struck him angrily down into the dust. There was a half crowd at the alley's mouth, a hard-breathing mass that shielded Dane Starr from guns farther off.

"Get in the lobby," said a wind-clotted voice. "Get in there. Nothing Benezet says is right."

Dane Starr moved from alley to porch, the miners close ranked behind. He walked into the lobby and halted, while all Dug Gulch slowly filed in out of the night and recruited behind him. Deeply puzzled, he stood in the center of a sullen, electric humming. Benezet was no fool, no faint-hearted man. Some shrewd and greedy impulse was behind his holding of the fire, some new thought born out of the volleyed crashing. What new move was the man proposing?

Dane Starr's restless mind cut forward and backward, and got no answer. The blacksmith shoved his way through the assembled miners to Starr, his smoke-black eyes wickedly cheerful. He had a twelve-gauge shotgun in one hand, two empty cartridges in the other palm.

"I had 'em flanked," he said, and laughed at the thought. "Nothing on earth can stand against buckshot at twenty feet. Makes no difference about pride. They give, and they run."

"You're a dead man," a miner said thoughtfully. "You'll be dead by tomorrow night, Guerney."

The blacksmith's smile was close, brilliant. "By tomorrow night, Billy," he said softly, "it won't be me that's dead." He looked up at Dane Starr's bronzed mask of a face, and the light of his eyes flashed more recklessly. "Benezet's had his thumb on us a good while. Why? Because his whip had a handle, and he's the handle. It takes one good man to stand up and say . . . 'Let's go, boys!' We never had that man. Listen! I'm from Fort Rock. I know this Dane Starr. I never saw him take a backward step. Here's the handle to *our* whip. I'll be damned if he isn't!"

The crowd grew. The word was out. The invisible telegraph was alive. They came in until the lobby was full, and tobacco smoke began to layer the room and the reek of fresh dirt and sweat to permeate it. Dane Starr remained silent, witnessing the heady anger working in all those rough faces — the sultry flash of a long-compressed rage. It was like opening the doors of a furnace; the angry heat rushed at him that suddenly.

Guerney, the blacksmith, laughed again and said: "What is it to be, Dane?"

"There never was a better time than now," a nearby miner interrupted, and shook a raw, roan head turbulently. "Never better than now!"

Starr spoke quietly. "We could whip them now." Silence arrived instantly. He had his audience.

The blacksmith grinned and addressed himself. "One good man. What did I say yesterday?"

"We could whip them now," Dane Starr repeated. "But why run into that waiting fire? Who wants twenty dead men scattered on the street? A high price to pay for the cleaning of a town that will be only another ghost camp, two years from now. Benezet stopped this fight. Why did he stop it? Think a minute. The man's no fool. Walk out there . . . and walk into the lead he's arranged to have spilled."

"Straight palaver!" said the blacksmith, and openly admired Starr with his eyes.

There was talk in the back ranks. "Benezet and Sullivan and this so-called Judge Haley . . . and Clare Durran. They're the ones we want."

"Yes," Dane Starr said noncommittally.

"All right. Let's go get 'em."

"Right into the guns," Dane Starr warned gently. "Wait a little."

"This man," the blacksmith exploded, "has got something up his sleeve. Stand fast and listen."

The cripple knocked a way through the solid mass. He seized a miner's arm, thus supporting himself, and his free hand shook violently in the direction of Starr.

"You're not straight!" he cried. "Listen, boys, don't be fooled . . . he ain't straight! Where'd he come from, and what for? It looked like a nice play, out there on the street. But Benezet's men didn't hit him, did they? Benezet stopped it. Why didn't any of those slugs reach him? Why did Benezet stop it? Here he stands, tellin' us to do nothing. I know why! That girl. . . ."

The blacksmith whirled in fury and grasped the cripple by the shoulders and shook him. He turned the cripple, smashed him back through the crowd, and dropped him by the doorway. "You're as batty as hell! Get out of here!"

Dane Starr's eyes followed those two swirling figures, and his bronzed jaws tightened and killed all expression. He said to those staring men: "Wait."

"How long?" somebody called.

"Why say something that will get right back to Benezet? He's got ears in this crowd. Tomorrow's a long day. Do you get it? Never play the other man's game."

"Don't trust him!" the cripple shrieked, and ran out.

That pondering silence had a depth to it, like calm water beneath which a wicked current waits to drag a man down.

Dane Starr shook his head and walked to the stairs. Three steps upward he turned.

"That's right. Don't trust anybody. I'm with you. I'm in on this. Never mind what happens, I'll be here till the last powder's burned. But don't trust me any further than you want. Why should you?"

He went on, the strain dying from his face muscles, once he had reached the darkness of the upper hall. A glowing streak crept beneath April Surratt's room, but he went on to his own, drew down the window shade in the darkness, and lighted a lamp. His first act was to reload his gun and to replace it under his waistband. Afterward he sat on the bed and rolled a cigarette and stared barrenly at the barren walls.

The cripple had the right of it. Somewhere in that half-mad head rested an uncanny perception that was like a drunken man's sharp glimpse of truth. He, Dane Starr, was with the miners. He had announced himself, and so had assumed an obligation that beyond denial would have to go the whole route until Benezet was down, and the stiff-jawed Sullivan, and the judge. Clare Durran, too. Nothing further mattered, for the lesser thieves would fade like all thieves bereft of support.

He drew in a great breath of smoke, crushed the cigarette between his fingers, and rose suddenly. *Well, it's as old as time,* he thought. *He who lives by the gun dies the same way. But there's Clare Durran!*

The cripple had the right of it, Starr thought again. *April Surratt wanted Durran out of this mess alive, and April Surratt would get her wish.* So he stood between two fires, having no illusions as to what the miners would do to him for protecting Durran, whose faithless smile and long-shown contempt had been so galling. Durran had dug his own grave.

Dane Starr's eyes widened on a segment of the pattern of the carpet. He was motionless until the thought came to him: *That's why Benezet stopped the shooting. He knows the girl has seen me. He knows I'll help Durran because she wants it so. That finishes me with the miners. I'm as dead as if he himself had put the bullet in me.*

He raised his head, eyes smoky and turbulent. "Not many men in the world with a mind that quick," he said.

He looked into the mirror, and looked away. *I ran away from this — and here we are again. It's a game where you can't change seats, or deck, or deal. So why complain? We play the hand out. Which isn't much of a brag, since there ain't any other hand.*

The street was very quiet. Reverberations of the crowd in the lobby came up through the flimsy boards of the hotel. Dane Starr grinned faintly and shut his mind. Then a rough and daring flame rushed diamond bright through his cobalt eyes. He dimmed the lamp. He stared over to the window shade and changed his mind, screwing up the wick again.

Opening his door, he passed into the hall and strode across to April Surratt's door in three cat-footed steps. He had meant to knock, but didn't, for a murmuring came through the panels — the girl's low murmuring instantly followed by a phrase from Clare Durran that was ragged and dissonant.

Dane Starr thought — *There's nothing in him.* — and pushed the door open.

The room was faintly illuminated by a lamp turned low. The rear window was open. Clare Durran stood in a sheltered corner, away from the light and away from the window. His face came around to Starr, thin and dark and shadowed by a moment's desperation.

April Surratt, bearing her trouble on proud and straight shoulders, was a poised shape in the center of the room. She said in a low, composed voice: "Please shut the door."

The rigidness, the shock, went out of Durran. The insolence returned. "Has knocking gone from style?"

"Your tongue can cut and hurt," said April Surratt. "Don't use it on him, Clare."

"Why not?" Durran challenged. He added bitterly: "Am I under obligation to him?"

She was watching Dane Starr, catching each bold line and each flat surface of that unchanging face. She merely murmured, "I think your fate is entirely in his hands."

"Have I asked for any help?" Durran demanded angrily. "Have *you* asked help for me, April? If I thought so. . . ."

"She didn't," said Dane Starr. He walked over to the window and looked into the utter blackness of Dug Gulch's unlovely rear. There was a ladder rising to the window. "She didn't need to ask. What has she been staying here for?"

"I don't need any help!"

But Dane Starr pointed at the window. "Think again. Why

122

didn't you use the lobby instead of that ladder?"

"Answer it yourself," Durran said impudently.

"It was all right while it lasted," Starr said. "Benezet kept you going. Benezet's power supported you. Benezet's hand cast a big shadow, and you walked safely in it. You could smile at men in a way to make them want to kill you, and you knew they didn't dare. Well, it's about over. You realize that, or you wouldn't have used the ladder. You're afraid, Durran."

"There is going to be bloodshed here," Durran said angrily. "It will be on your shoulders. Why didn't you stay away?"

"Speaking for the established order?" Starr asked gently.

"Why not?" Durran challenged. "If it wasn't Benezet, it would be some other thief. Did you ever hear of a mining camp on the level? No. And you never will. Let human nature alone, Starr. Benezet's a crook. Certainly. But he was good enough to pull me off a worthless claim and give me a chance to earn a living at my own trade."

Dane Starr framed the questioning word — "Honestly?" — in his throat, and killed it. For April Surratt's eyes were on Durran, heavily shadowed, the fine light gone. All her body was still, intent. She was absorbing every word.

Dane Starr thought: *Why does she want him?* Then he spoke to Durran. "Do you want to get away?"

"I'll get away."

"Not fifty feet without help. The stable is guarded by now. How far do you suppose you and this girl could travel on foot? It's starvation in the hills. Your way is toward Morgan Mountain . . . and they'd sight you on the prairie and ride you down. Horse or nothing."

"Where do you come in?" asked Clare Durran. Physically, he was quiet, but his thin cheeks went suddenly hard and homely. His eyes passed swiftly from April Surratt to the high-built rider, and back to April Surratt again.

"Do you want him away?" Dane Starr asked the girl.

She said — "Yes." — soberly, and met his level glance. Her next phrase was in a lower tone, and it seemed to shut Clare Durran out. "I like to finish what I begin."

Clare Durran laughed curtly, maliciously. "Your scruples seem pretty mixed, Starr. You want to reform the camp. But you're helping me . . . and double-crossing the men you're leading."

"If that's the way the hand reads," Starr said, "that's the way it's played. We do what we've got to do. Tomorrow, after dark, there'll be some horses in the brush . . . two hundred yards straight south of this hotel. Both of you get there when dusk comes, and ride on. You'll hear firing before you travel very far, but it won't be for you. It'll be for those left behind."

"*Three* horses?" the girl said.

Dane Starr's cheeks were expressionless. "Two will carry you."

"It will soon be known that you helped us. The camp's a whispering gallery. And you will be here without a friend. Three horses, Dane."

He said, after a while: "I'll be a little delayed."

"We'll wait, then," the girl said, and, when he looked directly at her, he saw the queer highlight shining along the straight brow. It was very plain, and very strange.

Beyond his vision, and beyond April Surratt's, Clare Durran spoke with a crackling dryness. "I suppose I should thank you, Starr. Maybe I will, when we're on the trail tomorrow night."

Starr was speaking to the girl. "It was Durran you came to get, wasn't it?"

"We will wait," she repeated.

"Three horses, then," Starr said gravely.

Durran motioned toward the lamp, and Starr reached the light and lowered it to a mere purple glow. Durran went through the window without a sound, and vanished.

Long moments afterward, when Starr had freshened the light again, April Surratt stood with her small, square shoulders in the same motionless attitude, her eyes waiting for him. But he turned abruptly to the door and went through it, saying over his shoulder: "When you reach Morgan Mountain, be sure that you've brought back with you the man you thought you'd find. Be sure of it. And don't go out into the street tomorrow."

Behind him was a sharp, swift sigh and a quiet phrase: "I know already what I've found, Dane."

V

"THE ULTIMATE DECEIT"

Clare Durran dropped to the bottom of the ladder and paused there, watching the light flare up again in April Surratt's room. His small hands seized a rung of the ladder. The breath went in and out of him quickly. He whispered, half in rage: "That was plain enough!"

Somewhere in the dark a foot struck sharply against a wooden box, making a brittle noise. A man spoke under his breath. "Tug, go back to the street and watch."

Durran's hand pressed down on the gun in his own pocket. He moved lightly along the opaque shadows, brushing first this rear wall and then that, until he arrived at the rear of the saloon. After a short pause, he let himself in with a rapid whirl of his shoulders, and slammed the door shut.

125

Benezet sat musing at the table and silently twirling an empty glass, his two ever-present bodyguards speechless behind him, the stiff-jawed Sullivan across from him. Sullivan looked at Durran, and let his eyes fade back across Benezet's face.

Benezet said: "Somebody posted out there?"

"Getting dangerous," Durran answered, absorbed in his own irritated thinking.

"Where were you?"

"At the hotel."

Benezet's small eyes, faintly amused, twitched to Sullivan. Then he said to Durran: "Stay out of there now, Clare. The lower half of the town belongs to the miners. We stick to the saloon."

"How long?"

"Till they get a notion to rush us."

"Is this the best we can do?" Durran said. "Hide behind a wall and admit we're licked? That's not like you, Benezet."

Benezet chuckled. "You don't know what I'm like. I take one thing at a time. Right now it's this. Maybe before curfew. . . ."

Durran reached for Sullivan's empty glass and poured a drink from the bottle standing there. He downed it, moved around the table, aimless and brooding. He was in a far corner, his back to them, when he spoke again. "No, not tonight," he said.

"All right?" said Benezet, a question in the words.

Durran turned toward him. "Starr's holding this fight off till dark tomorrow."

"Yeah?"

"Because he'll be out of here then with the girl. Lay a couple men in the brush two hundred yards straight east of the hotel, at that time, and you'll find three horses waiting

126

for them. That's straight."

"*Three* horses?" Benezet repeated.

Sullivan stared curiously at Durran.

"Extra one for relief, I suppose," Durran said, without emotion.

"So she dropped you?" said Benezet, deliberately overlooking the more important fact.

"She's been engaged to me for a year, and she met him just twenty-four hours ago," Durran said. "Is it because he's built like a tiger, or because there's something mysterious behind those damned black eyes? What makes a woman change in twenty-four hours, Benezet?"

Benezet rolled his palms on the table. Ironic laughter glimmered beneath the heavy brows.

"I don't know women," he said. "Not that girl's kind. But I know you."

"All right," Durran said, and jerked up his head.

"You're a dapper man, Clare. You got a manner, a damn' bright brain, and a ready tongue. In a settled community you'd shine. You'd be a big man. Up here, in this tough camp, you are only a small man with a day's whiskers on your face. See? It's law and order that makes you swagger. You got no nerve for rough and tumble. This Starr is a man anywhere. Maybe the girl sees it."

"Glad to have your true opinion," Durran said violently.

"I been pretty good to you, kid. May be an end to that . . . we'll never know."

"That bad?"

"Maybe. Maybe not." Benezet's frame was mountainously formidable in the hazy light of the room. "I'm a great hand to wait till the last fellow's fired before looking at my luck. Better get a drink," he added.

It was dismissal. Durran showed his irritation. His cheeks

127

were drawn and dark as he went out into the barroom.

Sullivan said to Benezet softly: "Three horses?"

"The girl asked Starr to help Durran, and Starr's that kind of a man. So the three of them have fixed it up for tomorrow night. But Clare saw something there between that girl and Starr. He's selling Starr out."

"Leaves it kind of tangled," Sullivan said.

"No. Clare'll be rustling around for two horses to cache at some other spot. He'll lie to the girl, and take her away. Starr's waiting with the other horses . . . and that's where we find him."

"Kind of stinks," said Sullivan.

"I always saw Clare plain and clear. This don't surprise me."

"If he's that tricky. . . ."

Benezet looked at his marshal. One swollen fist rose, and a stub finger pointed mutely from Sullivan to the saloon where Durran was. His palm made a gentle, erasing gesture against the air.

When Durran went out to the bar, he took a drink. Then he turned and hooked his elbows on the bar and stared vaguely around the great room now occupied only by Benezet's followers. His brooding eyes passed over them one by one, touched a particular man, and moved on. In another moment he shrugged his impatient shoulders, swerved out to the street. A mere trickle of citizens stirred along it, and these walked through the far shadows.

Under the porch roof of the saloon four idle Benezet hands remained very still, very watchful. Durran passed them. One said: "Mister Durran . . . not too far."

Durran merely nodded. A little farther he heard steps coming after him, and then he swung into an alleyway.

128

A figure cut the corner and halted.

"Tom? I got you out of some trouble once."

"Just mention it, Mister Durran. Anything you say."

"Two horses saddled to go."

"Not so easy, Mister Durran. But I will."

"Tomorrow, right after dark. Just off the trail that leads north to Placer, where the creek comes down." He ceased talking, and the silence was dull and heavy. Immediately he added: "Two hundred dollars to you when I step into the stirrup."

"That'll help, Mister Durran."

"More substantial than the deep gratitude you feel," said Durran with an irony so deft that the stolid figure in front of him missed it, and muttered: "Thanks!"

This was noon, and another day, and Dug Gulch's life blood seemed to have run out. At eleven the Morgan Mountain stage had stopped at the hotel, bearing two passengers, but the driver never got down. Two men came slowly from the hotel lobby and one of them said: "Water your horses, then turn back, taking your passengers with you."

There was no protest. The driver knew the country and its men.

The street was dead. One figure stood beside the saloon doors, and one figure leaned against the courthouse pillar. But between those two Benezet sentries there stretched an invisible line across which no man had passed since daylight.

The gutted ravines were still, deserted. A high sun poured fresh heat down from a cloudless sky, and on the lower prairie the returning Morgan Mountain stage kicked up a tawny ribbon of dust.

Dane Starr descended stairs to the lobby, and twenty-five men there showed a quickening interest. The blacksmith left a game of seven-up and came over.

He said genially: "There's this many across the street in the store. There's this many belly flat in the pines, all around the camp. If it's waiting, we can wait."

A raw roan head bowed beneath the hotel's door. It belonged to the miner who had spoken the night before. He strolled over.

"The street's safe enough to walk on," he said. "They're waiting. We're waiting. What are we waiting for?"

"You want four men," Starr said evenly. "How would you get them?"

"Go right where they are," said the redhead, his voice snapping.

The seven-up game stopped. A rustle of restlessness scudded around the room. The cripple swayed into the lobby and squatted near it. His burning, onyx eyes sought Dane Starr hungrily and stayed there.

Dane Starr's words hit the redhead like blows, one after another. "If you're in a hurry, walk down to the saloon and find them. The doors are open, and the street's wide enough."

The redhead's eyes glittered, and he pursed his lips and turned pale with anger. Yet he remained in charge of himself.

"Why dig your spurs into me? Whose show is this?" He stopped and scowled. "Now that I think of it, what's happened here? We were ready to go last night. Who's changed the tune here? What's the extra day of debating for?"

"Anybody can die," Dane Starr said.

"I'll take my chances."

"Take them," Starr challenged grimly. "There's the street."

The redhead's outraged pallor increased, and he threw his suddenly fired glance at Starr's stone-blank countenance. Pivoting, he walked back to the street. A tension snapped in the lobby. The seven-up game was resumed.

The blacksmith's admiring chuckle was resonantly hearty. He murmured: "You destroyed him, Dane. You could wrap this crowd around your finger."

"I want to see you for a moment in the shop," Starr said. Side by side, they moved to the door.

A man in the seven-up game looked up alertly. "It may be a safe street . . . but not for you, Starr. Benezet's sharp-shooter is in the courthouse tower."

Starr shook his head. "Benezet is a shrewd man, and he prefers to destroy me another way. It's an old game."

He went out to the porch. Half a dozen miners in the lobby turned instantly to the windows and watched him go idly through the drenching sunshine and swing into the blacksmith shop, Guerney beside him.

"Nerve!" somebody said.

The cripple said bitterly to the room: "He was pretty sure no Benezet man would fire at him. You fools! I know what the extra day's wait is for. Starr's helping the girl get Durran out of town. They'll be gone tonight. How do you know Starr won't be gone, too?"

One of the seven-up players said: "Get the hell out of here!" But in a moment his eyes sought the other players, and doubt was in them.

In the blacksmith shop, Starr stood slightly away from the arch and scanned the upper windows of the courthouse thoughtfully. High up in the bell-tower a mere porthole of glass showed a jagged break, and behind it lay something black and motionless. One of Benezet's hands marched from the courthouse door, touched the sentry on the shoulder, and took up his position. The relieved man went inside.

All this Dane Starr observed solemnly, other thoughts running through his mind.

Guerney moved restlessly back and forth.

Still watching the courthouse, Starr said: "Never mind what this sounds like. I need three horses."

He heard Guerney stop. The silence ran on. Two miners rolled past the arch, looked in, and wheeled back.

Guerney's speech was flat. "All right," he said.

Starr turned. "In the trees behind the hotel, tonight, as soon as dark comes. If the girl's come this far and waited this long for Durran, would you want to break her heart? Never mind what the crowd wants. Benezet's the only man we're after."

"*Three* horses?" said the blacksmith. He put his felt-black eyes on Starr and then turned his head away, a gray and unpleasantly disheartened expression seizing the broad face.

Dane Starr smiled at him. "She thinks so, Guerney. But I'll be here. I'll be right here."

The blacksmith's cheeks registered enormous relief. He grinned. "The horses will be there, Dane."

"Trust," Starr said, "is a wonderful thing."

Guerney spoke with some apology. "What's the extra day of waiting for? You could've got Durran and the girl off last night."

Starr hunted for his tobacco and sat on the end of an empty nail keg. "We could have taken the camp last night. It's a question of how much the taking is worth. A lot of those miners have families somewhere, Guerney. How would you like to be writing ten families this morning, telling each that a man was dead . . . killed in a fight to clean a camp that will be a crumbled relic overgrown with hazel brush twenty months from now?" His sigh expressed sadness. "I have had to do that. It's pretty tough."

"Tonight won't be no easier."

Starr said: "I hope you never have to know this game as

132

I know it. There's thirty men waiting yonder on Benezet's side. What are they? A bunch of pariahs, full of courage as long as the ground is solid, loyal to Benezet as long as he walks the street and rules it. But the ground ain't solid now, Guerney, and there's Benezet in his back room, never speaking a word. The easy days are all done, and here's eighty miners, full of bitter hell. Listen, Guerney, crooks fight when they're cornered, but waiting kills their spunk. And there's no loyalty in them for a lost cause. They've had twenty-four hours to think about it. When dark comes, Benezet won't have his men. Not all of them, at any rate. They'll be gone."

The blacksmith said: "Benezet . . . ?"

"I doubt if he'll run," Starr said quietly. "He's pretty proud."

"We'll find him!" the blacksmith said.

"Sure," Starr said. "But I don't want any of you boys to die, Guerney."

"Supposing that crowd don't run?"

"Always a little gamble. Nothing's very certain. Nothing's ever very clear."

It was half past two then. The sunlight was running like hot, liquid glass along a dead, empty street. Dane Starr sat on the keg, staring through the faint cigarette smoke, through wall and tree and hillside, to some vision far away.

Full dark folded down, and the moonless shadows took on body and thickness. Clare Durran emerged from a lightless alley, followed saloon wall and store wall as far as the hotel. Before him was a taut shape, very slim and very faint, and the thread of a voice.

"Clare!"

"We've had to change this to the Placer trail."

"Where's Dane?"

"Gone ahead," Durran said, and took the girl's arm roughly.

They went southward until the buildings ceased and the level ground dropped away. Fifty yards through brush and pine, Durran turned and crossed the Morgan Mountain road and struggled back to the higher area on the northern side of the Gulch. He was breathing fast, the muscles of his thin body were toiling.

April Surratt followed with a lithe, swift ease, profoundly silent.

Durran muttered bitterly — "All things change." — and came then to a trail.

But he followed it no more than a hundred feet, for a creek barred his way, and a man also barred his way. The man said: "Durran . . . off here. Don't stay on the trail."

The horses were in the brush.

"You're sure," said April Surratt, "that Dane's gone on?"

"Dane Starr?" said Benezet's man, a lagging reluctance in his voice.

April Surratt was in the saddle. Durran mounted. He turned his horse. He said to the man: "What do you care?"

"How about the two hundred?"

Then the man turned, and April Surratt saw his body crouch over.

The trail carried forward the muted drumming of riders, and in a moment a wraith-like line was abreast, moving by at a walk. One voice slid curtly back: "There's plenty of trails . . . why does everybody take this one?"

Then they were past, and the drumming died downgrade.

Durran's talk was unsympathetic, wholly indifferent. "Fleeing the wrath to come," he said, motioning toward Benezet's disappearing men. "There goes our side, Tom . . . and God help those left behind. Benezet probably doesn't even know."

"The two hundred!" said the man.

"Not for something I could have done myself."

The Benezet man emitted a rushing breath. "I thought so!" He whirled. "Ma'am, Dane Starr ain't down the trail. He's in town."

"I ought to kill you!" Durran rasped, and his thin body swayed.

But April Surratt reined her horse away from him, her talk swift and final. "You're free," she declared swiftly. "I said I liked to finish what I began, didn't I? Well, it's over now . . . and I'm not sorry, and I'm not sad. We won't meet again, Clare. Good bye."

She was on the trail, turned toward Dug Gulch.

Clare cried: "Come back here!" And that was all.

A shot burst furiously in the brush, its echo cracking the drawn stillness of the hills. April Surratt hauled her horse about, shuddering with the terrific pain and terror of that sound.

But Benezet's man was slipping past her, breathing hard, and his warning was enough.

"Never mind him! He drew on me . . . which I might have expected . . . no good, ma'am! He wasn't no good!"

He said something else, but it was overwhelmed by a rushing eruption of voices on Dug Gulch's street. Afterward, a pair of gun explosions lifted from the town, dampened by intervening walls.

At that, April Surratt once more turned her horse and spurred toward the street.

VI

"THE WAY A MAN DIES"

There was no more ease, no more card playing. The pulsing heat of the previous night ran through the crowd again, and, in the half-lit gloom of the lobby, men's eyes burned strangely.

A scout came off the porch and said: "No sound, and no sight. Nothing moved behind the courthouse lights that I can make out."

Dane Starr remained quiet. Yet the stormy and brutal temper changed his bronzed skin, changed the line of his mouth and the angle of his jaw. "I want you to do as I say," he said tensely.

The redhead was before him, speaking out of rebellion. "So far, what have you said? What have we got by waiting? It's another night . . . and the same crowd to meet."

"Steady!" said Guerney. "You'll soon enough know."

"When you hear a gun fired," directed Starr, "move out as you please." He turned a little to avoid the redhead; he started for the door.

The redhead swiftly put himself in front of Starr. "When and where we go," he said, civilly blunt, "you'll go, too. There's a little doubt here."

Starr's high shoulders rolled. He murmured — "Sorry, kid." — and drove his tough fist fully against the redhead's jaw.

The redhead's eyes turned full around, and he went slowly backward, to strike the floor hard.

Starr repeated himself, his talk running resonantly into the drawn stillness. "When you hear a shot, move as you please."

The cripple, his grotesque body hauled against a stair post, screamed: "Don't let him!"

But Starr was already outside, beyond them, and the black-smith was a black, massive barrier at the doorway. Guerney was grinning, wickedly pleased.

"Any remarks?" he called.

Starr turned at the alley, passed along its length, and traversed the tricky path beside the building walls. He was thinking rapidly: *Benezet's a proud man, and I believe I'll find him there. If there is to be dying, let a fellow who has seen enough of it take the proper part.*

He stopped then, his flat muscles very hard. The echo of a single shot looped over the false-topped buildings and shattered itself in the street, and all the long hush was disturbed by small whorls of sound.

Benezet's men had collided with the pickets, obviously. Well, this was the end of something — and the beginning of something. His running had been no good. Running never would be good for anything.

A full-lunged shouting slapped through the yonder street. A rebel yell wailed weirdly above that filling cry of the pack.

Dane Starr suddenly flung himself forward, as far as the pencil strip of light shining beneath Benezet's office door. There was no further need of caution, no more use for reason. He had the door knob in his palm, and he had wrenched the door open and crossed the threshold in the space of a full-drawn breath. There he stood like a firebrand, a high, flat-bodied shape who bulked large in the grisly, guttering semi-light.

Benezet was a sleepy-looking mass in the chair behind the one small table. Back of Benezet, caught in the act of turning, was Marshal Sullivan. Nobody else. The bodyguards had vanished. Beyond the office wall, the saloon room was as quiet as a grave. Beyond the saloon, the cries of the raging miners began to deepen.

"Power," Dane Starr said, "is a false light in the far desert. Benezet, your crowd's gone."

"I found that out a minute ago," Benezet rumbled. No emotion went through his body, however. His little eyes were inscrutable surfaces, like the blind orbs of an Oriental god. "That was why you waited the extra day?"

"The game is well known to me," Starr said.

Sullivan raised his arms so that Starr might see them, straightening and turning from his cramped position until he faced Starr directly. Two quick shots thickened the undertone of the crowd outside. Sullivan's glance whipped toward the door, and, when he looked back, Starr saw ferocious hope there.

Benezet's bland voice went on monotonously. "Consider it a compliment. I admire a tough man wherever I see him. I'd like to stand up."

Starr said gently — "All right." — and watched the great body lift itself above the table top.

All the light of the room came from the one lamp on that table whose edges were gripped by Benezet's ridiculous, puffed hands. Sullivan, half covered by the width of Benezet's enormous body, moved aside until he again faced Starr, each movement painfully slow. Boots slid tentatively along the floor of the saloon room. The crowd's hallooing grew in volume as it approached, but there was no further shooting.

"The trail, of course, always has an end," Benezet murmured. "You had courage, coming in here."

"Out of thirty men," Starr observed, "Sullivan was the only one to stick."

"Well enough," Benezet drawled. "I always saw these people plain and clear. It's been my observation that the men you can't buy are the ones to fear. The ones you can buy have nothing worth buying. The trail, friend Starr, always has an end." He paused. "Whose end?"

He said it — and then this prodigious mass of flesh found somewhere a flash of speed. A club-like arm blurred the air above the lamp. The light went out, and a chair fell over.

Dane Starr had it all like a flame-bright picture in his mind as he stepped aside and fired. He heard the actual impact of his bullet, and the wincing, punctured breath. The roar of the gun in this cramped space was like a dynamite blast, the sudden smell of powder strong in his nostrils.

Fury blazed again, and a long, screaming muzzle light licked the sightless quarters. By that pale muzzle light Dane Starr, selfless and impersonal, laid his last shot. Sullivan said nothing, but his body went down, audibly scraping the wall as it fell.

The next moment the full shock of the crowd shook the saloon building. The rebel yell wailed again, and the office door was smashed back by one single blow.

A man, full of wild foolishness, framed himself in the light and stared at the powder-ridden blackness inside. "Who's there?" he said.

"Light a lamp," Starr called.

A lantern bobbed forward, hand over hand, and the reckless one seized it and held it before him at arm's length. The redhead's hot face glistened for an instant behind the light, and then the crowd forced him in, and he was shoulder to shoulder with Starr, looking down at the two still figures behind the table.

When he stared back at Starr, the flash of unreason seemed to have gone out of his eyes. He spoke without heat. "Whose show was this?"

"Leave the game to those that play it well," Starr muttered.

"So you let them go?" said the other. But it wasn't in anger. It was something said out of second thought, out of awakening comprehension. "You let them go. And you saw Durran ride off with his girl."

"No, not Durran," spoke a man in the far ranks. "Durran's dead on the trail to Placer. Durran drew it too fine."

Dane Starr turned, rough and unreasonably harsh, toward that wedged mass in the doorway. He put his gun back beneath his waistband and shouldered through. He saw the blacksmith, and he spoke a farewell.

"Guerney," he said, "trust is a fine thing!" And then he passed into the street.

He stopped there, however, for April Surratt was waiting on the walk, tall and slim and pale.

"There's a lot of hurt in the world, April," he said.

"Never mind, Dane."

"So you found what you must have known about him?"

Her answer was a low melody, running through the shadows.

"What could I say now, Dane? Clare betrayed you. Don't you know why?"

Starr bent forward, his high shoulders coming down toward her. A great noise was running free through the doors, but the silence here seemed strong and full.

"April, three horses never have worked. Two horses down the trail . . . that's enough."

"Tonight!" she said, the melody turning eager. "Back to Fort Rock, which is your home, and will be mine. There isn't anything more for us farther along this trail. It would be sinful to expect more than we've found."

Blacksmith Guerney heard voices on the walk and came out of the saloon. But all he saw was two shadows passing back to the hotel. Guerney cleared his throat and said, to no one in particular: "It'd be pure satisfaction to go plumb to hell for that guy!"

NEW HOPE

I

"DOWN THE RIVER"

The buffalo coat he wore was thirty years old and showed how big a man he had been in his earlier life. It was loose on him now, and a little heavy. His sons and daughters and two of his grandchildren were around him, and most of New Hope stood on the wharf, and stevedores were loading the last pieces of cargo. The *T. J. Jackson* heeled gently to the Missouri's current, and smoke poured out of its twin stacks, and high up on the texas deck the pilot watched the scene with an impatient eye. A mate called: "Stand by." Henry Senn was going down the river to spend the winter with his oldest daughter in St. Louis.

There was a good deal of talk around Henry Senn. He kissed the grandchildren and his two daughters, although he was no man for a display of affection, and shook hands with Tom, the younger son. It was the older boy, Bob, who went up the gangplank with him. They climbed to the passenger deck and stood at the railing, overlooking the wharf.

Bob said, with a heartiness that fooled neither of them: "The winters get pretty cold here. You'll like it at Josie's. We'll see you in the spring. Don't worry about the business."

The throaty whistle of the *T. J. Jackson* burst over them, and on the wharf Henry Senn's youngest grandchild began to cry. Bob reached for his father's hand and turned away, but

Henry Senn called — "Wait!" — and watched his son turn back. "I have always been pleased with you. You have only one fault, which is to go along with the crowd. Remember this . . . it makes no difference what others say or do . . . don't you ever do anything that you personally think is wrong. Good bye." His son turned swiftly and went down the steps and across the gangplank. All the people were crowding the wharf, and the New Hope band had gathered in the background. The boat's idling engines pulsed steadily, and the deck crew dragged in the gangplank, chanting:

Way down, way down
Way down in Egypt land.

Wind came up the river strong and cold, and a sparkling winter mist lay over the housetops of New Hope, and the roofs and corners of the warehouses made a gaunt show in the day.

Henry Senn lit a cigar, seeing his family standing in line on the dock. His two boys were like himself, their cheeks held a half-severe expression — revealing nothing. Emma, always sentimental, was crying, but Alice, who was the youngest, showed him a still, soft face — as though she were dreaming of the years gone by.

Emma's voice was indistinct in the noise. "Father, don't smoke too much. You'll like it at Josie's. Be sure to write. Don't plan to come back before April."

Dike Miller pushed through the ranks, still wearing his leather blacksmith apron. Dike yelled: "Bring me some oranges when you come upriver, Henry."

"Sure," said Henry Senn. "Sure."

"Some men," cried Dike Miller, "sure get to lead an easy life."

"For bein' honest," said Henry Senn. "See you next year."

They were lying, and he was lying. He knew it — and they knew it. There would never be another spring in New Hope for him. He replaced the cigar and put his long, crooked fingers around the railing. His heart was a distant, sluggish murmur; the buffalo coat weighted his shoulders. That afternoon he had climbed the road to the cemetery to stand alone by his wife's grave and to say to her, in his mind, those last things a man thinks of saying.

Distant, in the core of the *T. J. Jackson*, bells jingled, and the mate was calling: "Let's go spring and stern lines!"

There were a lot of people on the wharf, and the band was going to play something. Billy McDermott, whom he had never liked, stood at the edge of the wharf. Looking up Custer Street, he saw the bare tracery of the locust trees in the courthouse square and the bronze statue of the Civil War soldier. Thirty-seven years before, he had pitched his solitary camp where the town square now stood. At that time a wild-plum thicket grew there, and no white man lived nearer than a hundred miles. All that New Hope now was had come to pass before his eyes.

Bells jingled again. The sudden thrust of the paddle wheels shook the *T. J. Jackson*, and the mate bawled — "Let go bow line!" — and the wharf began to slide by. People were calling to Henry Senn, their strong good byes floating across the widening water. Billy McDermott lifted his hat. Billy had fought him for thirty years, but that enmity faded now before the fact that both of them were saying farewell to a past that would soon be gone.

The New Hope band struck up "Auld Lang Syne," strong and slow, and the people on the shore were singing. Henry Senn removed his hat and held it against his breast, his white, close-cropped head motionless. Emma lifted her youngest child so that he might see his grandfather clearly this last time. His two boys never moved, and he was proud that they showed him no sentiment. Alice, who never cried, turned swiftly and vanished through the crowd.

The *T. J. Jackson* wheeled in the stream, turning about, and Henry Senn walked around the deck to have his last sight of the town. The shapes on the shore were diminishing, and he no longer saw them clearly. The band's music softened and died over the water, and the *T. J. Jackson*'s great whistle drowned all other sound. New Hope slid away.

A silver mist hung over everything. Chimney smoke spiraled grayly above New Hope, and the flag on the Central School whipped in the wind. From his position he saw the gridiron pattern of the streets, the oak groves and slim poplars along the Omaha road. Wexler's Meadow — where he had shot and killed the outlaw, Curly Ben — was a brown square in the distance; and above this was the low cemetery hill where lay his wife. Beyond this lay the open prairie, mist ridden and obscure.

The stages of his life were pretty clear. In the beginning he had been young and foot-loose, roaming these plains with his ears and eyes sharpened to the risks, with the strong savor of the land's wildness having a way with him. The frontier was his life. He had started with it and grown up with it, through the boisterous days of New Hope's youth. He had married and raised his family. Afterward, with his wife gone, his children matured, and, the needs of his life satisfied, the days had gotten slow and pretty long. This was the looking-back time in which a man had to live his life again, and compose himself for his ending.

The stern of the *T. J. Jackson* heeled around Sawyer's Bend and then, strangely and completely, the silver mist closed down, and New Hope was gone, and there was nothing on this prairie but emptiness. The intervening years were wiped away, and the prairie lay again, flawless and unexplored, as it had been in the beginning. It was like a last message to him — telling him that a man's life was this way, his little habitations and monuments fading and nothing remaining but the distant horizons that a man had to keep searching. There was always a frontier, here or somewhere.

He stood here, bareheaded and still, feeling the boat and the river bear him along, away from New Hope, away from this episode that had been his life, away from this earth. The land was a mist, and the sky was a mist, and he seemed to be released from all that he had been, and he felt quite free, and his eyes, old blue, sought westward, and distant excitement warmed him, as long ago.

The mate came by and said: "Pretty cold out here, Mister Senn."

He nodded, not really hearing. This was the end of one life, the memories and forms of which were fast fading — even the shapes of his children and the sounds of their voices. Probably they would not understand this, but his own mind was pretty clear. He was a stranger to all of them. He was alone and young again and a little anxious to be on his way, toward a fresh and misty land and its adventure.

II

"THEIR OWN LIGHTS"

I happened to be standing that afternoon under the arch of Billy Hope's Livery Stable on River Street when Leora Kadderly walked from the Bon Marche and lifted her parasol

145

against the drenching sunlight. Parasol in one hand and package in the other, she started north toward Belle Plaine Street which, in New Hope's social scheme, was the abode of the gentle born. Just beyond the Bon Marche store Herm von Gayl's double saloon doors opened on the walk, and von Gayl's roof extended over it, and, as she reached this area, I saw her pick up her skirts. I do not know why, but all the women of New Hope did this when they passed von Gayl's; it was originally a gesture of protest, I think, that at last had become a matter of etiquette. Her package slipped from her arm, and then Ben Tarrade, standing there, quickly recovered it for her and took off his hat. I saw her lips move slightly — thanking him, I suppose — and for a moment those two looked at each other, and then she went on; and, as long as she remained in sight, Ben Tarrade's eyes followed, his high body motionless, his blond head motionless.

Of all the incidents of my boyhood, this still remains, after fifty-odd years, the most clearly remembered. When I look back, I can see that this was the beginning; and I can acknowledge now that this was bravery. I was only twelve, yet I recall the touch of a feeling almost sinister in effect, for, young as I was, I knew that Ben Tarrade, a gambler at von Gayl's, had no proper right to speak to Leora Kadderly. Billy Hope, behind me, said — "So." — in a queer way, and I looked around and saw that his eyes were narrow and not pleased.

I think you should know New Hope, Nebraska, on the yellow river forever eating into its high, sandy shore line. There are no towns like that any more, for the time is gone, and the conjunction of that heavy-grained and rather somber 1880 man with a stubborn land no longer exists; or perhaps it is that boyhood's perception of color and smell and sound is gone. Reviewing that era, I can understand that New Hope's day was at a climax. To north and to south the railroads were beginning to take away much of its freighting traffic, and so it was like many another town along that river, middle-aged after two decades of brief existence. But of this, then, I knew nothing. To me, it was the exciting center of the universe, never dull, never the same. The big riverboats brought their cargoes to the landing, and the black boys sang as they filed up and down the gangplanks; the freighters — wheel, swing, and lead teams to each bulky wagon — moved out of New Hope in solid lines, kicking up the heavy dust as far as the eye could reach, bound for distant prairie points. This was only four years after Custer, and that yonder country was still wild, and beyond the far haze mystery still lived. By day the earth was copper and brass; by night the prairie undulated under the moonlight like slow groundswells at sea, pale and beautiful.

We were a trading town. I did not see it then, since a boy has little esthetic sense, but I can readily believe now a more unlovely place never existed. There were no grass lawns and very few trees, and the wind drove sand up from the south and turned daylight gray and ground the clearness out of window panes and left an ashy sediment on everything. River Street was the artery of town, solidly built of frame and brick stores and gaunt, three-story warehouses without the faintest grace of ornament. Palmer's tannery lay on the north quarter of town, and, when the wind hauled around, a stench swept over us. Slightly in the south was the brewery, gray tower dominating the sky, where I used to go to see the big wheel turn. There was a residual grace in those people, of that I am sure, for my own home life was gentle and serene; but men had little use for outward decoration. I think the land made them that way.

Of the day I speak, I stayed out too long, and, when I reached the supper table, I expected a lecture; but my father was playing the host, which meant that his customary reserve was put aside for an attitude half courtly, half genial. People in those days took their manners much more seriously, wearing them ceremoniously for the occasion much as we now wear our clothes. Leora Kadderly was there, and Jim Shugrue; and I knew immediately why. A boy's perceptions are much keener than elders realize, and in that day we youngsters had half the gossip of the town at our fingertips. So I was quite aware that all New Hope was trying to marry Leora Kadderly to Jim Shugrue, and that Mother was carrying on the game of match-making.

We always had wine at the table. My father raised his glass and proposed the toast. I recall it distinctly. I can even bring back the cheerful, humorous tone he used. He said: "To a certain happy event, which I hope will not long be delayed."

My mother showed a little confusion. She said to Father — "Why, Tod, that's too bold of you." — but I could see that actually she was a little pleased it had been put in the open. They sipped at the wine, pale and sparkling in the cut goblets that were heirlooms of the Tennessee Bowies, Mother's side. Then Jim Shugrue spoke. "If it does not soon happen," he said, "it will not be because I haven't asked," and he looked at Leora Kadderly. I had always liked him, perhaps because he owned so many of those heavy prairie freighters, and perhaps also because he looked a great deal like my father, who had a bold, broad face and a fine, cavalry-style mustache. Now that I recall it, many men looked like my father. In the 1880s the pattern seemed to be pretty uniform, mustache or beard on a sun-baked skin, a touch of severity about the eyes, and a slow way of talking. I can think of but one man in New Hope of that day who was clean shaven. This was the gambler, Ben Tarrade.

I think I remember a touch of embarrassment about the

table then; for it was always considered indelicate to discuss personal affairs publicly. But of them all, Leora Kadderly seemed least touched. She was looking at me, and she was smiling.

It seems rather merciless that the years should be this way: that they should drop dimming curtains behind us as the time goes on until in the end all that we know and loved remains only faintly — a fragment of a voice, a smile, a touch still felt — leaving everything else obscured and half forgotten. I do not think she was beautiful as we understand the word. But there was a power in her, a hunger that shone out through dark eyes and made every feature vividly expressive. It is as strong to me now as it was then; and so it must have been very real. There was laughter in her and gaiety, but it was subdued; it was something hard pressed by all that New Hope stood for. Little enough gaiety lived in that town, and, when I come to search my youth again, I remember but one other person whose smile held that same lurking recklessness, and again this was Ben Tarrade, the gambler. She was twenty-five, and a widow, and she lived alone; and so because in that land at that time an eligible woman was regarded as something useful and productive going to waste, New Hope laid its almost mandatory will upon her. This is what I know now.

My father said, more soberly: "I hear, Leora, that Ben Tarrade picked up a package for you today."

"I hadn't heard that," Jim Shugrue said, and his face sharpened.

My mother was rather angry. "The man should know his place."

"I thought it an act of ordinary kindness," said Leora Kadderly.

"It will be talked about," my mother went on.

But Leora Kadderly only smiled, and I can still feel the

wistfulness of it. They were all looking at her; and now I know that she was quite alone at that moment. "What harm can be in it?" she asked, with a softness I clearly recall.

They went on talking. Presently I was excused and went to the porch, and later my father and Jim Shugrue came out to smoke. Westward, beyond the end of River Street, the fires of the freighters' camps colored the sky, and the moon swam like a caravel on the low horizon. It was very still, and the smell of sage and dust and tar lay strong in the night. The shadows softened everything, even the talk of the two men.

"She needs a man to see that these things don't repeat themselves," said my father.

Jim Shugrue was a fair man. "I've always liked him for what he was, Tod. I have always found him square for a gambler."

"That will do, as between men. But he must know the line with womenfolk. If he steps over it, he shall be horse-whipped."

Their talk went on, very even, very sure; and in a little while I slipped away, crossed a vacant block westward, and came upon the margin of corral and barn and open space where were outfitted the freighters and freighting teams. I meant to cut past this to gain the quarter of town in which my particular band of boyhood friends usually foregathered; but, as I ran between corrals, I arrived at a wide circle of men, standing about a fire, and across and about this area two teamsters were wickedly fighting. I could see them very plainly — two huge, gaunt men bare to the waist, all muscles coiling and swelling in that crimson light, blood dripping down their bare chests; and I could hear the dull sound of their fists, the crush of bone into flesh. It was not the first fight I had seen, but all this red savagery chilled me; and, when I looked around the circle of bystanders and discovered the lust shining in those eyes, and the lips drawn back over heavy, yellow teeth, it was like coming upon a circle of wolves, and I pivoted and ran home.

Casting up accounts now, all the isolated pieces of this affair return in proper sequence; the years have given them meaning, and a clear light surrounds everything. It was the following Sunday that I turned the saddle shop corner at St. Vrain Street, on my way to Sunday school, and found Ben Tarrade standing idly by the shop wall. I do not know why I stopped, but I did — feeling half guilty and half charmed. I think the whole secret of Ben Tarrade lay in his eyes. He was a tall man, and he wore his black, broadcloth suit and stiff, white shirt with a certain easy flair, with a gentleman's indifference. His hands, I recall, were white and supple of finger; and underneath the black, loose-brimmed hat, edged by yellow hair, were features that at once gave you the impression of being responsive without the need of much facial play. But I think it was his eyes that smilingly encouraged you, and haunted you a little with what was behind them. He was, I know now, a very lonely man outside the circle of the genteel, yet aloof from the class that played at his table in von Gayl's. There was, I can understand, a need in him New Hope could not satisfy.

He spoke to me, and I remember being flattered by the equality of his manner. "Tod," he said, "you're looking rather sad for such a fine morning."

"I am going to church," I told him.

"Yes," he said, "I know." And his smile was very strong. "I remember being just as sad on Sunday mornings when I went to church. Older people forget how boys feel. But it's all right. Church is part of growing up, Tod. And the sun will still be shining when you get out."

I do not recall answering him. I stood a little in awe of this man. He was a gambler, someone I had been taught to distrust and abhor, and this he must have known as he stood there talking to me. Again it comes to me that this story lay in his eyes, in the gentleness of his tone. He said: "Like to fish, Tod?"

"Yes."

"I'll have to ask your dad if you can go up the river with me. Some mighty big cats in the upper channel. Well, you better not be late."

I went on, feeling a little guilty and a little honored. My crowd of boys slowly gathered, and we all went in to Sunday school, and after that joined our elders in the main church service.

Even now I can feel the dullness of those New Hope Sundays. Everything in that town closed, and everything became still and repressed. That day the elders put on their dark clothes and seemed stiff in them; and there was then a somberness and a quietness, and I can remember being a little shocked when one man laughed aloud on the church steps. We were a literal people with a literal religion. This was the Sabbath; this day we glimpsed the vengeful fires of hell, and in our pew, between my parents, that long hour of service stretched out with a dread monotony. Ours was a strict town in church matters, and it was a high honor to be an elder; and those people of our own class who missed the services were made to feel the evilness of their delinquency. The social hand pressed down.

I do not wish to cast any shadow upon the sincere devotion of those people; but it seems to me now there was in New Hope's Sunday a faint touch of the sadistic. For six days we lived in a raw world, a world of bald, Elizabethan frankness and frequent brutality on the part of the lower strata handling the heavy goods flowing from steamboat to prairie freighter. Above this were the men, such as my father, who made up the gentle class that governed the town with a certain dignified inflexibility. Yet gentility was a precarious thing, surrounded by heat and heavy dust and dusty evil, and so on the seventh day we went to church in a mood of self-flagellation and looked somberly into the pit. It was the land that made us so, I think, the land and the centuries of strict religion behind.

After church, Mother and Leora Kadderly went home while Father, as was his custom, walked with me toward the river; and I can remember the quietness of his manner as he spoke of the future. In front of the hotel we met Ben Tarrade. Father stopped, and it rather surprised me to hear a measure of affability in his voice.

"Ben," he said, "I heard you had high play at the table last night."

"A loser always magnifies his losses," said Ben Tarrade.

My father chuckled at that; there was always a sly vein of humor behind his reserve. "Mark Peachey would . . . that's true."

"Your boy," said Ben Tarrade, "ought to go fishing up the channel with me someday. You've got a fine boy."

"Why now," said my father, "perhaps we can arrange it."

We went on, and I tried to reconcile this meeting with all the things Father had previously told me. What he next said did not help — then. "You are growing up," he told me. "Some things you should know, Tod. A gentleman must understand all classes of people. It is the most valuable asset you will ever have. There's Ben Tarrade, a man with a fine classical education, from a first family in Kentucky. There he is, playing cards for a living, when he might have been a gentleman. It is very sad, Tod. Be generous in your judgment of the Tarrades of this world, but never grow sentimental over them."

I think now he was trying to tell me that there were many shades between the primary colors of black and white; I think he was. But the strongest impression I have now of my father is of a simplicity in ethics since quite vanished from life. The relations of man and man were in one compartment, the relations of man and woman were in another; and nowhere did they join. We went on to the river and turned into the brewery, and my father filled two glasses from the beer tap — one of which he gave me.

"I think it is time you knew the taste of this," he said.

I drank very little of it, for it was rather bitter, and I could not help feeling embarrassed in front of him. He said then: "A gentleman does all things in moderation. I hope you remember that." We turned home, and along the way he spoke of the early trappers and buffalo hunters whose names many of our streets bore. Sometimes I think my father vaguely felt that the generations were changing, and that I was growing away, and that he wanted me to know him before it was too late. Along the street, a great many men hailed Father, calling him by his first name, and he always replied in kind. Looking back I can see how intense was our lip service to the democratic ideal, and how untrue it was. For though he was "Tod" to the lowest teamster, familiarity ended here, and seldom was his quiet dignity penetrated. He knew his place; the teamsters knew their places.

Dinner was waiting at home, and we sat down. But my mother stared sharply at me and came to my place and bent over. And I shall never forget how instant was her suppressed anger. She turned on Father as if he were a stranger, and her voice shook a little.

"Are there not enough temptations in this town, Tod, without inviting him to share them?"

"He is growing up, Mother."

"I want no more of that nonsense," she retorted, and sat abruptly down in her chair. Leora Kadderly looked at Father, who seemed rather flushed and uneasy, and she said to Mother: "What harm is in a sip of beer?"

"Speak of the devil," said my mother.

I cannot forget Leora Kadderly's quiet answer, for I believe now it expressed all that she was. "The devil," she said, "is a monster only humans could think up."

My father said — "The discussion had better be deferred." — and I know they were all looking at me. But I doubt if I should have paid them much attention just then, for my small world had been unsteadied again. I think it was this night I discovered that my father's will was not absolute in our house, that behind the softness and deference my mother showed to him was a fiery will. The adjustments of boyhood are complex.

They took up another line of talk, but someone was at the door, and my father rose and went to it; and looking that way I saw Ben Tarrade standing there, yellow head bare. This, too, was astonishing. He had a long, paper box in his arm. "I should like to see Miss Kadderly for a moment," he told Father.

My father's voice was oddly unlike the one he had used on Ben Tarrade earlier. It was extremely formal, touched with coldness. "I doubt . . . ," he began.

Leora Kadderly got up quickly and went over, and Father turned on his heels, his face very dark. I wish now I had turned to see what expression my mother wore; it must have been one of utter shock. Ben Tarrade held out the box, and Leora took it. He said: "I had hoped to find you here, with company, so that it would not appear I had intruded upon you alone. You were very kind on the street the other day."

That was all. He went away, and Leora Kadderly came back and took the top from the box, and we all saw a spray of roses nested in fern. My father was silent, but Mother drew in her breath. She said: "This is . . . it's unthinkable. Leora, you should have thrown them in his face!"

Leora had lifted the flowers, and I saw on her features that strange, saddened glow I did not then understand. "I was merely polite, and he thought it was kindness," she said to us. "Omaha . . . he must have sent all the way there for them."

My father's answer was like the slamming of a door. "He has stepped over the line."

"What line?" Leora Kadderly asked, and as I review that scene I call up the picture of a dark and full-bosomed girl with aroused eyes. "You people are so kind and honest, and so cruel. Why is it you look at life as though it were indecent, and hate people who laugh? Must we all be miserable to be godly? Must we always turn from what little pleasure there is because it is unseemly? Must we all be plain and never wear bright clothes, and throw stones at a man like Ben Tarrade because he is the only one in New Hope to know that a woman loves flowers?"

My mother said to me — "Tod, leave the room." — and I went out and sat on the porch, hearing the three voices rise and fall behind me. Presently Jim Shugrue arrived, and the voices turned decorous again, and later Shugrue and my father came to the porch and sat there smoking, neither saying much. Both were greatly disturbed. Around five o'clock Jim Shugrue took Leora home; she was, I remember, carrying Ben Tarrade's flowers in one arm.

What happened thereafter happened swiftly, as was the way in our town. We were a people, I now realize, severely conditioned by the land. All nature was restless and extreme and quick changing. The mild seasons were so brief as to leave us with but a faint memory of mildness; for the rest it was heat and wind and sandstorm and great snows; it was drought or swollen river. This was the mood of the land, and this was the mood of its inhabitants, and nothing is fresher in my mind now than the bitter quarrels that at times broke through the courtesy affected by my elders. How soft and even were my father's words; but this was a deliberate manner adopted by him, as by the rest of the gentility, to avoid the clash of violent tempers. It was never wise in that town to stand in front of a man's will unless you were prepared to meet the farthest consequences.

It was within the week of Ben Tarrade's coming to our place, I remember, that I saw him turn out of River Street into Belle Plaine and lift his hat to Leora Kadderly passing by; and then, fascinated by a scene that I knew meant trouble, I watched them stroll on together. Old Colonel Lindsay at that moment stepped from von Gayl's, and he stopped, put back his head, and looked at the pair a long while. Afterward he wheeled about and walked, as though in a hurry, toward Messenger's General Store. My father came along presently, and we strolled home.

That same night, in the long, still period between sunset and full dark, I went out south of town to a pile of tar barrels that was the rendezvous of my crowd, and Nick Fallon told us the rest of the story. Nick was somewhat older than the other boys and had the gray knowledge of the world at his command. I think now his parents spoke too freely in front of him. We fired up a tar barrel and sat around it, and that image is indelibly stamped in my mind — of a great rush of blood-crimson light against the black mystery of the prairie.

"Ben Tarrade," Nick Fallon said, "came into Billy Hope's to get a saddle horse, and Billy Hope told him he'd get horse-whipped if he didn't stay away from Leora Kadderly. Tarrade just laughed at him. There's goin' to be hell to pay."

These were words, I suppose, Nick Fallon had picked up from his father. But Nick spoke them with a certain dramatic originality, and we all sat within the saturnine glow of the tar barrel and brooded over them. Boys are an odd compound of the purely primitive emotions; and I recall the mixture of fear and expectancy that shot through me. A little later we all left the tar barrel and walked to the courthouse park where the carpenters had just finished building the scaffold for a teamster by the name of Jeff Dann who was to be hung the following day because of a killing. It is another scene fresh and unblurred out of boyhood — the high platform, the heavy pole rising upward, the arm that was to hold the rope extending starkly into space. It stood there gaunt and grisly in the graying twilight, exuding a fresh-pine odor, the new timbers glowing faintly through this dusk like the pallid shining of a skeleton's weathered bones.

When I think of New Hope, Nebraska, in 1880, I am rather sure that only the boys of that town saw the delight of the world. We were a race apart; we were pure hedonists. The bitterness of the land was not for us, or the conformist ethics that — as I now understand — laid its iron obligations upon the elders. To us the outward manifestations of New Hope were eternally surprising. Life was rough and uneven but never dull. All colors were vivid, and all the contrasts of that land were fresh shocks, each shock leaving a deep impression. This scaffold in the twilight was only a dramatic event in a long chain of dramatic events, the very sight of which harrowed us morbidly and left us with permanent scars on the memory. Yet, being savages, we lived for this, and so we stood there a while and then drifted home.

The next day at noon, my father told me to stay at the house until after supper, and the direct glance accompanying the order stilled whatever protest I had. The hanging was at four o'clock, and I realize now it had been arranged as a public event, and that the hour was for the convenience of the roundabout ranchers who had to drive to town. In that public square the teamster, Dann, was to be hung before all eyes; he was to be the flaming cross of an outraged justice.

Law still is harsh, but it no longer possesses the extreme vengefulness of the years of my youth. There was something brutal in those kind, earnest people, and now that I recall all the brown and heavy faces, the unsmiling faces, the sad faces, I see the quality of spiritual somberness in each one. Sometimes I think it came from looking too long on the Original Sin of the race, from seeing so realistically the hell fire reserved for the condemned. The heavy hand of public opinion bore down on my elders unsparingly, and although we had a sort of individualism that is nowhere seen today — like that of Colonel Lindsay who always carried a sword cane, like George Faul who drank himself senseless each Saturday night and had one of von Gayl's men tie him into his home-going rig — we had very little of that true individualism that lies in the mind. You could not be a dissenter in New Hope; you could not violate New Hope's main body of morals and survive. If you did not conform, wrath descended upon you unmercifully in a dozen ways, from social ostracism to tar and feathers.

I remember that at four o'clock I stood in the parlor and held my breath, to discover how a hanging man must feel; and I noticed that my mother looked long and wistfully out of a window. I did not know what she was thinking; nor do I now. Her affection surrounded me for as long as I can remember, strong and changeless, but I have often felt inexpressibly sad in realizing I never knew her at all. Out across the many years I see only the seldom smile of a woman with her hair done straight back from a white forehead.

My father came home rather late for dinner, and, although his quietness was as usual, his features were sharp, and he ate little; and, when he said grace, he was unusually solemn. After we ate, he went into the kitchen, and I heard him speak to Mother in a guarded voice. Presently he left.

I soon followed, turning off River toward the courthouse square. Ten wild horses could not have dragged me away from the spot, yet I felt a strange dread; and, when I came upon the square, I brushed my eyes rapidly across the scaffold and looked away. Nothing happening then, I looked again. They had cut the dead man down, and the rest of the rope hung straight and motionless from the top bar; the trap door on the platform was dropped open. I do not know how long I stood there in a twilight that grew deeper and deeper while my mind gave the dead man life, put him on the platform, dropped him through the trap, and killed him again. I suppose I built up that scene a dozen times and would have done it as many more had not Nick Fallon come up on the run. His eyes were wide open and very bright.

He said, not stopping: "If you want to see something, go out to the tar barrels."

It was full dark when I passed across the square — touching the scaffold structure out of boyish bravado — and hurried down Colter's Alley. Beyond it, I saw a tar barrel blazing. There was a small crowd around it and a buckboard standing there with one gray horse in the shafts, that I instantly recognized as belonging to Ben Tarrade. I knew then; and that gave circumspection to my approach, for I realized a boy had no place here. But I went on until I was within the tinged shadows, on the edge of the circle of men, and remained there without being seen. In the center's circle stood Ben Tarrade, and I did not realize for a moment that he had been tied to the buckboard's tail gate. He was bare to the waist and he held himself straight, but his yellow head was bent over, away from us. Billy Hope was beside him, holding a bullwhacker's whip cut in half. I could see the flushed blood in Billy Hope's face. I could see the marble-like set to his lips.

He said: "Give your sort of men an inch and you take a mile. You been warned, which you laughed at. Now, by God, you'll catch on."

He stepped back, one foot straightening behind the other, and the whip slashed across Ben Tarrade's white back with a sound that twists my nerves now to think of it. I was rooted there in horror. I think Tarrade never moved out of his tracks, though his frame shook at each blow, and the long, red welts began to bleed. Billy Hope hit him a dozen times, cursed, and stopped; he was breathing hard, and the color had gone from his face. Another man stepped out from the circle and said — "That's enough, Billy." — and reached around to untie Tarrade's hands; and it was then that I looked about, the spell broken, and got a good view of those in the circle. I knew them all, yet they were strangers to me — strangers with hot eyes and the hardest lips I have ever seen.

Tarrade turned and held to the buckboard a moment. Billy Hope pointed into the farther darkness of the prairie. "Your trunk is in that buckboard," he said. "We took pains to see you got all your possessions. Now get out of here, and don't ever come back to New Hope."

Tarrade said nothing at all. His cheeks were the shade of ashes, and he moved as though he were dead tired. At the buckboard's front wheel he swung to look at us all; and I can say now, long thinking about it, that he had the best of those men. I do not know why, but he had the best of them, and I think some of them must have known it and felt shamed. After that, he got up to the seat, lifted the reins, and drove away into the dark. This is the last sight I ever had of him, bare torso red-streaked, yet square in the seat. The man nearest me turned, discovered me, and took my arm roughly, but, when he looked closer and saw who I was, he spoke with more consideration.

"You had better not let your father know you came here, Tod."

I ran all the way home and tried to conceal the dumb shaking of my body from my mother. But she saw it and said: "Where have you been?" All I could say was that I had been playing, and went immediately to my room. We always left the door open so that the cross current of night air might carry off the day's heat; and so I heard my father come in. He had not been at the whipping, that I was sure of, but he knew of it.

He said — "Well, he got what he deserved." — and my mother murmured, in a grieving voice, "Oh, Tod." Much as she disliked Ben Tarrade, that thought of punishment hurt her gentle soul. But lying there in the dark, the puzzling contradictions of my father's nature troubled me, and I could not understand. I do not fully understand now. He was always a kindly man and a fair one, and never would he have soiled his hands in such a scene as I saw that evening; yet he approved of what the rougher ones had done.

There was little sleep for me that night. I think I relived those brief moments of the tar barrels a hundred times. In the morning I was physically sick and could not touch my breakfast. Father was at the table; Mother was not. But as we sat there, she came in from the street, apron folded around her hands, as was her custom. Father looked up, and then stood up. He said — "What is it?" — in a concerned voice. Mother was crying, the first time I had ever seen her so.

"Leora left town late last night," Mother said. "She packed her trunk and gave her dog to the Sperrins and left on the

Omaha stage. Tod . . . oh, Tod!"

Father's whole face changed. He shook his head, and kept shaking it. What he said did not then make any sense to me at all. "Not to him, Mother! Surely not to him!"

"We will never see her again," said my mother. And her grief came out and touched me, and I felt very lonely and miserable.

There is little more to say. News came back to New Hope a few weeks later, telling us that Tarrade had married Leora, and then as far as the town was concerned they were dead. I do not recall either name ever being afterward spoken in our house, and a year later my family moved farther West. Time went by, and that old incident faded out as all things in time do fade. I never saw those two again, although one more fact belongs to this chronicle. In 1905, when I was a man grown, I passed through Omaha, and stopped off during a twenty-minute wait. Out of curiosity I looked up a city directory and followed the T column down, really expecting nothing, for in the West at that time we were a highly migratory people. But the name was there: **Tarrade, Ben (Leora), grain merchant.**

It was a tragedy out of my boyhood; it was to me then like a death. But the other day, reliving that affair, a feeling of unutterable relief went through me, as though I had come to the end of a tragic tale and had found triumph at last springing out of ruin. For as I look back into that far-off time, I see New Hope as it really was: a town of kindly people living in spiritual shadows, afraid of the light of life, cruel to those they could not understand. And for these two, who alone of all New Hope smiled because it was good to smile, the end was a happy one. The savor and richness and melody of the world were with them; and gaiety and understanding were with them — too powerful for New Hope either to comprehend or to subdue.

III

"THE MAN WITH THE

SMOKE-GRAY EYES"

My father lifted his cigar and spoke. "The Peach Creek stage was held up about an hour ago beyond Harriman's Ranch. Hank Lacey was driving. He was shot in the chest."

We were on the porch, watching summer's soft twilight deepen — my mother and father and myself, and Glory Harper who sat on the steps. This was New Hope's supper time, so still and peaceful an hour that the bell-like strokes of Rob Jenner's late-working blacksmith hammer came clearly from the far edge of town. A faint wind ran in from the west, bringing the savor of all that wild distance with it. This was 1881 when the world was young, and I was in a full and vivid boyhood that grows more and more strongly in my memory. Long ago as it was, I recall the quick turn of Glory Harper's shoulders as she looked up to Father and showed the worry in her eyes. She was twenty, and more inclined to silence than most women are.

She said: "Why, that's one of Jeff's stages."

"He rode out there immediately he heard the news," my father said and returned to his cigar. That sharp darkness that comes to the plains dropped swiftly; along our little street house lamps threw thin lanes across the tawny-silver dust. A sprinkling wagon came by, and all at once the mingled scent of water and dust and scorched boards and prairie grass was keen through the night.

Glory rose and stood a moment. Even then her presence and her personality were exciting to me, reaching out like the undertow of a current. Now that I am older, I can see that it was the inner richness of a full-bodied girl waiting for expression, waiting to be spent. Afterward, she said good night, and walked to the adjoining house where her aunt and uncle lived. Her own parents, we understood, had died long before in the East, and the Harpers had taken her as a child. They seemed to have money, for Harper lived a quiet, retired life. I recall him as a dark and kindly man who always marched in the Fourth of July parade with the Phil Sheridan G. A. R. Post, very straight and soldierly in his captain's uniform.

My mother's rocker creaked on the porch boards. I knew she was disturbed. "The Cameron boys again, Tod?"

My father said — "I suppose." — and smoked on. There was a shadow sliding along our picket fence, which was Johnny Dix waiting for me. But I held my place, for Father was talking again, and his tone was faintly sad and faintly bitter. "The war's put a curse on this country. It has made killing a noble occupation. It's made heroes out of desperadoes like Quantrell and the James gang. The Cameron boys are simply following the pattern."

After an interval I started down the steps. Mother's voice stopped and turned me around. My father had removed his cigar and was looking at me more sharply than usual. He said: "Let the boy go. He'll have little enough fun in another few years." I think he meant to speak to me. But he didn't, and it is one of my deepest regrets now that he so rarely broke through his long-maintained silences, that he was almost a stranger to me. For I have come to understand that his silence was the silence of loneliness. He was one of the few really educated men in a town that had little time or patience for education; he had nobody with whom to share his tastes, and, therefore, he fed upon himself. It is one of the tragedies of this world that people build walls around themselves and slowly starve inside.

I went out to Johnny Dix, and we trotted through the dark, back streets, on over to the south edge of town where the rest of our gang assembled. We had a ritual and a procedure, and presently we filed surreptitiously down the alleys of New Hope into the alien and dangerous territory along the river where the tough boys of Ward Two roamed. It is what comes across all the years to me, more real than anything else — the raciness, the freedom, the keen and sharp edge of that long-gone boyhood.

All the pieces of the story, so disjointed then, make a clear picture now. The next day I was standing on St. Vrain Street, across from the Beauty Belle, when old Henry Nellis turned out of a nearby store and stopped a man whose name I have forgotten. Nellis was very excited. He said to this other man: "Jeff McKay brought Hale Cameron to jail this morning. Lacey's dead."

I remember the chill that ran up my spine. It was always like this in New Hope. The humdrum days ran along, and then excitement and violence burst over us, as swiftly and unexpectedly as a heat storm out of the south. Nellis was saying something else, but suddenly stopped, chopping a word between his teeth. Both men were staring across the street to the Beauty Belle, and I turned and saw Big Bill Dolliver, who owned the saloon, come out of the swinging doors, shake his big shoulders, and pause to light a cigar.

I do not know a better way to describe Big Bill Dolliver than by saying that, although the width of the street was between Dolliver and these other men, they still feared him. I heard Nellis say in a bare breath, "I wonder what Bill thinks about it?" Afterward Nellis walked on, and the other man turned into the store. Dolliver had lighted his cigar; he crossed the street, passed me with one quick, stiff survey, and went toward Linenweber's Restaurant. I still feel the striking power of that glance and the taciturn, morose quality of Big Bill Dolliver's eyes. He was a central character in our town, and everybody felt that physical jolt of his presence. I think the knowledge and the sensation of fear were left out of Big Bill Dolliver, that neither his brain nor his nerves had any way of understanding them. He was not a big man, but he seemed tremendous to me; and there was about him always a massive indifference to the opinions of other people. It was as though a corsair spirit in him chafed at the small rules of a world he found himself in and did not like. The reflection of that was in his eyes — savage and smoky and domineering. He was about forty and finely built and kept bachelor quarters at the Occidental Hotel. But he went there only to sleep; all his waking hours were spent in his saloon, which was the most glitteringly luxurious thing in our drab and dusty town.

It was noon, and I ran home, bursting with the news, and found my parents at the dinner table. I said, all in one breath: "Jeff McKay brought Hale Cameron to jail this morning, and Lacey who drove the stage is dead."

My father looked queerly at me and merely said: "Yes." But my mother seemed very worried.

"He's growing up like a savage, Tod."

I sat down to eat. Then I saw Jeff McKay ride up to our front gate on his big bay, get off, and come up the steps, and eating became impossible. The hero worship of a boy is a strange and wonderful thing, and Jeff McKay, as he stood there in the doorway, was the sort of man I wanted to be. He was twenty-three years old, which was the age of a seasoned man in those days, with Scotch-gray eyes and a tall, rawboned frame and the quietest manners imaginable. There was a deference and a humility to him, but he had — as subsequent events proved — a Calvinistic conscience and a

Calvinistic will. It was these qualities that brought the storm down upon him. Like most Scotsmen he was full of ambition. He operated four stage lines into the West, and Lacey had been a driver on one of his coaches.

He bowed and smiled at my mother, and spoke to me in a way that bound me fast to him. He said to my father in his slow, careful manner: "I wanted to ask your advice."

Father motioned to a chair at the table, and Jeff McKay came forward and sat down. My mother got Father's eye and nodded at me. It was my signal to leave the table. But Father said: "Let him stay." I understood all that clearly now. My father would not preach to me, but he wanted me to see and hear for myself so that I might absorb the ways of the world.

Jeff McKay said: "Lacey died. But I got there and had a word with him first. It was Hale Cameron who held up the stage and fired the shot. I found Hale and brought him in. It's my testimony that will hang the rope around his neck. Have I done right?"

My father spoke in a wondering voice: "How did you know where to find him? When you found him, how did you get him away from the rest of the gang?"

"I found him," Jeff McKay said. It was softly said, yet behind the tone lay a terrible certainty I still remember. Then he repeated: "Have I done right?"

"According to your conscience," said my father wryly. "But conscience is a luxury in this country. The Cameron gang will never let you alone. Half the people in New Hope will hate you for trapping their hero, and the other half will despise you for not killing Hale out on the prairie where you found him."

Jeff McKay got up. "We have laws," was all he said, and went out. I was out of my chair immediately, following him to the porch, but he didn't stop this day. He went through the gate and led his bay horse to the Harpers' house. Glory was there, waiting for him, and I saw Jeff McKay bend a little and speak to her; they were both smiling, and I laugh now to think of the jealousy that flared up in me. He said something else, and they both ceased to smile. The sunlight cut down on them. They stood quite still, these two straight and robust people so much alike in their silence.

My father called me back into the house. He said gravely: "Whatever you have heard is something for our ears alone, Son."

My mother said: "It is a cruel, heartless country, Tod!" The anger was so unlike this soft-spoken woman that both my father and I were astonished. She looked at Father and seemed to accuse him. "I'm thinking of Jeff and Glory," she told him, and abruptly left the table. But in the kitchen she called back: "Why don't the men of this town do something?"

Father said: "What should we do, Mother?"

"You might start with Bill Dolliver."

I think something should be said about that wide and smoky land in that high-tempered time, if the fury that burst through New Hope is to be understood at all. We had some good blood in our town, some families grown wealthy from the freighting trade; we had our schools and churches and our gentility. We were a settled community. Yet we dealt on the edge of insecurity and violence. South of us in Kansas and Missouri the bandit gangs still scourged the country, and the border ruffianism of the war still smoldered. West of us lay the great prairie, reaching out its trackless distances; a hundred and fifty miles that way the cattle trails and the trail towns still roared. We could not escape the impact of that raw world. Orderly as New Hope tried to be, there was in it still a primitive concept of personal justice. If a man injured you, you took your own vengeance upon him.

All that Father had said to Jeff McKay was true. The jury was scarcely impaneled to try Hale Cameron for the murder of Lacey when New Hope began to burn with a strange fever. Boyhood impressions are keen, and I walked the streets and felt that excitement as clearly as though it were a hot wind rushing in from the prairie. I saw men in town I had never seen before, surly-looking fellows off the distant cattle ranches, impoverished homesteaders from the roundabout coulées. Our own teamsters and stevedores, who seldom loitered on St. Vrain Street, now ranged there restlessly. To a good many of these men Hale Cameron was a hero, a Robin Hood, as Jesse James still was; and to many of them Jeff McKay was a coward for not having exchanged bullets with Cameron as a man should out on the prairie.

There was no peace for Jeff McKay, and it was freely wagered he would die of a bullet from Dan Cameron, who was Hale's older brother, before the month was out. It was strange that the tidal wave of unreason would grip us so. But it did, and there were friends of Jeff's who dared not show their friendship for him in the bitter weeks that followed.

I recall walking down St. Vrain Street the day before the trial with Glory Harper. She wore a white dress with ruffles on the sleeves, and she held a parasol against the hot sun with a way of grace hard to describe. It was, I think, a rhythm inside this girl that flowed out of her and influenced whatever she touched. The street was crowded, as though it were a holiday, and this feeling of excitement was stronger than ever. There was a rumor in the wind that Dan Cameron intended to raid New Hope with his gang and get his brother from jail, and because of that the Phil Sheridan G. A. R. Post had turned out to guard the whole length of St. Vrain Street; every hundred yards we passed a pair of these men standing against the building walls, guns strapped at their hips, all looking very

170

solemn. Yet solemn as they were, they lifted their hats to Glory, and spoke to her.

Then somebody else spoke to her, and I saw Big Bill Dolliver standing at the curb. He had taken off his hat, and his black hair glittered in the sunlight and made all the rest of his face dark. He had a cigar between his teeth, but his lips were hidden by the long, heavy mustache he wore. I remember feeling fear as I stared into his heavy, round eyes; I feel the strike of them now. But I remember feeling hatred of the man, too, for I clenched my hands behind my back and stood at Glory's side. I had come to feel that somehow Jeff McKay's fortune lay in this stolid man's brain. Nor was I alone in that feeling.

He said: "Good day, Miss Harper."

Glory stopped and lowered her parasol, and I looked to see her smiling at him. She had no fear. She said: "I don't believe all the stories I've heard about you. Jeff needs help."

He took out his cigar and looked down. He brushed a flake of ash from his coat and lifted his head. "I hope you never will believe all the stories you hear about me. Don't worry about Jeff."

We went on and turned in at Jeff McKay's office beyond Linenweber's Restaurant. There were two men at the door, but they stepped aside for Glory, and we walked through and found Jeff sitting on a high bookkeeper's stool, writing in a book. I remember he wore black sleeve protectors, and that there was a gun lying on his desk. He got up and shook hands with me.

Glory said: "Mister Dolliver spoke to me."

Jeff's eyes narrowed. He wasn't pleased, I could see. "It was forward of him."

But Glory smiled. "He was very courteous. You have guards at your door. Will Dan Cameron try to rescue his brother?"

"We shall soon know."

They were face to face, absorbed in each other, and I felt completely excluded. So I went out, hurt by the exclusion. But I looked back once — and it is that one glimpse of them that comes to me now as a bright picture when I am discouraged. They were two fine people standing side by side, throwing a superb gallantry back at life. Their faces were sober, and they were not talking. Well, they were two people who had little use for words for they had a perfect understanding; they had the simplicity of faith.

I walked down the street, once more in the whirlpool of excitement. I stopped by the courthouse steps, but a G. A. R. man said — "This is no place for you." — and so I crossed to the south side of St. Vrain, and started home. Dolliver was under the board awning of the Beauty Belle, speaking to a man who stood still and very attentive. Dolliver's hand closed into a solid fist, and he said something that sent the man immediately away; then Dolliver went into the saloon with a ponderous swing of his shoulders and one sidewise glance that raked the whole street. When I came up, the doors were just swinging, and I saw the flash of mirrors and crystal chandeliers; there was a crowd in the Beauty Belle and a great deal of noise. A woman walked toward me, but she crossed the street to avoid passing the saloon doors.

That night my father said to me — "I want you to stay off St. Vrain Street tomorrow." — and I went to bed and dreamed of Dan Cameron's men riding into New Hope, shooting as they came. The next morning, which was trial day, I ran down to the corner of St. Vrain and Prairie Streets and climbed to the loft of Beekman's warehouse and lay on my stomach, watching the courthouse steps. I saw crowds there but no violence, although in the evening when Johnny Dix and I went prowling out through the freighters' camp, he told me Dan Cameron had ridden into New Hope alone, had vanished down an alley adjoining the Beauty Belle, and later had gone away. I said: "Why wasn't he arrested?" Johnny said in a mysterious way: "My old man says because Bill Dolliver didn't want him arrested."

The following noon Father came home to dinner looking very pleased. He sat down and said grace and glanced across the table to me. "I want you to remember, when you grow up, that occasionally your father's generation did the right thing. The jury convicted Hale Cameron. He will be hung. Half of the men in that courtroom were trying to intimidate Jeff when he took the stand. But he told his story, and, by God, they couldn't scare him."

"Tod," said my mother, "you swore," and then looked at me.

"It is time," said my father, "for our boy to learn responsible people sometimes swear."

We had a week's calm in our town, but it was a scary calm. For they were building this scaffold in the park block, and its skeleton shape did something to New Hope; it seemed to waken in all of us that latent, primitive savagery of which we were so afraid, against which our daily morals so constantly struggled. At night I used to walk by the scaffold and see its gaunt frame against the sky. They hung him August 10, 1881, with the Phil Sheridan Post guarding the park block against Dan Cameron's raid. No raid came, and Hale Cameron was soon dead. But before he died, and before they put the cap on him, he turned on the platform and looked down to where Big Bill Dolliver stood, and he said, so clearly that everybody in the block heard his exact words: "When you come to hell, Bill, I'll be there to watch you burn."

My father told us this when he came home in the evening.

He was speaking to Mother, but I can understand now he wanted me to feel and to see the picture as he saw it, that he wanted to harden me to the brutality of the world I was so fast growing into. I think he had been tremendously hurt when he had made the change from the dreams of youth to the realities of adult life, and I think he was determined I should not go through the same disillusionment. Certainly his training shortened my adolescent years and matured me early. Maybe I lost something; maybe I was cheated out of some of those golden days of boyhood. But at eighteen I was a man — and the education by my father saved me from many mistakes.

Mother was a gentle soul; the harshness of men always frightened her. Yet I remember how she lifted her chin at Father, and I remember the anger in her voice: "Then it is Bill Dolliver you ought to hang."

Father shook his head. He said: "You don't understand the rules of the game in our town."

Nor did I then. I was full-grown and had cut my teeth on the bones of goodness and evil, and most of the principal characters of my boyhood were dust blended with the shifting prairie soil before I understood either the rules of the game or that inscrutable, sultry-eyed man who walked our streets in silence and knew us so well and scorned us so much. The Beauty Belle made him wealthy, and wealth was a strong voice in New Hope, commanding the ears of even our best citizens. Yet the secret of his power lay not in his money, but in the circumstances that set him apart from the rest of us and shut the social door in his face. For, being a saloonkeeper, he stood on that borderline between good and evil that our town's conscience insisted on establishing. My father might drop in for a drink and a word. But the teamsters and the impoverished homesteaders and all those who formed the ragged edge of our life came there, too. The Beauty Belle was their lodge and their club, and Big Bill Dolliver, understanding them, was their leader. He knew the temper of that reckless, discontented group. He knew its secrets. He knew its lawless element. He was its spokesman and to him came our better citizens when they feared the multitude or when they wanted the votes of the multitude.

Even the outlaws came to Bill. New Hope long had suspected that Bill Dolliver shared the secrets of the Cameron gang, and, when Hale Cameron, standing on the gallows platform, had bitterly consigned Bill to hell, that suspicion became a certainty. I can understand it now. The Camerons were part of that world over which Bill ruled, and, therefore, to make his own authority more secure, Bill Big Dolliver trafficked with the Camerons. For he was a man brutally practical in his morals. I can see him now, swinging his bold shoulders down the street, his heavy-boned cheeks implacably turned to the world, his eyes scorning everything he saw. I think he admired only one thing, which was strength. Any other man New Hope would have horse-whipped and driven from town. But Dolliver walked abroad as indifferent as before while the cross currents of speculation and hatred and fear played around him.

Something happened, then, in our town hard to describe. There was a feeling along St. Vrain Street very strong to me as a youngster, a feeling of breath being held, of some catastrophe hovering over us. All the boys in my gang knew something was about to happen; it was so powerful an influence that we used to sit around the blazing tar barrels south of town, uneasy and afraid to prowl toward the river. And one night Johnny Dix gave it a name.

Johnny said: "Dan Cameron is goin' to kill Jeff McKay. My father heard it."

It is queer how the smell of blood goes with the wind, how the impulse of violence flows along the earth. It was a rumor only, without substance. Yet the following evening, just before supper time, Dan Cameron and five of his men whirled off the prairie into a half-deserted St. Vrain Street and poured a volley into Jeff McKay's small office adjoining Linenweber's Restaurant. They were instantly gone, leaving Jeff unhurt behind the desk; but a man just coming out of the restaurant went down with a bullet in the ribs. There was no pursuit.

We were all sitting on the porch, only two hours later, when Jeff and Glory came out of the Harper yard and turned in to our steps. It was dark, but our lamps made a lane down the walk, and I could see Jeff McKay's face clearly. I recall now that something had happened to his expression. It was the same, yet his features seemed to stand out, and there was a thin line at the corners of his mouth. Trouble hadn't broken him; it had toughened him.

"Has Sheriff Carrigan got a posse out?" asked my father.

"He wants a warrant to follow," said Jeff quietly. "I will not swear one."

"He needs no warrant," said my father. But afterward he added: "I understand why he wants an excuse to chase the Cameron gang. You are a marked man, Jeff."

"It is my quarrel. I don't wish a posse to go out and get shot up for me."

My father was long silent. Then he said: "It could be done simpler than that. The key to this situation, I think, is in one man's pocket. Go see Bill Dolliver."

"I can't do that," said Jeff.

My father stirred in his chair. I remember the quick, bright glow of his cigar tip and the smell of its smoke. "I believe I told you a month ago that your conscience was a luxury."

"It is the only thing I have to go by," Jeff McKay said, and turned away with Glory. I watched them stroll into the darkness, side by side, and without talk. They made tall silhouettes against the shadows; and something of that deep faith they both possessed seemed to remain behind on the porch, seemed to quiet the evening. My father rose. He said — "Come with me." — and we went out, crossed to St. Vrain, and turned toward the center of town. House lamps made golden lanes all along the way, and there was a bright-splashed pool of light in front of the Beauty Belle. My father spoke to me. "It is hard sometimes to know the difference between right and wrong. A man should be slow in coming to judgment." When we got abreast the Beauty Belle, I saw Dolliver standing beside one of the awning posts, smoking a cigar. He looked around as Father came up. He said: "Hello, Tod."

It was, for him, very civilly said. Father was a little-speaking man, but there was a quality in him. I think Dolliver respected it.

Father said: "Jeff McKay will be dead before the week is out."

Dolliver only looked at him. His cigar tilted upward, and his mouth thinned and disappeared beneath the sweep of his black mustache. I felt the power of those big, impatient eyes strike my father, and I hated Dolliver again. But my father's tone was even. I was, I recall, suddenly very proud of him.

"You haven't done enough, Bill."

Dolliver said: "I have done nothing at all, Tod."

But my father's voice was sharper than usual. "I disagree. You had power enough to save Hale Cameron from the rope. But you let him hang. It was a deliberate choice on your part. New Hope doesn't understand why. I do. When you let Hale take his punishment, you were backing up Jeff McKay. But it isn't enough."

The words came growling out of Dolliver's throat. "I am no reformer."

"No," agreed my father dryly, "you are not. Nevertheless

you stepped out of the part you have been playing in this town when you refused to protect Hale. I can see no other motive than a desire to give Jeff a chance. Yet the result is that you've ruined your own influence over the Cameron gang and made McKay's death as certain as the coming of night." Afterward he added very softly: "It is the penalty for allowing a kind instinct get the best of you, Bill. The situation is worse than it was."

"It may be," said Dolliver.

I understood so little of that talk then, yet every word made an indelible scratch on my memory, and every fragment of the picture remains clear. Dolliver seemed to grow more and more surly; his eyes showed greater restlessness. My father stood very straight and very certain there in the bright glory of the Beauty Belle; he was always rather handsome, with the small bitterness of unrealized ambitions whetting the edge of his words.

"You have always played your own game," he said. "It was not like you to step aside to support Jeff's game. If you meant it as a kindness, it is not enough. As long as Dan Cameron is alive, there is no hope for Jeff. It is not only Jeff. There's Glory Harper to be considered."

Dolliver's head came forward. "I heard she was going to marry him."

"That's right."

"He has courage," said Dolliver. "I admire courage." Then he was growling again. "Someday he'll have to learn to temper his high Scotch principles with a few practical considerations. This is a hard world for principles, Tod. I've never been able to afford them."

That was all. He turned on his heels and swung into the Beauty Belle, and Father and I went slowly down St. Vrain, toward home. My father walked with his head bowed and his hands locked behind. Something in his silence impressed me, and I did not venture to speak. A fine, full moon floated low on the horizon, and the deep dust of our street was shining like flaked silver. Jeff and Glory were returning from the far shadows, their steps echoing rhythmically together. At our gate Father stopped and stared at them, and he put his hand on the gatepost and swung his glance to me. He said in a queer way: "Don't be afraid of anything, and never be too quick to judge people." We went on into the house, and presently I climbed the stairs to bed. Not long after, before I had fallen asleep, I heard voices outside, and I sat up and looked through the window. Dolliver had driven up in a buggy and was speaking to my father who stood at the edge of the walk. The moonlight made our street very clear and lovely that night, and I could even see the details of Big Bill Dolliver's face as he bent down from his buggy seat. I do not know what he said, but my father extended his arm, and they shook, and then Dolliver drove away westward at a spanking pace, lifting the quick dust behind.

It is queer how sensitive youngsters are to voice inflections, how quick they can read meaning into simple tone; when my mother called up the stairs next morning, I knew something had happened merely from the way she spoke my name. It made me dress rapidly — for in New Hope all of us lived hungrily on the hope of the unexpected — and go down. My father was already at the table, his face extraordinarily dark, clearly sad. He said grace more solemnly than usual, and then looked over the table at me.

He said: "I think you should know, Sonny, that Dolliver rode out to Camp Creek last night and shot Dan Cameron through the heart. A Cameron man killed him before he could get away. The news came from Harriman's ranch a few hours ago."

My mother had hated Dolliver, but the gentleness in her soul nevertheless grieved. She sat with her hands folded, and I heard her murmur: "God be merciful to him."

"It is the end of the gang," my father said. "Hale was the brains of it, and Dan the whip. With both of them dead the rest will run to other parts. Jeff is safe enough now."

"He was a wicked man," my mother said, thinking of Dolliver.

But my father got quickly up from the table and shook his head. "I'm not altogether sure."

Well, it was a shock that literally ran from one end of St. Vrain to the other. I do not think New Hope quite realized how central a figure this inscrutable, massive, and savage-tempered man had been until it saw the black hearse carry him out to the cemetery on Locust Hill. It was a story that never died in our town as long as I was there. And it was a story that had the sort of moral New Hope liked. Big Bill had been a silent partner of the Camerons. But he had fallen out with them over some thieves' quarrel, and he had died. Once or twice I was with my father when somebody dwelt on this oft-repeated tale, and I noticed how quietly and sadly he listened to it, saying nothing.

It was a month or two later, I recall, that Jeff McKay and Glory were married. He had built a house on the western edge, one of the finest in our town at that day, and the ceremony was held there. Everybody knew the Harpers were comfortably fixed, but it was nevertheless a surprise when they presented Glory with a ten-thousand-dollar check drawn on an Omaha bank, that Harper explained was part of her people's estate long held for her. And it was also a surprise to the town when Harper, who had never worked, took a job as bookkeeper in the brewery. I remember his telling us the reason for that. "Raising Glory has been our only business for fifteen years. It's lonesome, losing a job like that. So I got another."

There is but one other thing to tell, and this I did not learn until many years later in the farther West. My father was growing old, and the memories of New Hope were increasingly dear to him. We fell to talking about the town one night.

"As to Dolliver," he said, "New Hope was only half right. He was a power there, and he had no illusions. He stood halfway between the good folks and the rough ones . . . and he controlled the town because he controlled the rough ones. To hold his power he wouldn't hesitate a minute to drive a bargain with men like the Camerons. I believe he went so far as to keep some of the money they stole in his saloon safe. When he fell out with them, it wasn't over money. It was over Hale, whom he let die in order to protect Jeff. So he went deliberately out to kill Dan, well realizing he had little chance to get away alive. But it was Jeff and Glory he was thinking about when he drove out to Camp Creek in his buggy."

I said: "Why? It doesn't sound like Dolliver."

My father said: "I was one of the men appointed by the court to open the Beauty Belle safe after he was killed. We didn't find a dime of money in it, though he was supposed to have been wealthy. There wasn't anything in it, except one paper. That was a birth certificate. There were four of us on the committee. After we looked at the birth certificate, we destroyed it and swore never to mention it. Bill had supported the Harpers for years. It was his ten thousand that they passed on to Glory. She knew nothing about that. She knew nothing about him at all."

My father was a man who hated to display his emotions. But that night I noticed how strong were the feelings beneath his customary reserve. "You see," he added, "Bill Dolliver was

181

Glory's father. But he knew himself too well, and he knew the world too well, to allow Glory to grow up as his daughter. It is why he chose the Harpers to raise her from childhood, many years before he came to New Hope. She never did know. Well, he was a crook, and he had no illusions. But he had no fear, either, and, when the time came, he played out his hand as he saw it to the complete end, without welshing."

To my father, and my father's generation, that covered everything.

IV

"AGAINST THE MOB"

The sound — scraping and sibilant — came out of the rear room again. Saul Trevick tightened the quoins of the page-four form and lifted his eyes toward young Johnny setting type at the cases. Young Johnny hadn't heard; he was a willing boy, but he didn't understand the mystery that ran below New Hope's placid surface.

"Go home now, Johnny."

"Ain't finished the White House ad yet."

Saul Trevick was remembering that when people crept through the back door of his newspaper shop from Wister's Alley they wanted secrecy. He said — "Never mind." — and waited. A partition separated the front office from this angular, high-ceilinged shop in which gas jets lifted pale blooms; another partition in the back end shut off Saul Trevick's bedroom. Light slid vaguely across the tables and type cases, across the skeleton shape of the Washington hand press.

Rain drove against the skylight with a gusty, intermittent

rush. Johnny said — "Good night." — and slid around the open end of the front partition. The trip bell tinkled when he let himself into St. Vrain Street. Saul Trevick shifted his cigar between his teeth; his lips settled, and he prepared to hear something unpleasant. He said: "All right."

He didn't look up from the table immediately, for he was thinking of the secrets of New Hope locked in his head with the detached indifference of a man who had no illusions about people — no faith in their goodness and no anger against their sins. He was forty-five, a dry and untidy and silent, little man in whom ambition long since had died, a spectator aloof from surprise and belief. The continuing quiet lifted his head. There was a girl standing in the opening of the rear partition — standing alertly there, wet haired and faintly disheveled. She trembled visibly, and her round breasts rose and fell to an irregular breathing. Fear darkened her face.

Saul Trevick made a distinct turn toward her. "What are you doing here, Lily?"

Her words ran breathlessly together. "We were walking down the alley, but the rain caught us, so we went into Marshall's empty stable and were sitting there when some men came after us. I ran. I didn't want them to know who I was."

"We?"

The girl watched him, her eyes blacker and blacker. She lifted her chin. "Jeff Huntoon and me. They thought we were bad, I guess. They were fighting Jeff when I left."

"They recognize you?" said Saul Trevick calmly.

"No." Suddenly she whirled around to listen, and turned again, rigid and poised for flight.

Trevick said: "Go out the front way. Your father know you keep company with Jeff Huntoon?"

She came on to the middle of the shop and stood before him, her hands lifted. Her mouth was white, and excitement had changed her prettiness to something stronger than that; it had turned her proud and angry. She was eighteen, Saul Trevick recalled, a motherless girl living with a father whose discipline was alternately severe and neglectful. She was a little wild — he could see that whipping across her face now.

"It wouldn't do any good. Please help Jeff, if you can." She ran instantly across the shop and vanished beyond the front office partition. Men's voices rose at the back end of the building, in Wister's Alley, and the front door's trip bell had only died behind the fleeing Lily when they flung themselves out of the alley into his bedroom and filed around the partition. Hands lying on the make-up table, Saul Trevick recognized each of the party of four. Tom Blaine, who was marshal of New Hope, said: "A girl come in here?"

"What's the trouble, Tom?"

"We saw Jeff Huntoon persuade some girl to step into Marshall's stable. We collared Jeff, but the girl's gone. She came this way."

"All right for people to step out of the rain, isn't it?"

Tom Blaine's glance held no sympathy. "You ain't that innocent. Jeff Huntoon's a chaser with a soft way toward girls. It won't do. Not in New Hope. Did she come in here?"

"No."

"I think you're lying."

Saul Trevick stirred his cigar between his teeth. His voice was dead level, enormously unkind. "Don't let me detain you from your pleasant pastime of followin' kids down dark alleys."

The four men showed discomfort. Tom Blaine took it poorly; his voice rode an arrogant note upward. "You wouldn't say that if you had a daughter. Your head's full of too damned many funny ideas."

Saul Trevick murmured: "This seems a strange committee to be enforcing the town's morals. How's the road toward

Peterson's ranch these days, Tom?"

Tom Blaine's mouth opened — and closed with force. He stepped on until his face was large and threatening against Saul Trevick. Blood pumped into his cheeks. He had an impulse to violence, but he changed it, and wheeled around. His voice was strange. "Jeff gets a warning this time. Next time he'll be whipped out of New Hope."

They were soon gone, leaving Saul Trevick with his hands on the page-four form, his chin tipped against his chest. He pushed himself away from the table and circled the walls, turning out the gas jets; and he stood in the darkness and listened to the rain beat against the roof. Afterward, he went into the rear room and struck a match to the kerosene lamp there. He washed his hands and laid aside his cigar to scrub his face, and put the cigar between his teeth again. Presently he thought to remove his coat and stoke up the little sheet-metal stove and draw a chair near it. He filled a water glass half full of whiskey from a bottle on the table, drank it at once, and settled deep in the chair. Light turned the contents of the bottle to heavy amber; narrow-eyed he stared at it, the smoky, burning color of the liquid shading all his thoughts. He was remembering Lily, the desperateness of her voice, the protesting stiffness of her body. Well, there was wildness in her. But it was the wildness of youth. Lily was eighteen.

"She'll break her heart," he said to himself. "New Hope will see to that."

He filled his glass again and solemnly considered himself. At forty-five nothing mattered any more except physical comfort. A bottle of whiskey and a cigar — he had reduced his existence to these. There wasn't any protest in him at the cruelties of this world; he had been beaten back to a silent acquiescence. Sitting there with a bowed, faintly gray head, he searched himself for some principle that would stir him to anger, and found none.

It was the following noon that Shiras Huntoon walked from a rain-driven St. Vrain Street into the Drover's for a drink. He was a harness maker, a big and heavy and very straight man with a Southerner's pride written over him plainly. He took his drink and was standing a moment at the bar when Billy Rees of the New York Store came swinging into the saloon, saw him, and walked over immediately. There wasn't any friendliness on Billy Rees's face. He said, in the shortest, bluntest way possible: "You better tie up your boy. If he keeps prowlin' around New Hope's alleys and back fences, he'll get his hide shot off."

"My boy?" said Huntoon in a dismal, dangerous voice. His back stiffened; the flash of his eyes was there for Billy Rees to see.

"You Southerners," ground out Billy Rees, "call it gallantry. Up here we've got a plainer name for it. If New Hope catches Jeff fooling around the women again, he'll get whipped out of town."

"Very plain," breathed Shiras Huntoon, and drew up his hand and slapped Billy Rees across the mouth. It knocked Rees against the bar. The noise in the saloon dropped away, and there was instantly a circle of still and attentive faces around these two men. Billy Rees hooked his elbows over the bar; he was raging angry, but he didn't make another move toward the cold Huntoon. "My boy is a gentleman. I'd break him in two if he wasn't. Young people need their adventure, and the filth you suggest exists only in your mind. I have remarked before, Rees, that you Northerners have no chivalry. Nothing but suspicion and fear of honest laughter."

He stopped and stared completely around him at the silent listeners. He had no friends here. He was quite alone. Yet he

186

said, in contempt: "Four men, led by Tom Blaine, followed my son and some girl down Wister's Alley last night. I can find no word to quite express the prostituted minds of those four men."

"You damned Rebel!" cried Billy Rees. "Go back to the South. Nobody asked you to come here!"

"As for being a Rebel," said Shiras Huntoon, "I at least fought for my side. Did you? But I understand the war is over, and this is again a country for all of us." Saying that much, he turned from them and strode out of the Drover's. Talk rose with a sudden, sullen quickness behind him.

It continued to rise; it continued to grow more and more angry. Shiras Huntoon, stung out of a discreet silence, had dropped a stone into the spuriously smooth surface of New Hope's life, and now the ripples spread outward from the Drover's, down St. Vrain Street, to the houses beyond. Coming along the street under a steady, slanting rain somewhat later in the afternoon, Saul Trevick saw Tom Blaine in front of the White House Restaurant. There was a group of men standing about him, and Tom Blaine's long jaws were grinding out talk. His arms swung, and his big chest rose and fell. There wasn't, Saul Trevick reflected, much wisdom in the man's head and no humor at all. But Blaine's loose lips and deep lungs were made for windy words, and he knew the things that struck home in his neighbors. Blaine saw him and called across the width of the street with a quick arrogance.

"Come over here, Trevick."

Saul Trevick merely shook his head. He turned in at his door and went back through the front partition to the shop. Young Johnny stood stolidly at the cases, setting type. But there was somebody else here, too. Jeff Huntoon stood in the background behind the Washington hand press. He didn't move. He said: "Thank you, Mister Trevick."

Saul Trevick faintly shook his head at the boy. He went across the shop to his room behind the rear partition. It was three o'clock, with little light coming down through the central skylight. Saul Trevick lit the lamp and turned on Jeff Huntoon, who had followed.

"Not wise for you to come here, Jeff."

"You're a gentleman, Mister Trevick. You didn't say anything."

"Maybe I'm a gentleman, Jeff . . . and maybe I'm taking the easiest way to keep out of trouble."

"Damn this town!" cried Jeff Huntoon.

"Or pity it," observed Saul Trevick quietly. He was watching the recklessness flame up in Jeff Huntoon. It was what he had seen as well in Lily. They were rash, and they didn't understand the brutal reasoning of New Hope.

"You like that girl, Jeff?"

"What can I do about it?"

Saul Trevick removed the shredded fragment of his cigar and studied it with a patient distaste. He dropped it down the vent hole of the stove and sought his vest for another. He didn't look at Jeff Huntoon; lamplight shone without mercy on the weariness of his face and accented the graying edges of his hair.

"You can fight back . . . and be hurt for your pains. Or you can lie low and wait for this nonsense to blow over."

"Let them hound me and do nothing about it?" breathed Jeff Huntoon. "Never, Mister Trevick. Never!"

Saul Trevick's arm made a slow gesture. "Perhaps you're right," he said, without emotion. "You'll be hurt if you fight back. At your age maybe it's worth the struggle. At my age it's different. You can't do much about people when they've lost their reason."

Jeff Huntoon turned through the back door, saying nothing

more. Wind came in, whipping the lamp flame. Saul Trevick walked back to the shop and found Johnny laying a column of type carefully into the page-one form on the make-up table. He seemed thoroughly blind to all things save his slow, painstaking work. Saul Trevick spoke with a degree of sharpness.

"People come to this shop either to get something in the paper or to keep something out of the paper. But whatever you see or hear in this shop . . . you haven't seen it, and you haven't heard it. Understand, Johnny?"

"Yes, sir."

Yet Saul Trevick wasn't quite satisfied. "Never betray a confidence. It's the only thing I can teach you. Do you understand, Johnny?"

Johnny said — "Yes, sir." — and looked around at Saul Trevick with a faint show of puzzlement. Saul Trevick's lips clinched the cigar stiffly; he pushed back his hat and picked up a composing stick and began to set type at a fast pace. But only half of his mind was on his job. The other half kept digging into the mystery of New Hope.

He felt the making storm. It was pretty definite to him. The Civil War was sixteen years in the past, but some of the war's resentment and distrust still lingered — like embers buried in the ashes of an old fire. The few Southerners who had drifted into New Hope understood this perfectly and had been wise enough to hold their opinions in silence. It was Shiras Huntoon, goaded out of discretion, who now fanned the flame to life again.

There was something additional here, Saul Trevick thought, that New Hope didn't realize. Living on the edge of the prairie, swept by summer's dust and winter's wind, isolated from the East and facing a Western wilderness, its people were touched by the wildness and the loneliness of the frontier that surrounded them. They had to be a dogged, hard-fibered sort to absorb the shocks of a raw land. But, tied into monotony and the grinding work of the day, there was in them a deep appetite for relief, and relief came to them only in vivid, violent, emotional outbursts: the election campaign, the murder trial, or the revival meeting that gave them their only relaxation from the discipline of the frontier. It was this deep and intense capacity for strong feeling Shiras Huntoon had released.

Saul Trevick heard the trip bell ring, but he went on setting type, his thoughts revolving around and around these people until he heard Tom Blaine speaking with an arbitrary command. He turned then and saw that a committee waited on him, the flickering gaslights sliding across the dark and disturbed set of each man's cheeks. He said mildly — "How do, gentlemen?" — and identified them all.

Tom Blaine could not keep his words pitched low. They rose and sailed across the shop, argumentative, ill-chosen, faintly ranting. "You're going to tell us who the girl was, Saul. We're satisfied she came in here last night."

Saul Trevick bowed his head a moment and ran his free fingers carefully over the type standing in his stick. The report of rain and wind flailed against the deep silence here. When he answered, it was with a detached wonder. "Why would you want to drag a girl's name down the mud of St. Vrain Street?"

Tom Blaine said brusquely: "So we can put a charge against Jeff Huntoon. She went willingly into Marshall's stable with him. What are you so considerate about? Who was the girl?"

"I don't know."

Tom Blaine lifted his long chin and shot the question at Johnny. "Who was it, Johnny?"

But young Johnny merely spread his arms. "I never saw nothin'."

190

Saul Trevick watched the men standing so darkly against him, and he saw something in their eyes. He knew what they thought then. Nor did he have to guess, for Tom Blaine's windy, bitter voice slapped at him.

"Do you propose to set yourself with the Southerners of this town? If you do, let's hear you say so. New Hope ain't big enough for any group of nigger-lovin' Copperheads whose sons chase around with decent girls. And it ain't big enough for a man like you, Trevick, if you think to support those people." He stopped, and afterward drove his threat home distinctly. "How'd you like to have somebody come in here and smash your shop?"

Trevick's head nodded quietly as though in answer to one of his own thoughts. He said very softly: "Let me remind you men of something you've forgotten. Other people have come into my back door before she did, bearing tales. If I were to talk, I wouldn't stop at that girl's name. I can go back eight years, and I can remember a good deal about a great many of you. You want her name now?"

Tom Blaine's cheeks showed change. Thoughtfully turning his glance along that row of men, Trevick saw some of them suddenly drop their glances away. "Money and politics and liquor and women," he murmured. "Where do you fellows get this sudden burst of moral purity? I recall. . . ."

"Shut up!" said Blaine. He turned on the others and said: "Let's get out of here." But at the partition doorway there was a discussion amongst them, and presently Blaine spoke again. "Trevick, you keep all this stuff out of your paper. Whatever happens tonight . . . don't print it!"

Then they were gone, slamming the front door violently behind.

Saul Trevick said to Johnny: "Get your supper and hurry back." He stood a moment after Johnny was gone, looking around his shop with the thoughtful eyes of a stranger and shook his head. He said — "It is hard to understand." — and went to the rear room. He lighted the lamp and poured himself a long drink. The rain made his bones ache, but the whiskey killed that. And the whiskey cleared his mind and turned all his thoughts logical. Somewhere an ancient ability to feel anger stirred from its long sleep. *I am ruined,* he told himself, and walked slowly through the shop and let himself into St. Vrain Street.

The moods of this town were like the moods of a woman. He understood them — and felt them; and before he had quite crossed St. Vrain to the White House Restaurant, he knew the night would be bad. There was that feeling of ugliness in the wind. He ate his steak and walked to the counter. Herb Marshall, who ran the White House, reached back to a shelf and brought out a box of cigars; it was a pattern that ran back eight years without variation. Saul Trevick filled a pocket with them, and paid his bill. There was something here that lifted his attention to Herb, who spoke evenly.

"Saul, take my ad out of your paper."

Saul Trevick stared at him, but Herb Marshall's feelings retreated and died behind the hazel screen of his eyes. Trevick's lips tightened about his cigar. "All right," he said, and went into the street again. The rain, driven by a higher wind, laid a silver net across the dark; and there was a crowd of New Hope's young men standing with some sort of visible purpose in front of Saul Trevick's shop. They saw him coming, but they didn't move, and he had to walk around them, through the forming mud at the foot of the sidewalk. There was one glaring word scrawled in blue chalk on his door, an epithet of the war that hadn't yet lost its stinging force: **Copperhead**. Saul Trevick's lips formed the word faintly, and he stood with his back to the group, knowing they watched him with an eagerness for trouble. But he put his hand to the doorknob and went inside, without looking around.

Johnny stood by the Washington hand press, wetting down paper; this was printing night, and all the forms were locked up. Henry Gray's youngster, Ted, had come in to his weekly chore of feeding the ink roller. Johnny looked about at Saul Trevick, stolidly troubled.

"They're going to wreck Shiras Huntoon's harness shop tonight."

"Mob logic," grunted Saul Trevick. He watched Johnny's big frame fall into the steady rhythm of presswork and afterward went back to the rear room and poured himself another drink and remained with his hand touching the table, his face bowed over a bottle almost empty. Most of his courage and most of his comfort, he reflected, had come out of bottles like that. They were his companions across a good many years, bringing to him a peace and a release from memory, and to him also an occasional brief glimpse of human magnanimity he had never seen on St. Vrain Street.

He dropped into the chair. *Some day,* he told himself, *men will not be afraid of generosity. But not in my time. The law of this world now is cruelty. People are blind. What good is the integrity of a man's conscience if New Hope stones him for it?* He was angrier than he remembered being in years; out of the long, gray emptiness of his life came a burst of rebellion that was strange to him. The hand press set up a steady clicking beyond the partition — and somebody was speaking there. But he paid no attention until a voice said: "Saul."

Ed McAleer stood before him, a big and solid man who understood people and still could laugh. McAleer smiled a little and for a while studied the disheveled, graying man sprawled in the chair. He spoke with slow emphasis.

"You're a queer duck, Saul. Never did give anybody a

193

chance to know you. Someday, when the town's calmed down, it will like you better for not speakin' the girl's name. Meanwhile, keep your shirt on. There'll be hell poppin' tonight, or I don't know New Hope. Shiras Huntoon said the wrong thing. The truth, maybe . . . but still the wrong thing. And Tom Blaine is politician enough to make the matter worse, to his own advantage. He'll ride into the legislature on foolishness like this."

Saul Trevick said: "Jeff Huntoon and his girl were walkin' in the rain, and went into Marshall's for shelter, a couple of youngsters dreamin' things that none of us feel more than once. Tom Blaine . . . and that pack out on the street . . . they're blind."

Ed McAleer said: "There's a streak of pride in you, Saul. Don't make an issue out of this. Whatever happens, keep it out of your paper. I tell you this for your own comfort."

Through the steady tempo of the rain along the building walls emerged the staccato break of outside sounds. The press stopped its methodical clicking. Ed McAleer turned from the back room, his feet striking solidly through the shop. Glass smashed somewhere; the voices of men lifted and fell. Johnny came rapidly to the rear room.

"Breakin' into Shiras Huntoon's shop. They're throwin' his goods in the mud."

"Mob logic," said Saul Trevick. Irony grated in his throat, but Johnny didn't understand. He showed his wonder and went back to the press. Saul Trevick pushed himself out of his chair; he started toward the shop — and stopped. The alley door burst open, and the wind sucked out the lamplight instantly. Then the door closed, and he heard heavy breathing across the darkness. He said: "Who is it?"

"Lily!"

He reached the table and lighted the lamp again. She had

her back to the door, her body pressed against it. Her face was distinctly white, and her breasts swelled with her violent breathing. Water dripped down her hatless head. Saul Trevick dropped his glance, afraid of the blackness of her eyes.

"It isn't only the harness shop. They're going after Jeff."

He said irritably: "Why do you come here?"

Her body slackened; her voice lost all its tone. "Where else could I go?"

He said — "Wait." — and went through the shop to the front office. Heat misted the window; he scrubbed off the film and put his forehead against the pane, seeing the crowd stir reluctantly away from the gutted harness shop. There was a heap of Huntoon's stuff lying in the middle of the street. He went back to Lily. She couldn't keep hope out of her eyes when she looked at him. How long had it been, he asked himself, since any human being had thought to come to him for support?

"Where's your father?"

"I haven't seen him in the house since dinner time."

"Wait," he said again. "Wait right here." He went out into Wister's Alley and sloshed through the soft mud. Two buildings farther on he ducked into the stable. A roustabout wheeled slowly beneath a suspended lantern and showed a dim, inquiring face.

Trevick said: "Doc Barnes has got to make a call. Get his sorrels hitched to a rig soon as you can." He didn't wait for an answer. He retracted, following the alley to Cottonwood Street, crossed over Cottonwood, and vanished in the thicker shadows of the residential section. He knew what he would find — and found it. Stragglers cut by him, through the rain, running ahead. A crowd had formed in front of Shiras Huntoon's house; somebody was breaking down the fence. Somebody was shouting: "Send Jeff out here!" They hadn't gone up to the porch, Saul Trevick saw; they hung back, afraid of something inside Shiras Huntoon's door. But the door opened, and the men quit yelling. Silence dropped, and there was only the slash of the rain — that and Shiras Huntoon's repressed words as he faced them.

"My son is not here."

It was a courage Saul Trevick suddenly admired; it was a quick flash of light in a dismal world. He turned from the forming edges of the crowd and cut back into Wister's Alley. Doc Barnes's team waited in the stable runway; the roustabout had disappeared. He seized the near sorrel's bridle and towed the team into the alley, as far as his own rear door. He opened the door swiftly — and stepped in. Jeff Huntoon stood opposite him with a revolver's cold, round muzzle lifted.

Anger gripped Trevick. "If you lose your head, I shall have nothing to do with you. Put that gun on the table, or New Hope will hang you for a killing."

The gun fell away. Jeff Huntoon's eyes were hard; they were old. He wasn't a youngster any more. He said, between tight lips: "What would you do, Mister Trevick?"

"You are through in New Hope. It's hard for young people to run when the time comes for running." He was trembling, and he felt his bones ache. "But go and find some place in the world where you can hold your conscience in peace."

"Yes," murmured Lily.

Saul Trevick emptied the last of the bottle's liquor into a glass and drank it. He put his back to them, but the silence went on. When he turned again, they were looking at each other in a way that struck him hard. Jeff Huntoon's voice ran low and humble: "You're wet, Lily . . . you're soaked." But she was smiling, and Jeff Huntoon crossed over, took hold of her, and kissed her. Once, Saul Trevick considered, he had

196

known what this was. It was a memory now; maybe it was only an illusion.

He said: "There's a buggy outside. It's twenty miles to Amity, and it's raining, and it's disagreeable, but what is that to you?"

The girl came over to Saul and grabbed his arm. She wasn't far from tears, but a moment later she went out the back door with Jeff Huntoon. He heard them drive away.

"Courage," he murmured, "comes easier to the young."

Yet there was something they had left behind in the room that shamed him. He felt it and turned into the shop where young Johnny doggedly worked at the hand press. He stood in the middle of the shop, watching Johnny's shoulders lift and fall and then went on to the front office and stared through the window, at Shiras Huntoon's goods piled in the middle of muddy St. Vrain. Men stood around it; men moved restlessly along the walk. He opened his door and looked at the **Copperhead** scrawled on the panel, and closed the door abruptly. Returning to the shop, his jaws tightened around the cigar.

He moved to a corner rack and found a cut of an American flag. His face changed a little then; a faint light broke through. He laid the cut inside an empty form on the make-up table. "Johnny," he said, "keep your conscience . . . it's all you've got." He lifted a stick, and for a moment remained still before the cases, his eyes half closed, bringing his bitter thoughts into line. The rain had freshened to a vigorous rush against the skylight, and the gas flames jumped a little from the currents prowling this draughty building. He pushed back his hat and began to set type.

Half an hour later he laid the type from his stick into the form, just below the American flag. He boxed in flag and story with column rules, put his paper's masthead at the top, slugged the surrounding white space with furniture, and locked it. He inked the type and got a sheet of paper and pulled a proof; he reversed the paper, staring at the flag and the story standing below it. When he read it, his lips moved:

Late tonight, moved by a spirit of insanity such as sometimes comes to this town, a mob of irresponsible men smashed into Shiras Huntoon's saddle shop, destroyed what they could, and threw what they could not destroy into St. Vrain Street, where it lies now as a monument to fools. All this was the result of Shiras Huntoon's speaking a few words of truth that New Hope didn't like to hear, in behalf of his son, Jeff, who had committed the unpardonable crime, in New Hope's estimation, of courting a girl down Wister's Alley. The flag at the top of this entry is supposed to cover all those who live under it. The war is sixteen years dead, and there is room for all of us in this great land. Yet New Hope seems to have forgotten. And forgotten, too, is that admonition of the Master, who said: "Let he among you who is without sin cast the first stone."

Saul Trevick

He turned then to Johnny who worked on at the press — and to Ted, the roller boy. He said: "Go on home."

Johnny stopped working. He said: "What?"

"Go on home."

"But. . . ."

"Go home," shouted Trevick. "Good God . . . get out of here!"

Johnny didn't understand. But he reached for his coat and looked at Ted and winked obviously. They went out of the shop together. Saul Trevick remained at the make-up table until he heard the trip bell jingle. Afterward, he took the printed sheet into the office, found a pastepot, and opened the front door. A man sloshing through the rain looked at him and went on; across the street by the White House a small crowd stood and seemed to be waiting. Trevick pasted the edges of the sheet and stuck it on his door, covering the scrawled **Copperhead**. Back in the shop he stared around him at the walls that had been his shelter for eight years and suddenly found them strange. His cigar was bad; he threw it away, got another, and lighted a match. His hands, he noticed, were not quite steady. Afterward he placed himself behind the make-up table, with his hands resting on it, his graying head pointed toward the front partition. He was standing like that when the crowd smashed through the front door and came violently around the partition into the shop.

They saw him standing there, small and without significance. Yet, for a moment, the leading man paused, not quite certain, and then more men came on and pushed through, and at once all of them spread through the shop and began to wreck it. He didn't stir. They lifted his cases and capsized the loose type on the floor and broke the cases beneath their feet; they ripped his furniture racks off the walls, tipped over his tables, and piles of paper. Four men upset the Washington hand press. They went to the rear room, and he heard his own possessions being scattered and rent. They came back to where he stood; one man pulled away the table by which he supported himself and threw it on its side. He saw the flash of their eyes and their heavy breathing. He looked around him and found nothing escaped from the ruin. They had said nothing; and they left the shop without saying anything.

But there was one man walking in from the alley. Saul Trevick turned, past curiosity, and found Tom Blaine there.

Blaine said: "It is a lesson you needed long ago. You'll never put together another paper in New Hope."

"No," said Saul Trevick, very slowly, "I never will. But I said what I had to say. That's the important thing, Tom." He looked thoughtfully at Blaine. "Been home yet tonight?"

Blaine studied him a moment. He said: "Why?" There wasn't any answer and then a change broke across his face. He said rapidly again: "Why?"

"Jeff Huntoon's gone from New Hope, taking the girl with him. The girl was your daughter, Lily."

He wasn't a fighting man. He had no defense to make against the sudden lunge Tom Blaine made at him. He stood still and took a solid blow across the face; it knocked him down into the capsized make-up table. One of its legs scraped across his side. Tom Blaine stood over him a moment, cursing him wildly. Then Blaine ran out of the place.

Saul Trevick got up and limped to the back room. The rear door was open, and most of his stuff had been pitched into the alley. He put his hands in his pockets and looked around him and pulled them out and reached down to recover the whiskey bottle. It was empty. He pitched it into the alley and went out there and scurried around the mud till he found his overcoat. He put it on and came back to the room. There was a small, cedarwood box thrown in a corner; he got this and carried it into the shop and wrapped it carefully in a piece of print paper. Going out the rear door again, into the alley's darkness, he held the box under his arm carefully. The few important relics of his life were in that box, the only thing he cared to rescue from the obscure vengeance of New Hope.

At the end of Wister's Alley, he swung into Custer Street and passed out of the town. A road ran due south to Amity, through the gusty, liquid blackness of the night. He stopped here, turning to look at the few, glimmering lights of New Hope. There wasn't any regret in him; there wasn't any bitterness in him. He said, in a way that was like elation: "Apparently I've got some deadline even New Hope can't force me beyond." It was personal triumph. "My conscience is clear," he murmured, lifted his coat collar, and swung into the muddy road, bound for Amity and the world beyond Amity, without a care.

V

"ONCE AND FOR ALL"

Always there was a short hour of beauty those summer nights in New Hope when twilight turned to dusk. Moonlight made this magic, changing the flour-gray dust of our street into a luminous, silver-rippled streak, softening the gaunt outline of our unlovely buildings. Peace and ease came then, and the voices of people rose from the front porches with a slow resonance, and heat released itself from the earth, and a small wind lifted from the west, bringing in the crispness and wildness and mystery of a thousand miles of plains. This was 1881, and I was a boy of twelve. Judith Grand and Chad Colpitt, pacing arm in arm along the walk, turned in at our gate. Their faces were dim to me, but I could see Chad's rash, reckless grin, and I could see Judith's soft smile.

"Well," said Chad Colpitt, "we are to be married."

My mother's rocker quit its squealing, and her murmur was as though a heartfelt relief came to her. Father rose and removed his cigar. He shook Chad's hand. "It is a thing we have all hoped for. When is it to be?"

Chad Colpitt's voice was like him, gay and pleased; for this man loved all the sensations of life and had neither fear nor quiet in him. "I have bought into Billy Ormes's freight business. I leave Monday with a wagon train for Dakota. It will be as soon as I return."

My father replaced the cigar between his lips. I knew that he was stirred by some thought deeply, for the tip of the cigar was a bright glow. He said: "You have come a long way since you were a wild boy of fifteen, Chad."

Chad Colpitt's laughter made a clean, strong wave through the twilight hush; and I could see Judith Grand's face, round and firm and fair in these shadows, tip toward him. Afterward they turned out of the yard, swaying in slow time as they went down the walk. It is strange how some memories die and some grow clearer as the years run on. The picture of those two, standing at the foot of our porch that summer's night, remains unforgettably with me, like the vision of a high-burning, signal fire on the back trail. There was laughter in Chad Colpitt, and a certainty of his own strength; and Judith Grand's silence, I know now, was a silence of pride. These people were in love.

My mother said in a strange, quiet way: "It is so good to know."

"Sometimes," my father answered gently, "life forgets to be cruel."

"Why, Tod!"

I remember being puzzled by that remark. I remember it sounded odd to me, violating my own youthful thoughts of life. But time has made it bitterly clear, and now my youth is a golden dream of long ago. Nevertheless, that phrase stuck with me like a burr, and next morning, walking down St. Vrain Street, I had it in my mind, silently repeating it in the way a boy will do — to get the sense out of it — when a voice stopped me, saying: "What would be the problem, Tod?" And I looked up to see Mr. Stanton in front of the Wells Fargo office, gravely interested in me.

I recall a feeling of swift satisfaction, for young as I was I knew that Mr. Stanton, too, had been calling on Judith Grand, and there was in me a boy's zealous and faithful worship of Chad Colpitt. That difference was between the two men. Everybody loved Chad, wild and laughing and indifferent as he was to so many things in those days. It was his way to bind people to him; it was his way to make people find excuses for him. I do not think Mr. Stanton was a day older, but I never saw him laugh, and in his presence I always felt exactly what I was — a boy. I remember that I felt a little stab of jealousy that morning as I looked up to him; for even in my prejudice I admired the solidness of his shoulders and the dark and wide and definite lines of his face. He was physically a bigger man than Chad, and I resented that. I can look back now and understand how unfair I was, for the years have taught me that Mr. Stanton was the kind of a man the world always unjustly deals with. Slow and steady, he had no way of binding people to him. All that he was lay beneath the quietness that covered him.

I said: "Nothing, sir."

He spoke carefully: "Don't grow up sober faced, Tod. You will come to regret it. Let others do the worrying. You have your fun."

I recall being unexplainably embarrassed. I stood there, not speaking. And then Judith Grand came out of the doorway of the New York Store, and Mr. Stanton wheeled and removed his hat. What stays with me these long years is the straightness of his body that moment, and the darkness of his eyes, and the softness of his voice that was like sadness.

"I have heard of God's good fortune, Judith," he said. "I wish you both all the happiness you may find."

The hot sun was shining down, and people were moving past us on the walk, and a line of freight wagons came creaking up from the river landing, the heavy horses straining against their collars. Dust came about us, and the voices of the teamsters were round and sharp and bold. I heard a steamboat, whistling hoarsely beyond the housetops of New Hope. Kit Maloney, who had been a scout with Custer just five years before, came riding by on his black mare. I thought then — and never have ceased to think — that Judith Grand was a beautiful woman. She faced Mr. Stanton and lifted her head with a slow, half smile, and I know now that she was sorry for him and that her eyes were telling him so. They were two fine, vigorous people with a grace and a binding honesty in their slow ways. Her lips were broad; they were generous; and there was a sweetness in them. Her hair was a fresh yellow.

"Why shouldn't Tod be grave, Charley?" she asked, changing the subject.

Mr. Stanton shook his head. "I should hate to see him play that part, Judith. I know it too well, for it has always been my part. There's no fun in it."

She wasn't smiling then. Her voice fell lower. "We cannot help being what we are, Charley. We can't help the things that happen to us."

"I wish you all the luck," he said.

She watched him a moment, and I thought she meant to speak again. But, instead, she turned and walked on toward Custer Street. Mr. Stanton stood quite still until she vanished around the corner, whereupon he wheeled away. He had forgotten me. He went on with his head down, not seeming to know where he was going. I continued on and came to the corner of Custer and saw Judith and Chad Colpitt, standing in front of the Emporium. He had his back to the wall and was leaning against it, with a negligence and a laughter that I clearly remember. People were coming up to speak to them, and all the group seemed very gay. Judith Grand stood quietly among them, her eyes on Chad in that still, proud way that seemed to fill the street with something strange and steadfast.

You must see New Hope as I see it now. A raw and prosperous and unlovely town sitting on the Missouri's bank with its face to the long, wild swoop of the western plains. You must feel its burning wind, its bitter dust, its isolation from the soft and pleasant memories of the East. For a boy it was always a place of wonder, of bold change. But as I call to mind the faces of my elders and remember the thin sweep of their lips and the settled gravity of their eyes, I at last understood they were afraid of laughter. There was a hunger in them they dared not express. The land, I think, had made them that way, for they had seen so much of tragedy and want, and their lives were so full of bitter work and sadness that they had steeled themselves to disappointment. And so the love affair of Judith Grand and Chad Colpitt was wonderful to them, a fire lighting and warming their own dark and half-forgotten dreams. Well, it was the story of youth and romance come to a proper ending. It had made my mother cry for gladness; it had made my father say that life sometimes forgot to be cruel. This was what the whole town felt. New Hope made that affair its own.

I saw them again that evening, walking through the soft shadows of our street, the echoes of their steps falling gently in time, and I heard Chad Colpitt's voice rise to soft, easy amusement. And then they were lost somewhere in the farther darkness. My mother said, in a way that was faintly displeased: "Why does he have to take that wagon train into Dakota? There's plenty of wagon bosses to be had for the hiring. I wish they were married first."

My father said: "Charley Stanton took the evening stage for a visit to Omaha."

My mother was a gentle soul. "I feel sorry for him, Tod."

But my father's tone was rather gray, rather grim. "Men like Charley were built to stand punishment. You'll hear no crying from him."

"I wish," repeated my mother, "Chad wasn't going to Dakota."

"He will always be doing things like that," my father told her. "And there's the difference between the two. Charley Stanton plows his furrow faithfully, but Chad has got to be forever seeing what this world is made of."

"Judith will change him," said my mother. "She'll bring patience to him."

My father didn't answer, and now I understood why. He was always a realistic man who saw the ways of men clearly; and I know that he felt Chad would never change.

This was on a Saturday. On the Monday next I went out to the western edge of town to see the freighters pull away. They made a long line on that smooth, sandy plain; great wagons with their canvas tops glistening under a fresh sun, and the heavy mules stirring up the flour-gray dust. They were ready to go, and nothing held them except the crowd formed there to wish Chad Colpitt good luck. I saw him standing beside his roan gelding with his hat lifted and his red hair shining and all his face alive with the glitter of high excitement. I feel it now, that powerful appetite for life that boiled in him and came out of him to agitate and lift the spirits of all those around. Judith Grand faced him, tall and still in this confusion, and then he reached forward and kissed her. He was smiling when he swung into his saddle and lifted his hand by way of signal. All the wagons groaned into a forward motion, with the lash of whips and the sound voices of the muleskinners rising. He waved at the crowd and looked again at Judith Grand. I saw the excitement fade momentarily from him. He spoke softly to her — so softly: "It will seem a long time, Judith. The days will be very long." And then he trotted away to the head of the wagon line. There must have been in me as a boy a preternatural sharpness of observation, for my eyes returned to Judith Grand, and I remember how straight and sober she stood and how her eyes darkened as she watched him go. He made a gallant figure on the horse; he made a picture. New Hope loved that man. I think it was because he represented the freedom and the gaiety the people of our town hungered for and never could find.

So he faded into the west, into the deep banks of copper and powder-gray haze lying all asmolder across that hot land. Beyond was the country of the Sioux, and the Black Hills where stormy Deadwood lay. That summer was a hard one, long and burning and bitter. The shapeless sun rose sulphur-red above the heat murk, and the south wind scorched us and clawed long clouds of dust across the housetops and through the street. By day we took to wearing wet handkerchiefs over our noses; by night we sat on the front porch and waited for coolness that never came. My parents suffered, and all the older ones of New Hope showed the shortness of their tempers and the raggedness of their nerves. Henry Tabor's feed store burned down. Mrs. Palmer took her three children one night and ran away from her husband. Two cowpunchers out of Plum Creek fought a duel, both dying of their quarrel. The Missouri showed its muddy bottom halfway out to Forby's sandbar. By long day I went with my particular boyhood friends to the willow bottoms along the river and lay there, hearing the mourning doves, smelling the rank mud odor of the river rise in steamy waves. To me my youth was golden.

And then Peter Braley rode back through the western haze, six weeks from the time Chad Colpitt's freight caravan had started, to report Chad dead. Somewhere along the banks of the big Cheyenne River, under the shadow of Harney Peak, the caravan had been attacked at night by renegade Sioux. There had been a battle, and Chad had charged out through the darkness and vanished. At daylight they found his horse shot through the head, and beyond was Chad's hat, streaked by blood, with a bullet hole in it. They had not ventured farther to find Chad because the Sioux kept potting at them with good agency rifles. Later a cavalry company had come up from Fort Laramie. But nothing more was to be found.

My father brought the news home that night. He came through the gate and stopped at the foot of the steps, looking over to Mother who saw something strange on his face and stopped her rocking. He told us then, and my own little world came crashing down about me, and I sat stunned. I heard my mother crying; I heard her rise and go into the house. I think I was crying myself, for I was a boy, and Chad Colpitt had been a hero to me. Father came over and put a hand on my shoulder. He said: "Never wear your heart on your sleeve, Tod. It is a thing you must learn."

It is difficult for me to describe what that news did to my town. But it was New Hope's tragedy; it was the brutal end of a dream to all those slow, grave people no less than to Judith Grand. All that they themselves hungered for was in that pair, the brightness of youth and love, the desperate hope of a happy ending that came so infrequently to their lives. But now that was done, and the ending was dark. It was as my mother said a week later, so sadly, so wistfully: "It was too good to be true. I feared for them." That was the way New Hope felt.

I used to watch Judith Grand stroll down our quiet street

those long evenings of late Indian summer, passing alone through the shadows where she had often before strolled with Chad Colpitt, and, young as I was then, something filled me to bursting and went away, and left me very empty. I think this summer the shadowy intimations of life's mystery first disturbed my boyhood world. I think it was there and then boyhood's implicit belief in goodness and security went away. She walked alone those evenings, a fair figure in the dusk; and sometimes she stopped at the gate to speak to Mother, and I saw how grave her eyes had become, how still and sober were her lips. And then one night I saw Mr. Stanton walking with her.

They were married in the late fall.

I hated him then, for the loyalties of boyhood do not soon die, and I still remembered Chad Colpitt. And I recall one evening, after Judith and Mr. Stanton had stopped by a moment to speak to us and gone on, that Mother rose from her rocker and looked long at Father. "It isn't right!" she said, and went into the house. I can understand that now. She had nothing against Mr. Stanton. She respected him. But it was the treachery of time she would never forget; it was the swift brutality of life that grieved her. I think New Hope felt that way about it, too. My elders had allowed themselves to believe in a miracle; and they were sad now.

Yet we were a practical people and believed that life was meant for use and for work. In New Hope in 1881 it was proper to grieve and to cry, and then it was necessary to be done with tears. Ours was a land that had little place for single women; it was wives we needed, and children. And so New Hope put away its dream of what might have been, and Judith and Mr. Stanton settled in the big, stone house at the corner of Belle Plaine and Prairie Street. We paid them a formal call soon after they were married, and all uncomfortable in my

209

good suit I sat in their high-ceilinged room and listened to the talk go on. I remember that scene well, with Mr. Stanton standing with one arm hooked to the fireplace mantel, a fine, tall figure of a man browned by the weather, with a slow and silent way about him, with a manner of looking now and then toward his new wife. Long as it has been, I still see the fairness of her features and the sweetness of those long, generous lips, and I still feel the vigor and melody that seemed to flow from her like a tune. One thing I recall my mother said as we went homeward that night. It seemed to be a reluctant admission; it seemed to come out of her under protest. "They make a perfect-looking couple."

My father went walking along with his head down. He had no answer. Mother turned her eyes to him. She said: "What are you thinking?"

He said: "They do not smile." And neither Mother nor Father spoke again on the way home.

Indian summer went by, and the wild geese began to go south. I used to lie awake at night and hear that faint, high, wild clamor overhead; and sometimes I thought the strange, dark thoughts of a boy, my mind running out into those windy, gray mists that are the mysterious boundaries of all our lives, and then I would feel an echo and a fear — I knew not why — and lie, staring at the dark shape of the window. We had an early winter, with ice on Beechey's pond in November. Just before Christmas, Colonel Cliff, riding back from New Hope to his ranch, thoroughly drunk, fell off his buggy and was found dead in a drift of snow. A revival meeting came to our town and unsettled it, and miser Joe Scott's eldest daughter married against his persuasion.

It was on a windy afternoon in March, I remember, that I came out of the New York Store with a package for my mother and found Judith and Mr. Stanton, talking there with

Father. Something had been said, and Father was strongly laughing, a rare thing for him to do, and I could see Mr. Stanton's brown, solid face show pleasure. Judith said to me — "Why don't you visit me, Tod?" — and, afterward, Mr. Stanton half spoke and half grunted a word that turned my attention to him. He was looking down the street, and then I observed Judith's cheeks whiten from a pure pain. It thrust me about on my heels. A man yelled clear across the street: "Chad!" And I saw Chad Colpitt ride forward on a long-jawed, Indian pony that had only a piece of rope for a bridle. He came up to where we stood, and I saw the eagerness of his grin flash behind the full beard that covered his face. He was a thin man, and his clothes were ragged, and a scar ran down from one temple toward the point of his nose. But he came before us, still hugely pleased, and got down; and he said to Judith, as though he had never been away: "Hello."

Nothing in my life has ever been like that since. I heard her breathe in a strange way. She swayed toward Mr. Stanton, whose own expression was all dark; and she was asking him to take her home. They turned, and my father let his arm fall across Chad Colpitt who moved to follow. I looked back to Chad. He had stopped smiling.

"You were supposed to be dead, Chad," my father said. "Missus Stanton thought you were." He repeated her name in a stronger voice: "*Missus* Stanton, Chad." Then he looked at me and said — "Come along." — and we left Colpitt standing that way. There were people running up from all parts of the street, and voices were rising fast, but my father said not another word. His mouth was peculiar to me, being thin and dismal in its set.

I had another errand to do before reaching home — and so I do not know how my mother took that news. But when I did get home, I saw that she had been crying again, and that the old hurt was once more fresh. My father had gone, and it was late before he returned. Something sat heavily on his mind, and he was not pleased. He said: "Chad went up to Charley Stanton's house." And then, after a silence that was uncomfortable to me, my father burst out: "What did Chad expect? I am disappointed in him."

It was my mother who found an excuse for Chad, just as so many people in our town found excuses for him, because they could not help it. "It is a hard thing to come back to. I cannot blame him too much."

But my father's sense of right was always a stern thing, many times impelling him to make decisions that were harsh, that were uncomfortable. "You could have blamed Charley Stanton six months ago, if he had interfered with Judith and Chad. But Charley is a man who takes his punishment. He took it then. Chad should take it now."

My mother had a woman's answer for that. "This is different," she said.

My father looked at me and held his tongue. My parents were this way: they never argued in front of me. It was dusk then, and I slipped away, going out around the western edge of our town where the big freight park was, and found my young companions there. Boyhood has its own telegraph, its own sources of information, and I found that Nick Fallon, one of the more knowing lads in the group, knew the story my father had withheld.

Nick Fallon said: "Chad Colpitt went up to the Stanton house. He was pretty mad. Semus Curtiz saw him go in, and heard some loud talk. Then Mister Stanton and Chad came out and crossed to the alley behind Blagg's stable. Semus Curtiz saw the fight. Mister Stanton beat hell out of Chad."

The very thought outraged me. I said: "That's a lie."

Nick Fallon was a wicked boy, the son of a teamster who

let him run wild. I remember that Nick slid off the tar barrel he had been sitting on. He wiped his mouth with the back of his hand and came at me, and the other boys stepped backward into the shadows to give us room. I felt very cold, for I was afraid of Nick; and then he hit me, and I wasn't afraid any more, and I struck him on his lips and ran against him and hit him in the chest and threw him down. He got up and cursed me, and his fist sliced the skin from the side of my face. I was very confused and missed him completely and stumbled past him, and he caught me a hard blow on the back of my head. I remember turning with a wild swing that knocked the wind out of his stomach. He went down again, and that was all of our fight. We both stayed as we were. I wanted no more fighting, but this was one of the great moments of my boyhood. I had been afraid of Nick Fallon, and now I wasn't afraid any more. It changed the night for me; it changed me in front of my crowd. It is one of those things that sometimes happens. I stood over Nick then, and I would be forever standing over him. I do not recall any other moment in my life when one long minute ever meant so much to me.

The other boys came toward us. None of them spoke of the fight. We were all crouched down in the semi-darkness, and Henry Dix was speaking.

"My old man heard Chad Colpitt tell why he didn't come back sooner. The Sioux captured him and meant to kill him. But Chad said the Indian leader was superstitious about red hair. So they didn't kill Chad because he has red hair. Chad said they were afraid the soldiers would be after them, so they went away up into Montana, almost Canada. He was adopted into the tribe. Pretty soon they didn't watch him very close . . . and he escaped."

I got up without saying anything and went home.

It is hard for me to describe New Hope's emotions during that long winter. I felt it then and did not understand it; I feel it now — and the years have made me wiser. It was a restlessness, a sense of a thing gone wrong. It was a kind of a wound that would not heal. The news of Stanton's fight with Chad soon got out — for our town was too small not to know people's secrets — and I think New Hope thought the better of Stanton from that moment forward. He had done only what any honest man would do; and it was strange to all of us to observe how this wild Chad Colpitt turned his ways inside out. I remember meeting him on the street one day. He stopped me, and he spoke to me — and I waited for that old-time, famous smile to break across his face. But I never saw it; there was a change in him. He used to play seven-up at the White Palace in the evening with old Judge Menefee, and he used to take his horse and ride away from New Hope. But he was a tame man those days, a quiet-spoken man. He never went to the Stanton house again, yet we wondered about that, and we always watched when Mr. Stanton met him on the street. There was a kind of friendliness between them that New Hope could not understand, and sometimes the people of our town would stop and turn and watch Judith as she passed by Chad Colpitt's stage office. I think now it must have been an ordeal for those three, yet nobody ever saw behind that strange reserve, that unsmiling serenity.

Remember, ours was a strict town. We didn't know what divorce was, and we believed in the hard and fast ways. Yet the winter went along, and our blustery spring broke, and the sense of wrongness still was strong. New Hope once had thought to see the story of young love work out. But that dream had died, and New Hope had laid the memory aside. And now Chad Colpitt walked the street to mock the hope our town had put away. It was, as I say, like a wound that wouldn't heal. There was no cure; there was no answer. Young as I was, I often watched Judith walk along the street, a fair woman in all her ways, a woman vigorous and serene, with a sweetness in her lips — and I used to feel a hatred for Mr. Stanton that made me old.

It is something I regret now. For in June of that year Mr. Stanton, riding out to one of his leased ranches, was thrown from a high-strung horse and fatally injured. A rider came in with the news on a noon of that day, and Judith was driven out to the ranch where they had taken him. He lived to see her come, and New Hope saw that scene through the eyes of Dr. Gillespie who was there.

Judith came to his bedside, and it must have been plain to her that he was dying. She bent over and took his hand, and she kissed him. But she didn't cry.

Mr. Stanton said: "Luck was with me once, Judith. It's against me now. It comforts me to feel you will never know want. I wish I could live long enough to see our child."

She said: "Charley, I want you to know this. . . ." But we never knew any more, for Dr. Gillespie turned and left the room. When he returned again, Judith was kneeling at the bedside, and Mr. Stanton was dead.

There is so little left to tell of this story, and yet in that little lies all that is wonderful to me. It would be a cruel thing to say that New Hope felt relieved at Mr. Stanton's death, and it would be an untrue thing, for our town was kinder than that. Yet, I know that there was a change, and I know that people were quietly talking again of that long-interrupted courtship between Judith and Chad Colpitt. I know it because my mother, gentle soul, said it to my father.

"It is almost too much to hope," she told him. "I pray God is kind this time."

When my father was deepest moved, he spoke most softly, as he spoke now. He only said: "I should not pray too much."

But my mother's hope was the hope of our town. Even then I knew it. There was a kindness surrounding these two, there was a gentleness around them — and above all that, a quiet insistence, as though my elders meant to have their way at last. Yet we were a seemly people, and we held our tongues until the baby was born, a boy that some said looked like Mr. Stanton, and some said looked like Judith. I saw it once and could see no resemblance anywhere, but that is a way people have. And then the gentle conspiracy grew, and our good matrons made it their business to have parties that included a Chad Colpitt now turned grave and a Judith whose eyes seemed to smile above those quiet lips. And once I saw them, walking at dusk down our street, down it and into the yonder shadows as they had done in that past day which seemed so far back. Once. Never again. And nothing happened. That night, I like to think, they laid the pattern of their lives for the time to come.

She came to our home one day to visit Mother. I was there and heard some stray talk between them. Then, all by impulse and energy, Mother said: "You have a man waiting for you, Judith. A fine man to make you happy."

I still see Judith, standing there so sweetly, with something in her eyes deeper than serenity; I still hear the soft, grave melody of her voice.

"I was Charley Stanton's wife, and I have his boy. It was the choice I made. Well, we choose our parts only once. There is never a second choosing. It has to be this way."

That is all. She never married Chad.

I see the world so confused now, so puzzled about its ways. I see people seeking happiness and crying out for it and walking away without compass or light, eager to hear whatever little stray whimper may come to their ears. And then I think back to my boyhood and recall Judith Grand, walking along our street, a woman instilled with the grace and vigor and sweetness of life. I was a man fully grown before I realized what she had done to our town, and what she had done to me. Many times, in darkness and in doubt, I have felt the touch of her personality upon me; and I know now it touched our town as well.

It was a steadfastness that somehow showed me what dignity life could hold — a shining light coming all through the long darkness of the world.

VI

"PROUD PEOPLE"

It was always like this in New Hope those far-off days when I was a boy, and the world was so young. The weeks ran on without event until, it seemed, time stood still, and then excitement would burst across our town like a sudden prairie storm.

I stood on St. Vrain Street in front of the Western House that morning at the moment old Henry Bland, a tall and genteel man with an old soldier's brisk carriage, wheeled out of his bank and walked toward the courthouse with more haste than was usual. The freighters were rumbling up from the river landing, their great wheels dipping and dropping the dust like water, and the Omaha mail stage rounded the corner of Prairie Street at a very reckless clip. Mr. Wackrow stepped from the Western House, spoke to me, and went on toward the bank. And just then Mark Morrison, Henry Bland's cashier, came from the bank with his cheeks set like marble and hurried into the adjoining alley. Henry Bland was returning from the courthouse with our sheriff, Tom Blaine, and Mr. Wackrow had stopped on the street to look at them. And at that moment I heard one shot break through the alley.

Mr. Wackrow said — "My God." — and ran into the alley, and the sheriff jumped away from Henry Bland, trotting after Mr. Wackrow, and people began to run out of the buildings on St. Vrain Street. I do not know why, but for some reason I watched old Henry Bland who seemed to walk more and more slowly, as though there was a weight pushing on his shoulders. Suddenly there was a crowd in front of the bank, and Tom Blaine came back from the alley. I heard him say: "Mark Morrison just killed himself." Afterward he followed Henry Bland into the bank. Through the glass of the door I could see Mr. Bland lock the door and put the **Closed** sign across it. As young as I was, I knew then what that meant.

These things are so clear in my memory. Camilla Bland came from the Bon Marche, a startled expression in her eyes. She called to me: "What is it, Tod?" On hearing her voice, young Phil Hendry turned from the edge of the gathering crowd and went directly to her. "You've got to go home, Cam," he said, and took her away. My father appeared from his office, and pushed through the crowd, rapping on the bank's door. Henry Bland let him in. Dr. Gillespie turned from the White Palace directly into the alley. By this time St. Vrain Street was full of people, and Johnny Dix slid beside me, his eyes as round as plates. He said: "Mark Morrison blew his head off." I was shocked and a little sick, and turned away. Somebody was carrying a canvas tarpaulin into the alley.

My father came home late that night. Mother and I were on the porch, and I noticed the roundness of his shoulders in the twilight and the heaviness of his step. My mother just looked at him, not speaking.

He stood on the steps, one foot above the other, and I recall now that I was suddenly aware of his age. There was a faint gray along the edges of his black hair. He was looking at Mother, quietly shaking his head. He said: "The bank examiner dropped in today. Mark Morrison wasn't expecting him."

"I always trusted Mark," said my mother.

"So did Henry Bland," said my father. "Too much. Mark was speculating." He so seldom swore, but he swore now. "Damn him, he's left half the families in this town in trouble!"

"Tod."

They were looking at each other, and, afterward, Father's glance seemed to rise and run along the front of our house, and my mother said instantly: "Oh, not that, Tod."

"I'm one of the stockholders," he said. "I'll have to stand the assessment."

There was a long, long silence, and then my mother, gentle soul, said in a soft voice: "I'm so sorry for Henry Bland."

Father said: "You had better be sorry for a good many other people."

After a moment he left, and a little later I went roaming down St. Vrain Street and saw the lights of the bank shining through the cracks of the drawn shades, and I knew Father was in there with the other directors. Tom Blaine guarded the doorway. This news had spread like a grass fire, and half the farmers of the county had come in, and the teamsters and river roustabouts choked the street, and the talk was sullen and a little wild. Father came home long after I was in bed that night. His voice and Mother's voice made a murmuring below me until at last I fell asleep.

You have to see New Hope clearly to understand the havoc

that failure wrought. Sitting beside the Missouri and facing the long swells of the prairie, our town depended on the freighting trade for its existence. Its wealth sprang from the traffic of all those great wagons pitching westward with the land's long undulations. In the beginning old Henry Bland had pioneered that trade; he had supported and encouraged most of the others who had grown moderately wealthy in the trade. The river and the wagons and the far-off settlements — and Henry Bland. This was the way of it; and, when the bank closed, the life of our town fluttered.

I could see care and anxiety deepen the lines of my father's face that following week when the big stockholders and the leading merchants of our town met to apportion their losses. And I remember how bitterly he said one thing: "Alex Hendry is a damned hard man!"

My mother said: "The law says he must stand his assessment, doesn't it?"

My father looked at her. "We've got to shoulder more than that."

She said: "I don't understand."

Neither did I. But I was soon to learn. It was the next night that Belle Mellish, the widow of a teamster tragically killed, came to the porch. I was in the house, but I heard her say to Father: "It's little I had in that bank, and, if I'm to lose half of it, how do I live? There's years ahead of me, and now I've got to take my boy out of school and put him to work. How am I to live?"

I didn't hear my father's answer, but, after she went away, I did hear him speak to Mother. "There's a hundred like her in New Hope. We've got more to shoulder than just our assessments. But Alex Hendry won't assume a dime more than the law compels him."

My mother spoke in a softly wondering way. "What will

Phil Hendry do . . . and what will Camilla Bland think?"

At thirteen my boyhood world was widening in a queer way, with strange things creeping in to disturb it, to make it less secure. I thought of Camilla Bland and of Phil Hendry, who was old Alex's son, the day they auctioned off the Bland possessions. Everybody said that Bland had turned all that he ever owned over to the creditors; and this was the last he had to give. Legally he didn't need to; but, if you knew Henry Bland, you understood he could have done nothing else.

I remember the auctioneer's voice crying through the rooms of that big and pleasant and homely house, and I remember how crowded the place was with people I had never seen before — farmers in from the prairie and bargain hunters from adjoining towns; and I remember, too, that of the Bland family's friends only my father, who represented the bank, and Phil Hendry were there. It was a sense of courtesy, I think, that kept the others away. And I remember Camilla standing alone in a corner, tall and a little pale and not showing anything out of her eyes but a bitter pride while all the things that had been a part of her life for so many years slowly melted away. Later, in the yard, I heard my father swear faintly to himself when a Dutch hardscrabble settler from Sage Coulée bought the two, matched, gray mares Henry Bland had driven for so long.

My mother cried when Father told her how the auction had gone. He said: "I would rather have been horse-whipped, but the creditors wanted me to be there. I don't know why Phil Hendry put in his appearance."

And then I remembered that Phil Hendry had stood across the room from Camilla, a big, yellow-headed young man inclined to laughter and to indifference, but who hadn't smiled that long afternoon and who had only looked at the girl and had never gone over to where she stood. It was strange to me, for all New Hope understood those two were to be married.

In the end the bank was reorganized and my father made president by the stockholders. After the assessments had been paid in, there was, I think, about fifty cents on the dollar; and then the leading men of the town went their own personal notes to assure the small depositors another twenty-five cents. My father's share of that extra assessment was, I recall, five thousand dollars.

Often in later years I wondered why they had gone beyond their strict responsibilities, why they had so quietly and so calmly assumed that added debt. And I was a man fully grown before I saw those bearded and slow-speaking and rather stolid men in the proper light. Well, there was something in them they could not help, a taciturn sense of duty they could not escape. A hundred or more little depositors, like Mrs. Belle Mellish, had suffered in the crash, and the extra money raised was to relieve them.

Alex Hendry had been one of the big operators of our town, a wry, taut New England man with a shrewdness for trading that was marked even in a country of traders. But he had not joined in the extra assessment. All the way through he had fought for his pound of flesh, threatening to liquidate the bank if his interests were pushed, and in the end the other stockholders, with an indescribable bitterness, had made their hard bargain with him. The Bland block on St. Vrain Street was turned over to him to satisfy his share of the lost deposits, and a working interest in the brewery as well. A month after the crash I saw a painter put a ladder to the arch of the Bland Block building; when I passed that way later, it had become the Hendry Block. My father had been this man's friend; and Henry Bland had been his banker and his advisor. But it made no difference. From that day forward I never saw my father speak to Alex Hendry. And once when Henry Bland happened to be walking down Prairie Street, I saw this shrewd and foxy Alex stop and speak quite civilly to Bland. There was no answer. Henry Bland, grown terribly old, looked at Alex Hendry in a way that erased the man from existence.

I think from that day on Alex Hendry, as rich as any man in our county, had no real friend. I can look back now and see our town with wiser eyes than I had then; and I think something came to New Hope it had not possessed before. I cannot see them as romantic figures, those slow and solid and heavy men who ran our stores and owned the stage lines and lived in the big sprawling houses out along Prairie Street. They were hard men, and they were drivers; in a rough and sometimes cruel world they were extreme realists, all of them. Yet, they had a sense of duty they could not voice — a kind of pride in their obligations to this town and to the people in it. It had pulled them together; it had shut Alex Hendry out.

It was just after the bank reopened that New Hope noticed Camilla Bland had returned Phil Hendry's ring.

I remember the night my mother told this to Father. He was reading the paper, but he put it aside and looked over to her a rather long while, as if considering what he ought to say. I see her so vividly now — a quiet woman with sweet lips and a way that was soft and gracious, filling all my boyhood with a gentleness that comes to me now like a fragrance. He said, soberly and cheerlessly: "It's better that way."

My mother protested. "He was always a good boy. They were so nice a couple."

My father said: "He'll get his father's money . . . which is tainted. I think Camilla wants none of that."

Often, in the months that followed, I wondered. For these were the days when the world was opening for me, and I was thinking of things I felt and feared — and could not under-

223

stand. I saw Phil Hendry go down Prairie Street one evening after dusk and stop at the little house the Blands were then living in; and I saw her come to the door, her white dress shining in the faint moonlight. I could not help myself. Stopped in the shadows I watched those two. She came out to the porch, closing the door, and for a moment they stood near each other, and some brief word was said. Afterward, she went back in the house, and he walked away. A laughing, careless man, this Phil Hendry. But he wasn't laughing then.

In our town it was inevitably a matter of speculation. All of us lived close together, and our lives touched and became common property. We had manners, and we had a strictness of belief that seems to me now to have been narrow; but below that was a curiosity so frank and real and earthy. Some thought Camilla wanted nothing to do with any Hendry, but there were others who thought Phil Hendry, seeing the obligation that hung over Camilla Bland, was afraid to assume it. There was evidence to favor this belief, for the whole town knew that the aging Henry Bland had laid upon his daughter the obligation of paying off his debts. The debts he didn't legally owe and yet could not forget.

None of us knew the truth, though all the sharp eyes of the town were upon those two. It was a little after the bank's crash when Camilla went to Omaha, leaving a neighbor woman to look after her father. And it was around that time, too, that Phil Hendry bought himself some wagons and started a freighting business. I remember the town had its skeptical thoughts about that, for Phil Hendry had never been a serious man, and it made no sense that he, who would one day inherit old Alex's wealth, should be striking off for himself like any other moneyless boy. Six months later Camilla Bland returned from Omaha with a teacher's certificate, and that fall she took the third grade of the old First Ward School — the first woman to teach in our town.

I used to see these people walking their lonely ways along our streets and be possessed by a wonder that would not diminish. Old Alex, turning into the stairway of his building, dressed more poorly than any stable roustabout, with a sly and strange backward glance at whoever might be passing behind him; and Camilla, going soberly down Custer Street in the morning, with an inner grace that was like a light shining; and old Henry Bland, passing the bank without ever looking at it, his age coming upon him like quick winter; and Phil Hendry sitting up on the box of one of his wagons, his big shoulders bowed over against the sudden slant of our March rains. I used to watch them and wonder, and I know now that all New Hope was also watching them — trying to resolve this puzzle.

In the middle of the following year old Henry Bland died, and, when they lowered him into his grave on Locust Hill, I could look up and see all the people I ever knew standing bareheaded there, crying or near to crying. In his young years he had been a strength to our town; in his tragic years he had been a strength. I can still feel the emptiness of that day. He had left behind twenty thousand dollars in life insurance that was, for our time, a large amount. And he had said to Camilla as his last words: "People trusted me, Cam. You remember that."

When the insurance company's check came, Camilla Bland turned it over to Father, to be applied to the old debt. I remember Father telling it to Mother that night. He sat in his accustomed place on the porch, gently rocking; and then he stopped rocking, and his voice went out on a note that I can still hear — deeply stirred and proud, and regretful in a way that hurt you to hear.

My mother wasn't happy. Just and fair as she was, she

could not find it right to balance Camilla Bland's life against old Henry Bland's stern sense of honesty. She said: "It has gone too far."

"Perhaps," my father said, "it has."

Mother said: "Is she giving you part of her teacher's pay, too?"

But Father never answered that question. I knew other people wondered about it, and I know that he was often asked. But Father found a way of stiffening against talk he thought improper. Without speaking he had a way of drying up curiosity and leaving the silence uncomfortable. I recall that we were still grouped there in the soft, spring night when Phil Hendry came down Prairie Street on his big, high-wheeled freighter — headed outward toward the west. He had his hat off, and his blond head swayed a little to the wagon's motion. He sat in freighter style, bowed on the seat, his heavy hands clasping the reins. After he had gone on, my father said something that surprised me: "Perhaps that's gone too far, also."

He said no more, and after all these years that silence is what comes back to me, freighted with a thousand memories. My town was like that — realistic and hard and often brutal. But with a deep silence covering the kindness that ran beneath all that stubborn life. All those people look across time to me now, stiff in their clothes, tight-lipped, and almost grim in the way they faced upon the world. I know now I misjudged them. There was somewhere in them an imaginativeness almost wild, a strain of hidden sentiment, an honesty they were afraid to reveal.

I remember Phil Hendry stolidly riding his freight wagon through that summer and that fall. There were parties in New Hope — hayriding and skating on Beechey's pond, and dances, and long trips out to Buttermilk Farm during the hot spell. But Phil Hendry, who once had lived this way, never went. I think the younger crowd avoided inviting him. Once, under the arch of the Bon Marche, I saw him come face to face with Camilla; and for a moment they stopped, stepped suddenly back from each other, and stared in a way that even to me was somehow bitter and hopeless and strange beyond belief. In a moment he bowed his head and turned.

This was the way it went, all our eyes upon that pair, with nobody knowing and nobody satisfied. With the feeling of something unfinished in the air. And then Alex Hendry, who had moved so obscurely through New Hope that year, came to the end of his time and, like a shadow, passed out. He had a moment with his son, a moment in which all the misery of his life seemed to break forth. He had sent Dr. Gillespie from the room so that he might have his word with Phil. But Gillespie heard the old man's voice, high and strident, come down the length of the hallway.

"It's your money now, and you can do what you damned please with it."

Gillespie heard Phil Hendry speak in a slow, sad way. And then old Alex broke in, still bitter. "No, you'll find out what I found out long ago. I can't tell you . . . it's something you've got to learn. But you'll never buy a dime's worth of happiness that way. It's pleased me to see you turn to work this last year, though you've been a fool in the way you've used what you made. I know you like a book, Phil . . . and I see what you're going to do now. It won't work. You'll find out."

When the Menefees' big, black horses drew the hearse up Locust Hill, there was only one carriage to follow, and only Phil Hendry there to see his father buried. The resentment of our town was that strong, its memory that hard and that unforgiving. My mother cried a little; she could not bear to think of this anger following Alex Hendry to his death. But my father had no pity.

"He lived his life the way he wanted. Never gave any sympathy and never asked for any. I give him credit for consistency. That was his one virtue."

A week afterward, with soft dusk falling out of the sky, Phil Hendry came down Prairie Street and stopped at our gate. My father went out there, and the two of them talked for a long while. When Father returned to his chair, he lighted a fresh cigar and smoked it entirely through, so silent that my mother gathered up her sewing and went to bed. How indelibly stamped upon my memory that scene is.

There was something in the wind. I felt it, and our town felt it. And then, a month or more later, I turned into St. Vrain Street and saw Camilla Bland come out of the Bon Marche and pause deliberately and turn to wait for Phil Hendry who had been standing across the street. He came over and lifted his hat, and for a little while they stood like that, with a graveness deeply covering both their faces. She said something in a low voice and lifted her cheeks, and I noticed how fair and pale and proud she was at that moment. I was almost fourteen then and not particularly an observing boy. But these people I watched, because I liked them, and because I wanted them to like each other. There was something in Phil Hendry's eyes, like pain, and his lips came together and were very thin. They walked down the street together.

One day, a little after school had started in the fall, they were married without announcement in Judge Rawl's office and left on the next stage for Omaha. They were gone about a month, I remember, and, while they were gone, my father announced that Phil Hendry had made a settlement of the bank's old debt, clearing up each depositor's account and assuming a share of each stockholder's assessment. I do not think New Hope realized until then how large Alex's fortune had been; for Phil had paid out in that transaction over a hundred thousand dollars.

I remember that, when they returned and had settled in Syl Connoyer's house at the end of Prairie Street, all the friends of the Bland family went there to see them; and I remember my parents talking about it on the porch of our place, later in the evening.

Mother said: "I'm happy for Camilla. She looks lovely. But I didn't see Phil there."

My father said gently: "He was playing seven-up in the back room at Dolph Oliver's saloon."

"Tod!"

But Father made an impatient gesture with his arm. His face wasn't pleased. "It's Camilla's friends who called to pay their respects. Not his. That's why he wasn't home."

She said: "That's over, Tod. Nobody's holding Alex Hendry's sins against Phil."

"Perhaps not," my father said. "But perhaps Phil is holding New Hope to account for its sins."

I didn't understand, and I know my mother didn't. And as the months went along, New Hope had no answer for that puzzle, either. For there was a strangeness here that nobody could explain. They had returned from Omaha — two tall, fine people who once had been in love and who once had been so quick to find laughter in living; and who maintained now a reserve New Hope could not penetrate.

It was like a riddle that wouldn't leave you alone; our town perplexed itself more and more with the little clues that furnished no answer. We all knew that Alex Hendry had secretly bought the old Bland mansion, and that it was now Phil Hendry's. Yet the Bland mansion remained empty, its windows scummed with the dust blowing out of the deep prairie and the iron sage in the front yard half overgrown by the upshooting weeds, while Camilla and Phil remained in the little place at the end of Prairie Street. It would have pleased New Hope to have seen those young people move back into old Henry Bland's big house; it would have been like the happy answer to a troubled story. But there was something here between Phil and Camilla too bitterly remembered; some pride stung beyond forgiveness, some thought that, married though they were, built its barrier between them. We could see it. We could feel it. We could watch it grow.

At times they walked the pleasant dusk together, which was a habit of the folks in our town. From my porch I could see them pacing along the uneven boards of Prairie Street, saying little and very grave; as though each was deep-caught in some loneliness that could not be shared. A big, blond-headed man with a growing solidity about him that caught your attention, and a tall, slender woman who had a beauty hard to describe — a beauty that came from some deep and steadfast place. At times they strolled this way.

Otherwise New Hope saw them seldom together. She seemed to stay habitually in the little house at the end of Prairie. As for Phil, he had his office in the Hendry Block. Now and then he liked to take over the reins of one of his freighters and make the long week's trip westward. Sometimes in duck season we would see him ride out along the Missouri and disappear behind the long banks of autumn haze hanging a lovely color across the horizon; and sometimes we saw him, late at night, come slowly back. Somewhere, through all this time, he had kept two or three of his oldest friends, and, if there was need to find him in the evenings, it was best first to look in the back room of Dolph Oliver's saloon. Ordinarily he'd be there, playing seven-up in his shirtsleeves, an old pipe clenched in the deep corner of his mouth, his heavy eyes thoroughly unreadable.

I saw them once meet at the stairway entrance of the Hendry Block. He was leaving the building, and she was turning up the street in company with Fay Stayton, who had just been married. And I recall with what exactness he removed his hat and looked down at Camilla, giving back to her the same measure of thoughtful, steel-hard courtesy she was giving him. I heard her say: "I'm giving Fay and Billy a dinner. What night would be best for you?"

He said: "Whatever night you choose."

She said: "I do not wish to interfere with your plans."

He said: "They are not important."

That was all. The women turned away, leaving him paused there.

There was that antagonism, clear to me and clear to all of the people in our town, something as cold and hard as steel that made their courtesy to each other painful. It was an unnatural thing — a thing that in time would break their hearts. This was what New Hope, more and more irritated, felt and said.

I think my mother mirrored the sentiment in our town. Kindly and tolerant always, she watched this affair until she could no longer be still. There was a desire in her to do something about it. She told my father so.

"They are both so proud. They'll go on like this . . . never making up." And then, because she felt, as all New Hope felt, that Father knew the roots of this affair, she challenged him directly. It was a thing she seldom did. Yet, as I say, she could no longer look idly on. "What is it, Tod?"

He was a long time answering. I can see him now, seated quietly in the rocking chair, his face rather grayly fixed. Shadows were running across the housetops of our town, and the smell of summer drifted in from the prairie. He said: "Maybe she wonders if it was a fear of assuming her debts that made

231

him drop away from her when the bank crashed."

"Then why . . . ," said my mother, "why did she marry him?"

My father said, so softly, so deeply regretting: "She told her father she'd pay the debts he left behind. Maybe Phil went to her, when the money became his, and offered to pay off what she owed. Maybe it was a bargain."

"Tod," said my mother, completely outraged. "Don't say such an indecent thing! No man would want to buy a woman."

But my father said: "They were in love once, and then they got caught in the crash. A man might have things in his head he couldn't speak . . . particularly if his father was hated like Alex was. Who knows what Phil thinks . . . what he thought then, or what he thinks now? We can't tell. There's the chance he thought he had to do it this way, to correct the wrong old Alex did. And now maybe he's remembering what old Alex told him. The money will buy him no happiness."

Mother said: "Is that what he thinks?"

But she could press Father no further. He put his cigar between his lips and fell into a deep silence, leaving Mother restless and unhappy. I recall how mild a woman she was, and yet how injustice and pain could sometimes lift her to action that left my father astonished.

It was the way all the town felt, seeing tragedy work its way with two people who had a right to something better. Looking back now, I can feel that sense of smoldering dissatisfaction burn through New Hope. And yet there was nothing to be done, for Phil and Camilla Hendry held New Hope away with that gravity, that cold and distant pride.

Perhaps it might have gone this way for the rest of their lives, the laconic habit of our times, holding tongues still and real thoughts hidden. Our days ran along, slow and uneventful, until it seemed the world stood still. And then Belle Mellish took to her bed and called in Dr. Gillespie; and late one night Gillespie sent Belle's fifteen-year-old boy down to the end of Prairie Street to summon Phil Hendry.

All this New Hope had from Dr. Gillespie, a man who had attended our town from its beginning. There was a sharpness in him that punctured our pride when it suited him to be that way, and a knowledge of our secrets that made him a little bit feared. He was like my father, faintly grim and past the stage of hoping for very much out of life. And yet, if he knew how to hold his silence, he knew also when silence was no longer good. And so he spoke of that scene, so that New Hope might understand.

When Phil Hendry came into the room, Belle Mellish said: "I want you to take my boy. He'll not bother you long, but he needs care the next three years."

Hendry said: "I'll take him, Belle."

She said: "You're a good man, Phil, and the town has treated you poorly."

Dr. Gillespie said: "What's that, Belle?"

"The day the bank closed," said Belle, "Phil Hendry came to me with a promise to make good what I had lost. That's why he drove freight wagons, Doctor Gillespie. He's got old Alex's money now, but it was his own, not Alex's, that I got. There's others on Custer Street that can tell you the same."

Gillespie said: "You hear that, Camilla?"

She had been on the porch, and she had heard. It was the way Gillespie later told it that made my mother cry. For pure happiness. For sorrow at all those two fine, proud people had gone through. Camilla came into the room then. Pale, Gillespie said, pale and her eyes terribly dark. Phil Hendry stood there, looking at her in the way a man might look when

233

desperately hungry and desperately hurt.

Camilla said: "The day of the auction I saw you standing across the room . . . and I thought you were afraid of what I might cost you as a wife. I thought you didn't want me at that price. How could I believe anything else? You never said anything."

"There was nothing to say," said Phil Hendry. "I couldn't shame my father by letting New Hope know I took on a debt he refused to recognize."

"Then," said Camilla, "you inherited his money, and it seemed to me you thought you could afford me as a wife."

He said bitterly: "You took up my bargain."

"Yes," she said in one breath. "Yes, I did."

They were all so still. Belle Mellish and Belle's boy and Gillespie who had turned his back to them because, he said, he had a little decency left in him, even after forty years of practice. But he heard Phil Hendry say: "I'm awfully proud of you, Cam."

When Gillespie turned around, Phil had taken his girl solidly between his big arms. Gillespie told the story to Mother many times because she so loved to hear it, and always at this point Mother would say with an eagerness she could never suppress: "And then, Doctor?" And always Gillespie would smile a little and shake his head. "What," he would always say, "do you suppose a man would tell his wife after years wasted? I think they forgot there was anybody in the room."

A day or two later, in passing down Prairie Street, I saw men cutting the weeds of the old Bland mansion. The door was open, and Camilla was inside, a towel around her head, sweeping like fury.

I look back to that town and that time, and I can understand why Phil Hendry could say he was proud of her for having made that deliberate bargain. There was love between them, long delayed and hard used, but it was another thing that made him smile and reach out with his big hands — a sense of stubborn honesty that could silently applaud what she had done. In my boyhood people were like that, doing what they had to do without crying and without explanation, hiding the heat and the strength of their lives so often behind silence.

VII

"AN INTERVAL IN YOUTH"

This was in 1882, the year before the big fire destroyed most of New Hope's First Ward. At that time the Central School stood on a rise of ground just beyond John Gentner's meadow, and, as I ran down the clay-slick slope that late afternoon, beneath a steady rain, I recall I stopped at the meadow's bottom to wade my new boots into a collecting pool of water. In another month this would be a shallow pond covering all the lower part of the field.

The homeward trail went through a stand of scrub oak. A cottontail skipped before me in no great haste, with the earth-stained pads of his hind feet showing as he ran. Rain scuffed steadily against the oak leaves, the earth's mold scent was very strong, and the freshness of a wind-cleansed sky was around me. I tramped through the small puddles of the trail and dragged my empty, lard-pail lunch bucket along the battens of John Gentner's barns as I passed by, so coming into Bridger Street. There was a small town wagon backed into the walk before Mr. Himmelmyer's empty house, and two men were unloading some trunks.

A girl stood at the edge of the walk, looking down, and, as I came up, I saw that she had dropped a paper-wrapped bundle into the wheel-furrowed mud. In matters of this sort I was a backward boy, and I do not know what impelled me to reach down and retrieve the package. When I stopped, the top of my lunch bucket fell into the mud, and this accident so embarrassed me I handed back the bundle without meeting the girl's eyes or answering the small — "Thank you." — she gave me. At the corner of Custer Street I paused and looked behind. A woman stood in the doorway of Himmelmyer's house, and the girl said something to her and afterward pointed toward me. More embarrassed than before, I walked home, hitting my boot heels on each interstice of the board walk.

After all this time it is odd how clear that whole scene is to me. Her picture is in my mind now, fresh and colored and living. She was around thirteen, my own age, wearing a checked dress and gray, ribbed stockings that made her seem long-legged. Her hair was amber-blonde, braided in back, and her eyes were a soft and sober gray. I remember that the tone of her voice was very distinct, yet softened by shyness.

That evening at the supper table my father said: "A Missus Alice Stuart moved into Himmelmyer's house today. She has a daughter, Elizabeth, about Tod's age. Apparently no husband. I think she said she was from Maryland."

My mother said to me: "You must get acquainted with her, Tod. It is hard for a new child to change schools."

The new girl was in my school room the next day, sitting in my aisle, and, when I pulled myself straight, I could look over Ben Jettson's head and see the straight part running through her hair. That night I waited until she had crossed Gentner's meadow before following. I wanted to speak to her, but the obscure pride of boyhood held me back. At the edge of the oak copse I saw her make a short, swift turn of her head and then hurry on.

Within a week we were walking together, and stopping at the pond in the meadow. Sometimes she held my pail while I waded in the deep water. I remember that she watched me with a great soberness. I seldom saw her laugh.

One night I said: "Where is your father, Elizabeth?"

She had a quick way of walking that I never have forgotten, with her shoulders swinging a little and her glance fixed ahead. After I had asked the question, she said in a level, hesitant voice — "I am not to answer that." — and walked on. The eyes of boyhood are sharp. I saw her lips tighten and didn't know why, although I do now. She turned in at her gate without saying anything more.

It was the next night that her mother came out to meet me. She said: "Tod, it is nice of you to walk home with Elizabeth." All I can think of in describing Mrs. Stuart is that she was like my mother, with the same sweetness. Her voice had a sustaining gentleness in it. It was a tone that carried you up and made you feel better; and behind the tone you felt something calm and firm. In New Hope, in 1882, there were many women like that. Remembering back through the years, piecing together the sharp images of boyhood, it seems to me now that my mother's composure came from a strong, self-nourishing spirit. There was cruelty, and there was tragedy in our world. Her eyes saw it and reflected it. Yet, she had a faith that kept her steady and a courage that made our house a warm, secure place.

That same night I heard my father say: "I understand Missus Stuart will do dressmaking."

We were in the living room. Mother sat by the center table, patching my clothes. The lamp's yellow light coned down on the table's red, checkered cloth; its glow faded out along the room. The isinglass eyes of the stove made four ruby squares in the corner shadows. My mother looked at Father, her white fingers pausing with the needle. She was on the edge of smiling, as though amused by his late knowledge. "I have already left some things with her. She has an eye for design, like a Frenchwoman's. She is well bred, Tod."

My father said: "It is somewhat odd for a woman of her refinement to be so far from home. I have wondered. . . ."

Mother said: "You needn't wonder." She spoke one more word, but she spoke it without sound, framing it on her lips. The word was: *Divorced.* And then both of them were looking at me as though something unseemly and evil were here.

There is something you need to know about New Hope as it was then. It sat on the bank of the muddy Missouri, facing the endless, unfilled prairie westward. Ours was a rich, little town built on the freighting trade. Up the river came the cargo-laden steamboats, and out onto the prairie, day after day, the great, high-wheeled wagons rolled. Along St. Vrain Street stood a row of gaunt, unlovely, three-story warehouses with their high-arched doors and windows; on Custer were the stores and saloons and shops that supplied the surrounding prairie. This land was fresh and still raw; hot by summer and bitter by winter, and all its contrasts were violent. Now and then at night at the end of St. Vrain Street a great, round, sullen plaque of flame marked the campfire of the freighters. On Sunday a long silence settled, and the bells of the two churches rode a bronze, sonorous summons all across the housetops, and stiffly and solemnly we went to church.

One evening I rounded the corner of Custer and saw Hugh Sutherland come by the Himmelmyer house and pause and lift his hat to Mrs. Stuart on the porch. I heard him speak, and I heard Mrs. Stuart's slow answer, and for a moment these two faced each other, and then Hugh Sutherland replaced his hat and came on. When I passed him, I saw that he didn't notice me. There was a half-excited cast to his face. Afterward, in the closing shadows, I stood and watched the doorway of the Himmelmyer house. Mrs. Stuart had gone inside. I could see Elizabeth through the front window. She sat before a table with her head bent over, as though reading, and I waited until I knew she wouldn't come out. Down by the brewery, so still was this night in New Hope, I heard Ben Jettson calling. I turned slowly that way.

These are memories that come across those years, bright and crowded and so little dimmed by the intervening time. That week the rains filled the pond at the bottom of Gentner's meadow, and I made a raft of fence posts and old battens from Gentner's barn and floated it. Elizabeth sat in the center while I poled the raft around the shallow pond. When I put the raft over toward the shoreline, Elizabeth jumped and sank to her knees in the water. I stepped into the water and pulled her ashore, and for a moment I had my arms around her and felt the quick beat of her heart. She was a speechless girl, but she looked at me with a shock on her face, tore free, and ran through the oaks toward home.

Ben Jettson called from the school side of the pond. "Come on back, Tod." But I left the raft and tramped into Bridger Street and up Bridger to Custer, traveling toward my father's office. Mrs. Hugh Sutherland's buggy and two white horses stood hitched in front of Sutherland's law office. I stopped to scratch the nose of the near mare and was this way when Mrs. Sutherland came out. She was a tall, common woman, always heavily dressed, and she was laughing at something, though the tone of her laughter was hard. I turned around to see her look long and carefully at Hugh Sutherland who had come to the door. Her face was red, and she laughed again and saw me. She said — "Tod, you are a little man." — and reached into her purse.

Hugh Sutherland said in a downward tone — "Nellie." — and then Mrs. Sutherland bent toward me and put a half dollar in my hand, stepped into her buggy, and ran it recklessly down the street. I didn't look at Hugh Sutherland, feeling strange, and went up to my father's office and waited in the doorway. It had begun to rain again, slow and fine, and twilight moved down from the lead-colored sky. Mrs. Stuart appeared from the Bon Marche, walking toward Bridger Street, and immediately Mr. Sutherland came out as though he had waited and watched for her, and the two of them were face to face for a moment. I saw Mrs. Stuart step away and lift her head, and I saw Mr. Sutherland's arms go behind his back and remain there. Now that I think of it, I recollect that he was a good-looking man, and in our town he had always been respected. My father came to the street and saw this scene, and I knew, from his silence, that he was displeased. Presently Mrs. Stuart went down the street, Mr. Sutherland walking beside her. My father said no word all the way home. In the house I told them about the fifty cents. My father's eyes, so very black, showed a rare anger and he said: "Tomorrow I wish you to return the money to her, Tod."

I slipped out of the house after dinner and stood again in the shadows of Bridger Street, watching the shine of light in Elizabeth Stuart's window. I saw her move around the room and stop at the window and place a hand against the pane. As long as she stood there, I watched the silhouette she made. At last, when she turned away, I went home through the steadying rain. As I got inside the door, I heard my mother say: "A grown and married man. He has no right to spread his unhappiness on others."

Then she stopped, and both she and Father looked at me. Father said: "What's the matter with you, Son?"

But Mother spoke to Father in a quick and gentle way: "Tod."

He looked at me more carefully, and then both of them knew. I understand that now.

But it is strange that time does this to us. I look back with a kind of tolerance, with a kind of amusement for the boy I was that short, fall season. There is no way for me to bridge the gap, to live again the alternate misery and wild self-confidence. I am older, and my boyhood comes to me only as a warm memory. But that fall when Elizabeth Stuart lived in our town, I was in love; and to boyhood love is a shyness, a torture, and a fierceness. It is strange that we forget this. I recall that I lay in bed and remembered her silhouette in the window. I remember wishing I were a man.

That fall rain fell heavily along the prairie. Mud lay deep on our streets, and the muddy river rose in yellow turbulence and tore huge chunks out of the banks near town. Geese turned south early, and at night I used to lie awake and hear their high, thin murmuring and was touched by this wildness. It stirred me in unnamed ways. The steamer, *Old Vincennes*, blew up at Sawyer's Bend. Jack Lyle and one other outlaw were killed in a fight at Blue Bonnet crossing, fifty miles west. Mrs. Hugh Sutherland was fined twenty dollars for driving her team through St. Vrain Street at a gallop. One night, pacing down Bridger Street, I saw Hugh Sutherland standing directly across from the Himmelmyer home; he was a tall shape in the shadows, and I went by without turning my head, not wishing him to know I had seen him. There was a rumor around town that he had asked Mrs. Sutherland to divorce him; and a rumor that he had proposed to Mrs. Stuart. Now and then, by day, I used to see him stand in the center of his door, fastened to deepest thoughts. I recall that he was not more than thirty-five, although in boyhood that seemed old. Clark Williston, in my grade at school, said — "Elizabeth ain't got a father." — and I tore the shirt from his back and fought him until he fell on the ground. Mrs. Williston talked to my mother about it. My mother said nothing to me.

A boy is a harp whose strings are plucked by the fingers of many strange winds. There was a dread in those short, dark days, a dread of a future that was so slow in coming, and a feeling stronger than any feeling in the world when I walked across Gentner's meadow with Elizabeth.

Even then a sharp social line divided New Hope, and on each Friday night those who belonged to the right of that line dressed and drove to the german at the Masonic Hall. Now that I look back, I think it was a ritual to preserve the gentility and the manners of an East our people would never see again and yet wished never to forget. Or it was a way of breaking the hardness and loneliness of this fringe of life, facing the edge of the smoky West. Clear through my boyhood that bright memory runs, of my mother's dress stiffly rustling as she walked and of her face, normally so serene, a little flushed beneath her auburn hair while my father looked down at her with an expression faintly puzzled, faintly amused. My father was not a big man, but his eyes were blacker than any eyes I have ever seen, and there was a kind of austerity at the edges of his long lips. When I was young, I thought my father was made of iron. But I know now that the austerity was a mask to keep a secret. After all these years the strongest impression I have of him is of a lonely and imaginative spirit lost in the wrong world.

That Friday night I left my father and mother and went to a corner of the hall and sat beside Max Beal and Clark Williston. I saw Elizabeth Stuart, standing with one of the Gilstrap girls nearby, and then I noticed that Mrs. Stuart had

242

come to the dance with James Pelky, who was a friend of Father's and not married.

There is a color in this world that is seen only in boyhood and never again; there was a grace and a dignity in that age of my youth that is forever lost. The bracket lamps along the walls sent a soft shining across the floor, the violins and guitars made a melody that rose and fell in steady waltz rhythm, women's dresses wheeled beautifully by, and the sound of talk was gay and very strong. My father and mother came by and smiled at me, and I saw them look at each other in a way that was odd and young; it was an expression that shut me out. Mrs. Stuart came by with James Pelky who was earnestly talking to her; and Hugh Sutherland came by with his wife, his eyes turning and following Mrs. Stuart with a continuing insistence. Mrs. Sutherland's face was quite red. Once she lifted her face and caught Mr. Sutherland's straying glance. I heard her strident laugh. She said something that seemed to hit him hard; his shoulders fell. I heard him say: "Nellie, please."

Elizabeth was in a chair farther down the wall. I got up and went toward her, feeling awkward and hearing Clark Williston's low laugh behind me. Elizabeth's dress was white and came up to a collar around her throat. The light of the hall shone on her hair and made her eyes very gray. She looked at me, dropped her head, and I saw her hands move on her lap; and then she looked at me again, and smiled.

I said — "Would you like some punch?" — and turned away before she answered. The music had stopped. I worked my way to the punch bowl and waited my turn. Howard Fitz-Lee came up, wiping his forehead. He was a short, huge-shouldered man with red hair and a red beard that fell down against his white shirt bosom like a crimson waterfall. My father came up, and Hugh Sutherland came up, and Howard Fitz-Lee

243

laughed in a great, deep way and said: "Hughie, next time you go shootin'. . . ."

But Hugh Sutherland wasn't listening. He had turned and was looking at Mrs. Stuart across the hall; and on his face was an expression I had seen before — sharp, compressed, and stirred. He went directly to her and bent over to speak, and, when the music started a moment later, she rose and wheeled away from him.

I took up my cup of punch, noticing how soberly Fitz-Lee and my father were at the moment. Fitz-Lee said in a low voice: "Trouble here, Tod." Walking across the hall, I saw Mrs. Sutherland waltzing with James Pelky. She kept turning in Pelky's arms, turning her hard, discontented cheeks so that she might watch Hugh Sutherland. I reached Elizabeth and handed her the punch, more embarrassed than before. Elizabeth's voice was slow; it was soft. "Thank you very much, Tod." I heard Clark Williston laughing behind me, and I walked down the hall to the rear door, knowing that I would fight him before the week was out.

The door led to a wide, second-story porch behind the hall. I went through the doorway and stepped out of the yellow lane of light into the dark shadows of the porch's corner. From the porch I saw the lights of the Derby Saloon on River Street and beyond that the high smokestack of the brewery; and I was thinking of sliding down the porch post when I heard Hugh Sutherland's voice behind me.

I was trapped in the black corner of the porch. Hugh Sutherland held Mrs. Stuart's arm and drew her gently out of the hall until they were two tall, vague shapes silhouetted against the lane of lamplight. After all these years I remember the way his words rode the shadows, so hopelessly, so forlornly.

"Alice," he said, "if there is any hope for me, you'll have to give it."

Her answer was breathless and afraid: "Take me inside, Hugh."

"How much should I give up? I love you! Is there nothing to do?"

"Take me inside, Hugh!"

And then he said in a long, dying voice: "There is some happiness possible for us, Alice . . . if we take it."

Her voice was only a murmur. I scarcely heard the words. "I have not known much happiness, Hugh. But how could we be happy by being cruel to somebody else? I want you to know. . . ."

Mrs. Hugh Sutherland was in the doorway, and her voice was high and arrogant; the sound of it made me cringe; it made me ashamed for her. She said: "Mister Sutherland, if you are through with Missus Stuart, take me home."

It seemed to me that the music got louder, as though to cover this. Mrs. Sutherland went inside, and Hugh Sutherland took Mrs. Stuart's arm and followed. From my position I heard the swell and fall of the music and, later, its ending. I went back into the hall and across it. The Sutherlands were gone, and Mrs. Stuart and Elizabeth were gone; and the pleasantness had gone out of the night. My father and mother took me home a little later. Long after I had gone to bed, I heard them talking in their room, and knew what they were talking about.

Next morning, which was Saturday, I drifted down Bridger and stopped at Elizabeth's gate and waited until she came out. Mrs. Stuart came to the door and said: "Not too long."

Elizabeth and I walked on toward the river. We cut through Fitzpatrick's Alley and stopped to watch the huge wheel of the brewery spin around until its spokes were a blur. Beyond the brewery stood the high warehouses, out of which came the strong smells that carry across the years to stir me now

— the smells of coffee, of burlap, of molasses, of flour, of whiskey. Wagons and horses were parked in a solid tangle along this street, and men moved in and out of the dark building runways, sweaty and deep voiced. And these men were my boyhood gods. Stables adjoined the warehouses, and Nippert's blacksmith shop stood here, with Nippert's huge, leather-aproned shape poised before the glow of his forge fire. This was New Hope in my boyhood, raw and strong and busy — with a kind of excitement stirring all of us.

We drifted along, Elizabeth and I, past this quarter of town and past the shanties and sheds and corrals until we stood by the open edge of the river. Westward lay the open prairie, marked here and there by a house and a windmill's trestled shape; and on and on until there was only a blueness and an emptiness. The yellow river, swollen with a thousand miles of rain, swept by. It rustled against the bank at my feet, undercutting the soft soil; I could feel the earth shake at the water's impact. A tree moved downstream, turning around and around. The *T. J. Jackson* came about Sawyer's Bend, throwing black smoke from its stacks as it labored against the current. The expelled blast of its engines made a steady *chuuu-chuuu-chuuu* across the quiet.

I took up a dead branch and threw it into the river, and bent at the crumbling edge of the bank to watch it whirl away. There was a pressure pulling me back, and I turned and saw that Elizabeth held the tail of my coat. "Tod," she said, "I wish you would be careful."

These are the things I remember. They come out of that far, stirring past as bright as any memory a man will ever have. She wore a heavy coat whose collar tucked in at her chin. She wore a round, flat, fur hat on one side of her yellow-blonde hair. She was a leggy girl with deepest gray eyes and a composed, grave expression that seldom changed. We were both thirteen, and yet she was older than I. In the things she said. In the things she thought.

The river shook the ground beneath me, and the westward horizon was an invitation I felt in my bones — and something in me was hard and desperate. I did not know what it was then, but I do now. It was the desperateness of being too young. For the dreams of youth are greater than the body of youth — and waiting grows too cruel.

I said: "When I'm sixteen, I'm going to drive a freighter."

She said: "You'd be away a long time."

"Well," I said, "I'd come back."

But she kept looking at me, and I remember now the grayness of her eyes. She said: "Maybe you'll change, Tod. Maybe you'll want to work in your father's office. Three years is a long time."

Something in her voice brought a dread to me. For in boyhood there is only uncertainty — and the fear of it. I said: "You'll be here, won't you?"

"Maybe not, Tod. My mother. . . ."

Young as I was, I knew what she knew. The *T. J. Jackson*'s great, throaty whistle sounded for the landing, the echo riding all across New Hope. We turned back along the muddy road leading into Custer, not saying anything. I saw Ben Jettson over behind the courthouse square, and he waved at me and made a secret signal. I went on with Elizabeth, past my father's office. Somebody ran down from River Street into Dr. Gillespie's office, and in a moment Gillespie came out with the man, carrying his small satchel and walking very fast, back up River. When Elizabeth and I turned into Bridger Street, we saw Mr. Sutherland at the door of the Himmelmyer house.

Mr. Sutherland had been hunting. He held a pair of ducks in his hand, and he was smiling at Mrs. Stuart who stood in the doorway. Mrs. Stuart wasn't smiling. She put up a hand

and touched Mr. Sutherland's chest, and she said something to him that took the smile from his face; and then both of them were still and gray. I recall that expression on Mrs. Stuart's face so clearly, even now. And I know now that she had let herself love Hugh Sutherland. But she shook her head at him, and the pressure of her arm pushed him gently back. I hated Mr. Sutherland then. Because he was a man standing on Elizabeth's porch.

The town marshal, Lot Graves, came down Bridger with his long legs moving fast. His arm removed me aside from the gate, and moved Elizabeth aside. He went up to the porch and said something to Mr. Sutherland, and Mr. Sutherland said — "My God!" — and came back with Lot Graves; the two ducks were still swinging on his arm as he passed around the corner into St. Vrain. Mrs. Stuart's face was pale, and something smothered her voice. She said: "Come into the house, Elizabeth."

This was Saturday, mid-morning. My father came home earlier than usual. He said: "Missus Sutherland took laudanum, but Doctor Gillespie has her out of danger."

My mother caught her breath. She said — "Oh." — in a sad and gently diminishing voice.

My father said: "I am going to talk to Hugh Sutherland. I want you to go see Missus Stuart now."

My mother said: "She loves him, Tod."

"I am sorry for her," said my father, "and I pity Hugh." They had forgotten me for the moment. But I knew what my father meant. I knew he was thinking of Mrs. Sutherland with her bitter voice, with her intemperate anger. He said: "But it is his life, and he can't run from it. It would be worse, for all of them."

"Why?" asked my mother.

My father looked at her in some surprise. "Because he is

an honorable man. Because his conscience wouldn't let him forget. You go see Missus Stuart."

My mother looked at me. "Go outside, Tod. I want to talk to your father."

My father said: "Let him stay. It is time he learned some of the hard things."

My mother shook her head. "He will learn soon enough."

I turned out, put my feet on the gate, and idly swung it back and forth. In a little while my father went to his office, and Mother came out and walked down Bridger, going into the Himmelmyer house. She stayed through noon, and, when she came back, I could see that she had been crying.

There were things happening in New Hope. I felt them and did not fully understand, but I was afraid. I ate dinner and walked along St. Vrain Street and stopped by the stage office. My father came from his office, and Howard Fitz-Lee came from the store and joined him, and both of them stood a while on the walk, very solemn as they talked. Then they went down to Hugh Sutherland's place and went in. Ben Jettson came from Wister's Alley and said from the side of his mouth: "You hear about Missus Sutherland?" We idled along the street and stopped at the bank. Pretty soon my father and Howard Fitz-Lee came out with Mr. Sutherland, and my father put his hand on Mr. Sutherland's shoulder and said something, and then Mr. Sutherland came across the street with his head down and his face blank, and I thought then that he was an old man. I hadn't noticed it before. He went on up Bridger, but he didn't turn in at his house. He kept walking until he was lost in the scatter of buildings at the edge of town. Once he stumbled over a loose plank.

Ben Jettson and I walked out the Omaha road and came down to the tall bluff and hooked our feet over its edge, watching the Missouri roll heavily by. Ben Jettson said something, but I do not remember what it was, for I was thinking of other things. At five o'clock that evening I came along Bridger Street and saw a wagon backed into the walk by Himmelmyer's house. I knew then what was to happen. I sat on the steps of our porch.

Grayness swept over the prairie and turned the town dark. I watched the Himmelmyer house until my mother called me in to supper. There was little talk. I sat before my plate and didn't eat, and my father said: "Do you feel sick, Tod?" But I saw my mother shake her head at him, and nothing more was said. In a little while I went back to the gate and stood there. My mother went down the street to the Himmelmyer house again.

In these side streets, I remember, darkness lay soft and thick. Down St. Vrain the store lights made long patterns across the mud and at the corner of Herm von Gayl's old saloon there was a solid brightness. The Omaha stage came up from the stables and stopped in front of the bank; and then I saw my mother come from the Himmelmyer house with Mrs. Stuart and Elizabeth. I heard Elizabeth speak, but I didn't leave my gate; and pretty soon she came up and stopped in front of me. All these memories are bright and real and some of the old hurt comes back, even now. The gate was between us, and she was saying: "I am going away, Tod."

I said: "Where are you going? Maybe I can visit you when school's out."

She said: "I don't know."

"Well," I said, "maybe you can write me a letter. I'd answer it."

"All right, Tod," she said.

Mother and Mrs. Stuart had stopped over on Custer Street. I remember how quiet Mrs. Stuart's voice was when it called back: "Elizabeth."

Elizabeth said — "Here, Tod." — and placed something in my hand. I could only see the faint glow of her face in this darkness, but I heard her crying. That was all. She turned away, and I saw her walk across the street to her mother and go on toward the stage. I remember this best: the way she walked, with her shoulders straight and swinging a little. From my place at the gate I saw Mrs. Stuart kiss my mother and step inside the stage with Elizabeth. The door closed, and the driver made a complete turn in the street and drove down Custer. I saw Elizabeth wave; afterward the stage vanished in the yonder dark.

My mother was coming back, but I left the gate and went down Bridger. A light came out of Clark Williston's house, and I stopped in its beam to see what Elizabeth had given me. It was a small tintype picture, of herself. I turned into the Himmelmyer yard and sat on the steps. I heard my mother call my name, but I didn't answer it. There was the sound of wild geese overhead, and away out at the end of Bridger Street the teamsters had lighted a fire that burned its red glow against the black. Somebody came through the alley by the brewery and walked forward, and I made out Hugh Sutherland's shape. He stopped by the gate of the Himmelmyer house, and I heard him breathe once, deeply. I was in the thick shadows of the porch, and I don't think he saw me. I sat very still and hated him. Afterward, he walked on up Bridger, very slowly and with his shoulders down.

There was a little spatter of rain on the walk. Down at the landing stevedores were unloading the *T. J. Jackson*, with tar flares burning. I sat on the porch of the Himmelmyer house, feeling its emptiness as I have felt no emptiness since, and was this way when my father came down the walk and turned in. He came to the steps and was silent for quite a while, and this is one of my strongest memories of my father now — the silence that understood. Presently he said — "All right, Tod." — and we walked home. I recall that his hand, resting across my shoulders, was heavy and warm. It was a strong support to me as we walked through the night's black shadows.

These were my people, and the memory of them now is warm and sustaining. Their voices follow me, kind and steady; and their faces, so grave from what they knew, are watching me though the dimness of time. What I remember best is their fidelity to the truth, as they saw the truth.

The End

THE HUNTING OF TOM HORN

WILL HENRY

Lively, action-packed, exciting, this is a collection of short masterpieces by one of the West's greatest storytellers. The characters in these tales—be they cowboy or bounty hunter, preacher or killer—are living, breathing people, people whose stories could be told only by a master like Will Henry.

___4484-6 $5.50 US/$6.50 CAN